THE JUSTIFICATION OF JOHANN GUTENBERG

Blake Morrison is the author of the bestselling memoir
And When Did You Last See Your Father?, two collec-
tions of poems, a children's book, and a study of the
Bulger case, *As If*. He lives in London.

Blake Morrison

THE JUSTIFICATION OF JOHANN GUTENBERG

V

VINTAGE

Published by Vintage 2001

2 4 6 8 10 9 7 5 3 1

Copyright © Blake Morrison 2000

The right of Blake Morrison to be identified as the author of
this work has been asserted by him in accordance with the
Copyright, Designs and Patents Act, 1988

First published in Great Britain by in 2000 by
Chatto & Windus

Vintage
Random House, 20 Vauxhall Bridge Road,
London SW1V 2SA

Random House Australia (Pty) Limited
20 Alfred Street, Milsons Point, Sydney
New South Wales 2061, Australia

Random House New Zealand Limited
18 Poland Road, Glenfield, Auckland 10,
New Zealand

Random House (Pty) Limited
Endulini, 5A Jubilee Road, Parktown 2193,
South Africa

The Random House Group Limited Reg. No. 954009
www.randomhouse.co.uk

A CIP catalogue record for this book
is available from the British Library

ISBN 0 09 928529 0

Papers used by Random House are natural, recyclable
products made from wood grown in sustainable forests. The
manufacturing processes conform to the environmental
regulations of the country of origin

Printed and bound in Great Britain by
Cox & Wyman Limited, Reading, Berkshire

JUSTIFICATION *n*: 1 The action of showing something to be just, right or proper; vindication of oneself or another; exculpation; verification, proof. 2 The action whereby a man is free from the penalty of sin. 3 The action of adjusting, straightening, levelling or arranging exactly, in typefounding and printing.

'Having many things to write to you, I would not write with paper and ink: but I trust to come unto you, and speak face to face ...'

Second Epistle of John, 12

Prologue

Something of me as I am.

I have hair on my head, thinning, but no beard.

I am tall, five foot six inches.

I have skin white as vellum but less tough.

I am past sixty, one of the few hereabouts to live so long.

I speak German, read Latin and Greek, and struggle with English.

I have no children I know of.

I owe money to none in Mainz, though some in Strasbourg pursue me for loans and have set the imperial court of Rottweilers at me.

I keep in health by eating plentifully of herbs – sage, rue, tansy, marjoram, southernwood, lemon-balm, mint, fennel and parsley.

I do not trust my doctor, who for an aching tooth prescribes mutton fat mixed with sea-holly.

I have eased my work to half a week.

I am poor in sight and growing worse.

I have no fear of dying.

What I fear is that death will rub out what I have done, till not a trace of me is left upon the earth.

Which is why I sit here, so that I, Johann Gutenberg, otherwise known as Gensfleisch, print master and citizen of Mainz, in the fourteen hundred and sixty-fourth year of our Lord, shall furnish this my vindication, a history of Work, Love, Faith, Pride, Deceit, Devotion and Art, which I commence herewith from Eltville, in the house of my late brother Friele, whose widow has made generous with an upper floor overlooking the Rhine, than which no setting could be more fit, since through the duration of my life and no matter how wide my journeyings I have rarely ventured far from its course, and though much has altered in the fortunes of men clustering its banks, yet the Rhine itself displays the same strong brown current as ever, a current which your author, mildly failing as his heartbeat is, observes with a certain poignancy, the river being an emblem of God, in whose swiftness we are sticks carried along, an image, now I have hit on it, which cannot help but raise doubts about the purpose of this testament – the hubris of it! surely all men do is swept away! – but which doubts I must set aside, the time left being short and the need burning in me to *justify* myself to the Lord my Maker, whose goodness fills me with hope that if I unburden myself I will, at the conclusion, feel lighter at heart than when I began.

In other words, I plan to get it off my breast. To make a clean bosom of it. To wash my inky linen in public.

When Mainz was torn apart two years since, and the men from my old printshop flowed out into the world, I hoped my name would spread with them. In idle moments, I have dreamt of a stream of visitors seeking me out, eager to see Gutenberg, the man who minted Bibles, the dung that grew the flower. Many times I have rehearsed the scene. A knock below. A stranger announces himself to my trusty servant, Frau Beildeck. Is this, he asks, where the Print Man lives, the Press Master, he who conceived *artificial writing*? Indeed it is. Frau Beildeck ushers him up to where I sit among my books. Cap in hand, he looks ready to kiss my feet but contents himself with bowing. He is sorry for the lateness of the hour, but he has journeyed far, and it was not easy to find me. He is bashful at first – until I offer him a jug of Rheingauer, which Frau Beildeck fetches from my cellar, and his tongue is loosened. He has lately set up a printshop, he says, but is bedevilled by difficulties. If I could spare an hour speaking *mechanical* with him – on how to secure blocks of type on the coffin of the press, what consistency of ink to use, what quality of paper, and so forth – he would happily pay me. Perhaps a fee *should* be paid me for the dispensing of advice. Years of my working life were spent in debt, and now men come to plunder the riches of my retirement. But instead I give myself freely, and an hour becomes two or three, and with my visitor too merry to care to leave, I fetch a second jug, offer a bed for the night, and ask Frau Beildeck to make us rib and sauerkraut. Over supper will then emerge the pilgrim's purpose in seeking me out, which touches less on his present ambitions than on my past: he wishes to know where I began, how the idea came, who helped me, what difficulties I met, and so forth. It is the difficulties I lay weight on: the sermon is entitled My Struggle. I sit there like some ancient ferryman of the Rhine recalling the ice-maroon of '38, the storm of '44, the rapids calamity of '56. Reminiscence is an old man's folly. But I have earned the right. My hair is white like goosedown and my face as cracked as summer earth. I am old.

So the visitor hears me out, and in the morning, enlightened, departs, ahead of the next visitor, to whom I tell my tale again ... Alas, though, these visitors are but phantoms. Tired of waiting, I dreamed them up. Now I am close to death – the vale from which none return – ghosts are my only guests. Last week my old friend, Nicholas of Cusa, went by in the garden, although some six months dead. It must be my grieving raised his likeness from a sunbeam – that and my eyes, which are so poor these days they could mistake an angel for a pig. Yes, I am haunted by phantoms. But theirs are not the visitations I crave. I would prefer the company of flesh and blood.

You will think me vain, but I am certain that a few print-pilgrims must at least have set out in this direction. Perhaps indeed they have come as far as Mainz. It is only because I have moved here to Eltville, some leagues downstream, that they fail to find me. Even then they might succeed but for my enemies telling them lies. My old print-works in the Humbrechthof is now a pit of adders – all slipperiness and forked tongues. Any visitor who calls there asking for the Press Master is told he need seek no further. A rule has been laid down, and even the humblest worker sworn to observe it, to this effect: that my name must on no account be offered up; that if a visitor should raise it, it should be deprecated or denied; that after a generous tour of the premises, the departing pilgrim must be handed a parchment giving the 'history' of the works, with the colophon of my usurpers (that lying misprint) underneath. Thus do truth-seekers run up against a wall of silence. Thus am I stripped of the honours due me. Not that honours themselves – laurel wreaths, citations, the ceremonials of patronage – matter a fig to me. But when a man has been first, the world should know it.

Deeds, not words, are what we are judged by. But if another says my deeds were his, if he steals them from me, then I must resort to words to repossess them. Hence this my justification.

If I were able, I would write it myself. But my hands being shaky and my eyes half-blind, I have hired a scribe to do it for me. Anton his name is, a boy of fifteen, whose late father was a charcoal-burner and whose splendid *noisy* mother is famous here in Eltville for raising thirteen children on her own. When Frau Beildeck sent word out that her master sought a scribe, this mother fetched her Anton to me, proclaiming loud and long that despite his occupation – six days a week he tills and hoes at the manor – he had been taught to read and write. The family being in need of pfennigs, he could, she said, come scribing on Sundays and never mind what was said against it by priests. The clucking mother pushed him out from under her wing. I stared him in the eye, at which he blushed. Blond hair, brawny shoulders, chestnut eyes – I liked the look of him, but doubted his writing skills, five other boys from Eltville having come ahead of him and none fit to hold a quill. But Anton sat straight down and proved me wrong, copying without blemish a page I gave him from Saint Augustine – and with such grace and swiftness too. Where had he learned Latin? I asked. At the chaplain's house, he said. He had also borrowed books from there. If ever he saved the money, he would like to study in Erfurt or Cologne. A boy like Anton is wasted in the fields, I thought, and told his mother I would have him. We fixed a sum. She hugged and goosed me in delight.

Here then, one week later, Anton sits with me, transcribing my impressions as fast as they leap out of my mouth. He has been told to set down each word I speak, even those just now spoken of him. For though to see his own name may discompose him, these words do not compose themselves. And though humility may be a virtue, to be effaced, as I know myself, is a painful wound. I will not play that game, Anton. Without you, this manuscript cannot exist. Without you, there is no hope of making it a book. (Nor would an old man have the pleasure of sitting with a handsome boy.) Let your presence be admitted here – you are Anton, not Anon.

Be careful, then, you do not skip or nod. Nor must you leave words out or write them twice over, as scribes are wont to do. My invention sought to correct such error – in metal, books should read as God intended. But for drafting this testament I put my trust in your ear and hand. Be sure, then, you copy me in good faith.

You lost your father, Anton, and I have never had a son. Perhaps by sitting here, we can console each other. I always wanted a child – a son or daughter I might have looked after and who now would look after me. At the Humbrechthof, when word came that any printman's wife had given birth we used to stamp feet and bang chisels, then take the lucky father to the tavern. In my heart at such times was always a sliver of envy. It is there still. My friends have children. Even my enemies do. The injustice of this world! It is not enough for my enemies to have robbed me, they must be given children too.

Words are my only children – the only heirs I can trust to preserve my name. I have given my life to seeding them, raising them, hardening them, straightening them, watching them grow. Now, in return, while there is time, I ask their help. One final kindness, that is all. A favour owed to me and to these ghosts I here address: you my readers, my brothers and sisters in tribulation, the unseen visitors of time to come.

I would like it to be known what I have done. Come, words, and stake my claim for me.

Part one

1. Gooseflesh

I was born in Mainz on ... But let me not trot the usual river-bank path. Honest though I am pledged to be, I may surely be granted this omission – whether it springs from vanity or a fading memory I leave to you. For neatness' sake, I could offer 1400, so my birth and the century's are joined. To add a flourish, I might give a saint's day, John the Baptist's, June twenty-fourth. But those are games for chroniclers. I am past threescore but less than seventy. You have an abacus to work it out. Closer than that I will not come.

My first years were spent ... Can I ride straight past them, too? Since I have kept few impressions of infancy, better that page of life stay blank. Only a single early memory will I own. It is dusk in the kitchen, and I am lying contented in my crib. Overhead, clothes are drying from a rack. By the hearth, my mother is telling the maid how to sew britches and nagging the cook to add more pepper to the stew. Beyond the door, a horse clops by, carrying some bearded wool-trader from market. The click of hooves without, the clank of pans within, the drift of woodsmoke in the rafters, the murmur of women absorbed in homely tasks – I feel at peace among them, as though still wombed or cauled. Suddenly, at the side of the cradle, a moon rises – my brother Friele smiling palely down. Pleased to have his attention for once, I smile back. Next thing my smile is wider still, for at the other side of the cradle a second planet has risen, the shining crimson of my sister Else. Sun and moon, sister and brother: how blessed I am to live beneath their playful orbit! Soon my cradle, which had been stirring only gently before, as from a breeze, begins to sway this way and that, like a boat moored on the Rhine. And as I laugh to be thus swayed between my siblings, so their eyes shining down at me gleam a little more sharply, and the swaying becomes a rocking, and the rocking becomes a bucking, and the bucking becomes a gale, and the gale a storm, and the storm a tempest, till the wooden vessel I am encribbed in is being tossed wildly to and fro. Now my content has turned to panic, and my laughter to fear. Too shocked to find my voice, I am at first a silent howl of rage, until my screams break open and drive the planets from the sky. Stirred to action, my mother hastens over, snatches me from the waves and takes me to the harbour of her bosom: 'Oh, Henne, poor little Henne,' she croons. Through my sobs and tears, I cannot find her nipple at first, but soon I am feeding and content again – my little voyage happily concluded in a lapping haven. Or so it should be. But in my memory there is more to come. The maid pricks her finger with a needle. The cook upsets a pot and scalds her hand. My mother, rushing to help, parts me from her breast and I am thrust half-fed back in the cradle – where I sob and bawl at being so rudely cast out. When my eyes clear from weeping, what I see is Friele and Else come back again – not to taunt me, but to take up residence at my mother's breasts, one to each teat, she (between scolding the maid and bandaging the cook) calmly allowing it. And so night falls in the kitchen.

With what clarity that episode is *printed* on my memory! Even now the impression returns unwilled whenever I see a starlit sky, as though the galaxies were the profligate spray and scatter of all the milk intended for me but given to my siblings instead. And yet, in all honesty, I distrust the recollection. No infant can see back to the cradle. Friele and Else must by then have been long past weaning. And surely my mother, however distracted, would not have missed their roughness with me nor forgiven it so easily. No, that this is the sole picture retrieved from my first five years on earth suggests to me, when I study it cold, not a real event but a sentiment which infected my childhood – the feeling that I, as the third-born, came last in my mother's affection.

Best call it not a memory but a dream – though one dreamt for good reason, since in dreams lie the achings of the soul. Whatever the truth of that episode, from it was formed this firm resolve: that since I came last in the family, I would be first at something else.

As for the rest of my infancy, it is a passing lantern-show of swaddling bands, sore gums, wooden rattles, tops, hoops, rods, whips, tears, tantrums, messed underclothes, pulled hair, grazed knees, teeth left under pillows, burning candle-wax, stone flags, water-rats, whiskery old aunts, causeless laughter and unreined grief. I do not mourn the loss of such detail as would make these phantoms live again in all their vigour. Once his forelife has been closed off from the mind, a man becomes free to pursue more profitable meditations. To recollect infancy would be to dwell perpetually in its foetid prison. Since it prefers to forget itself, I choose to forget it too.

What did I get at my mother's bosom? I am tempted to say nothing of sustenance, but that would be unjust.

Letters and numbers: she taught me those. Writing, too. We had a goosequill in the house, and an inkwell to draw from, and she inducted me in the art: which angle to hold a pen at so the ink flows freely from the nib; how I should bend and raise my wrist so as not to smudge the script; what pressure to exert so as to keep from blotting or making holes in the paper. She also taught me how to write down who I was. Since we lived at the Hof zum Gutenberg, which had been in the family for generations, Gutenberg (according to custom) should have been my name. But because the house was not legally ours, in writing, I was called after my father's ancestors, Gensfleisch – Gooseflesh. Even my first name caused me confusion. On paper, I wrote Johann. But my parents called me Johannes, Johann, Hengin, Henchen, Henne, Hans and Hen, according to their whim or my behaviour. The shorter the name, the fonder they said it.

But I could not foretell, at any moment, which one I would be.

The difference that a name makes I learned one winter afternoon, when coming home in a jerkin stained with blood. Our favourite game in those days was to kick, pull, drag, harry and bully any new found rat-corpse we came across, which we did often enough (the city fathers, long *plagued* by rats, had begun to lay down poison in cellars and yards). The older, stiffer corpses swished drily over the cobbles, like a stone across ice. The newer and softer, being plump with lately arrested blood, were less obliging in that way, but had the advantage, if prodded with a sharp stick, of springing generous leaks. That day, I was out playing alone when I discovered a large rat-corpse in the snow. Prodding the stomach open, I then gripped the tail between finger and thumb, and dragged the corpse along the street, observing to my delight the even flow of red blood across the snowy cobbles, as straight as if drawn with a ruler. At the end of this line, I made bold and swirled the rat about, in a circle, so that a decorative red stain, or curlicue, was deposited, like an illuminated letter at the head of a page.

My first experiment in printing? If you must read it so. But for me the episode had another meaning. The hour was late. My britches were torn. I had lost my cap somewhere in the dusk. I suspected I might be in trouble, and as I neared home the sound of my father (in his sternest voice) calling 'Johannes' confirmed the thought. I turned into our street. There he stood at the open door. Seeing my messy clothes and hands, he ducked inside a moment, then emerged holding a horse-whip. I dropped my head, and – as I reached the doorstep – adopted the most piteous attitude, like a pickpocket silently pleading for his life. My father stood unmoved, testing the whip on his open palm, and I resigned myself to a thrashing. But then my mother appeared beneath his raised arm, saw my expression, shrieked loud at the sight of blood, and snatched me from the jaws of chastisement: 'Hen, Hen, who has done this to you?' she cried. That the blood splashed about my hands and clothes was not mine, nor even human, my mother could not know. Grasping this as firmly as I had the rat's tail, I forced a sob from my throat and let her imagine I had been set on by a gang of older boys and sorely injured, these being conclusions which my mother's frightened babble led her to: 'Dear dear ... scraps with lads ... little Hen ... so small to be doing battle ... come to Mutti.' For fighting with other boys, my father might still have given me a whipping. But having no answer to my mother, he put the whip down and left us alone.

I had thought to go to bed bumsore and hungry. Instead, when she had at last done cooing over me, my mother bathed me, gave me a fresh peach (no small treat), and nursed me to sleep by singing lullabies. Oh happy outcome! I put it down to my discovering how to wheedle. And also how to lie – not by actively propagating falsehoods but by letting others talk themselves into a position of untruth.

Lying and wheedling I used later in my business dealings. This is what I learned at my mother's bosom.

꓿

My father was stern, but also unruffled. Tall and thin-faced, he never rushed at anything, nor worked himself into passions, having the ease of one in a stained-glass depiction of Calvary, who stands apart and quite unmoved. Though we children saw little of him, and that only at night, he seemed at ease with who he was and how he lived – unlike my mother, who was more of a Mary Magdalen, wearing her unhappiness like a shroud.

Her misfortune was to have been born to a family of *shopkeepers*. To be precise, her father Werner ran the 'stone-built store', so called, I assumed (grandpa Werner was by then long dead), to give it airs, the stores around it being lowly wooden shacks. My mother was sensitive about her ancestry. If ever the subject arose, which she took pains to ensure was rarely, she would narrow her eyes, draw herself up to her full 4 feet 10 inches, push out her bosom, and boast that her mother had first been married to a Fürsten-berg – 'practically *nobility*'.

I could not help but notice my father's condescension at these intimations of high birth. Not that he uttered a word. Not that he bothered to enter his own more solid claim. But the raising of his left eyebrow, the faint smile across his lips, the feigned attention to some other more weighty matter – these spoke volumes. His relations – our *true* relations, so we understood – were wealthy patricians to a man: silk-merchants, brokers, judges, long-distance traders, compan-ions of the mint, with houses in the best part of town and country estates (to which they would retreat in summer) running over with wheat and wine. Our affluence was almost level with theirs, but our standing fell below, on account of my mother.

My father, some fifteen years older than she was, had been married before – and had a daughter, my stepsister Patze, to show for it. Like the stone-built store, this earlier marriage of his was not a theme my mother discussed, but we understood that his first wife had come from a rich family and that when she died her wealth had been added to his. With this behind him, and rich relations working alongside, my father could afford his lofty air. He was the wry, almost indolent half of the marriage, while my mother scurried about and constantly got into a stew. Though we were comfortably off, with several servants, she contrived to torment herself with anxieties – the roof was leaking, the cook was stealing, the chimney smoked, rats were in the cellar again, the slop-pail needed emptying, we children were foul-mouthed and lazy, her lungs were choked with dust, her head ached from running the household budget, God only knew what was to become of her. My father would return from the cloth-warehouse or the mint in expectation of a quiet supper and jug of Rheingauer, only to be met by this torrent of woe. He would listen patiently, and suggest remedies, but my mother refused all help, in part because she judged domestic matters to be the sole province of a wife, in part because she thought that sorrow was her lot. I was too young to grasp it then, but see now that her tears and frettings betrayed a deeper misery about her station. Because she did not feel the true or equal owner of it, she thought the house was falling apart. And because my father had been married before (and to a rich, tragic, beautiful young woman), she thought she came a poor second in his affections.

As the years passed, my father's face, as he came through the door, no longer wore the expectation of a peaceful evening ahead – indeed, he took to coming home as late as possible, having consumed his jug elsewhere. With no one in whom to confide her worries, my mother was forced to cry alone. I remember once coming upon her in an upper room. 'Oh, Henne,' she sobbed, her voice mingled with the ring-doves (those most self-pitying of God's creatures) moaning and glooming in the eaves. 'You would not understand,' she said, hugging me close to her salt-smeared cheeks. It was true. I did not. But guessed it had to do with shopkeeping. Her tears ran down my neck in a little stream. Poor Mutti. The weeping martyr of her father's stone-built store.

That I too would pay a price for family shopkeeping neither my father nor my mother told me. Perhaps they thought me too young, and meant to tell me later. But soon, thanks to my cousins, I found out.

𝒟

My cousins were Frilo and Ruleman, whose country house I was sent to each summer so that my mother be spared some weeks of having to care for me. They were twins one year older than myself, gold-haired double selves I had trouble telling apart till Frilo got the bigger mouth and became leader. Being close in age, we played together. And what we played at was being knights. For swords and daggers, we had beech sticks. For lances we had reeds from the banks of the Rhine. For horses, we had our own galloping legs, though sometimes, if a servant could be nagged to spare one, we rode an ass. Our crusades took us far and wide, through Christendom and beyond. Many a dragon lay bleeding in the orchard. Many a haystack was scaled so that a maiden might be rescued from a castle tower. These were our triumphs the long day. Then when we lay abed, Frilo and Ruleman would spin stories through the night – the conquest of an Infidel army in the Holy Land, or of a lady's heart in France.

When we were young, talk of fighting stirred us most. Shining *lances*, azure *bucklers*, broken *baileys* and burnished *swords*! Our fondest wish was to crusade against the Muslims. Closer to home, we had the Jews, who despite being scarce in Mainz since my great-grandfather's time (when some hundred of them had been burned to death on suspicion of having spread the plague), were rumoured to poison wells, carry tails under their skirts, drink the blood of infants, and commit other sins, such as usury, which we in service of God should ride to war against. (I had never seen a Jew, since they kept to their own quarter, but believed like any other Christian what was said against their faith, and later in life made a policy not to borrow from them, for fear of being deceived.) Such were the enemies we dreamt of trampling under our hooves. But as I grew older, my thoughts moved to another kind of conquest. What kind of lady would I win when I grew up? How did one lay siege to a panting heart? The heads of Frilo and Ruleman also ran with such mysteries, and they would trace for me the blessed features of girls they knew – cherry lips, swelling bosoms, cascading locks – who after such fanfare could not help but seem disappointing if later I met them. Once, we roped a girl called Gretchen into our play ('rope' being no idle metaphor, since we had tied her arms about with strands of hemp and placed her up against a tree, telling her she was a Rhine maiden unjustly accused of witchcraft and that we would deliver her from being burned at the stake). Afterwards, we lay in the grass with her and each of us in turn essayed a kiss. It was me she resisted most fiercely, which since her teeth were crooked and her breath smelt like cabbage I did not much resent. But I minded Frilo and Ruleman laughing at me for it later.

'It is because she thought you too young,' said Frilo.

'And because you are not one of us,' said Ruleman.

Frilo glanced at him sharply, and Ruleman at once looked bashful and put his arm round me. I think their parents – my aunt and uncle – must have set a rule that they should speak as though we were family together and all alike. But now Ruleman had let slip that whereas my cousins might be knights riding to battle, I came of humbler stock. I pressed them to tell me where the difference lay: why was I not one of them? They blushed and would not speak at first, but it came out. To have power in Mainz, a man must be one of the *Münzerhausgenossenschaft*, a Companion of the Mint. So my father was. So their father was. So would Frilo and Ruleman be. But thanks to the stone-built store on our mother's side, neither I nor my brother Friele could be admitted. Never to belong! Never to shine where coins were struck! Friele being the first-born would at least inherit our father's cloth business. For me the loss was greater.

'Have no fear. We will strike coins for you,' said Frilo.

'As many gulden as you like,' said Ruleman.

'How many to buy a Gretchen?' I asked.

'Gretchen you can have for nothing,' they laughed, and we chased off across the orchard hoping to catch her.

I feigned a carefree air, but the shadow of grandpa Werner had fallen, shutting me in darkness and blotting out my sun. Years later I would look on this confinement as a sweet release: if I did not fit in my own class, then I would find another, or live outside all groups. But that summer, it felt like punishment and exile. When we played at being knights in the orchard, I kept always a little apart.

Pale-skinned beneath the shade of fruit-trees, I watched my cousins turn gold in the summer heat. They were mint-boys, born to strike coins and ride fast stallions. I was the heir of grandpa Werner, born to be left out.

I had my father's face, everyone said so – pale and thin and rather studious. But I did not have his hands. Gensfleisch hands are large, with fingers crooked from raking in coins. My hands were small, with long straight fingers. How I had come by them no one knew, since they were nothing like my mother's or those of any relation. Pickpocket hands, a teacher once called them. Others said I had fingers like candles, like needles, like arrows, like knife-blades. But I preferred what was spoken by Brother Erhard (of whom more later): 'They are hands like the pens of scribes – as though they could write by themselves.'

The more men talked of my hands as something uncommon, the more I looked at them, and in private held them up to my face, to tell me what to do. I would move my ten fingers in turn, each like a single tongue wagging, then wiggle them all together, like a cacophony of voices clamouring at me. Each advised a different course in life – to do *this*, or then again *that* – but they agreed that whatever I did my hands were my greatest asset. 'Use us,' they cried. 'We were given to you by God.'

My hands became objects of private study for me, and meditation on them a form of prayer. I would contemplate the back of them. New moons rose in my nails. Veins lay in puffy blue tracks across my wrist, as if a mole had burrowed there. Or I would gaze on the cracks in my palm, which ran like rivers till they fell off the edge of the known world. I had been raised to think that working with my hands was below my dignity. 'Let a servant do it,' said my father, if anything needed making or mending. But I had read in the Bible that the sleep of a labouring man is sweet. And I was taught that in Ancient Greece and Rome engravers were prized even more than poets. I wanted to make things with my hands.

The boys I mixed with at school had fathers who were tanners, smiths, carpenters, cobblers, rope-makers, linen-weavers and masons. They were rough-tongued boys compared with me, and had no head for learning. Yet when they talked of their fathers I would listen with envy. One of them, Martin, befriended me, or so I thought. His father was a carpenter, and during prayers, as we knelt, I would whisper questions about the art – what tools were needed, which woods yield best to blades and suchlike. He had no answers, and looked puzzled at my asking, but one day, after lessons, invited me to watch his father at work. Leaving school, we bore left towards the work district. A broad lane led us, till Martin tugged me off into an alley, and then another, and another, each one narrower than the last, my excitement growing at each turn. Somewhere ahead, like a grail or altar, lay the workbench of Martin's father, whose glory – the shine of his chisel! the glow of his wood shavings! – I was impatient to behold. In an alley danker than any before, a huddle of boys stood barring our path, Martin's brother Matthias among them. They were like a knot meaning to tie us – or rather tie me, for Martin slipped from my side to join them, part of the plot.

'Where are you going, Gensfleisch?' said Matthias, stepping out from the ruck to jab me in the ribs.

This Matthias was a hulking carrothead two years older than myself. Though a dunce in lessons, he ruled the schoolyard like a tyrant. Till then I had escaped his notice. But Martin must have told him of me. His hands were like paddles now, pushing me back.

'What do you want here?' he asked.

'Anyone can pass along these streets.'

'Not you,' he said, taking hold of my arm. 'Your skin is too white. Look at it, boys. Look at the Gensfleisch.'

By now he had ripped my sleeve, and was plucking at my freckled arm, as though pulling feathers from it. The other boys laughed. In the midst of them was a red-faced tubby, loudly chanting my name:

'Gooseflesh, gooseflesh, gooseflesh.'

I stared down at my arm, the hairs standing from shock, the skin pimpled with fear. Lifting my head, I looked up straight into Matthias's face, waiting my fate. The red-faced tubby was urging 'Beat him, Matty'. But perhaps Matthias felt pity for me, as too small to merit the torture they had planned.

'Stay with your own gaggle, Gensfleisch,' he said, letting me go.

I turned and ran, out of his hands, away from sneaking Martin and the red-faced tubby. Lost among the maze of alleys, I came out at last by the river, and from there could navigate myself. My arm hurt from Matthias's grip, but my hands were undamaged. Next day I did not speak with Martin, nor he with me. But it was truce between us. Nor did Matthias trouble me again. The only injury was to my pride. Gooseflesh – and that red-faced tubby chanting out loud.

The mint-boys liked looking down on me. The guild-boys hated looking up. Well, then, I must live in limbo, in between.

2. School

In brief, before I continue, since it came only this morning, I must mention a letter from Herr Doktor Konrad Humery, one of those in Mainz who loves me still. He writes that my house in Mainz is free to return to, the students who were given it for lodgings having been forced to leave. He hopes I will think about returning – we could then see more of each other, which my being in Eltville prevents: 'Most of us who were sent out have since come back. Will you not do the same, Johann?' Well, I shall pay a visit in secret perhaps. But I will not again settle in Mainz. I am too bitter. This amnesty comes too late.

For I have not been candid about my circumstances here. 'Retirement' I called it. Exile would be closer. Two years ago I was banished – not from my native land but, a worse fate, from the town of my birth.

A summons to the Dietmarkt. Eight hundred of us, coralled there like sheep in a pen. We have come expecting to be made to swear allegiance to our enemy, the new Archbishop. Instead of which, we are told that we must leave, that our homes and possessions will be forfeit, that we are banished. Soldiers to the right and soldiers to the left: the Swiss with their crossbows, the others with their swords. To walk between and hear them curse – 'heretic', 'traitor'. To walk between and feel their spit. It does no good to turn the other cheek when both are wet. Tears, phlegm, anger, shame: I am too old for this. I have suffered enough already. I deserve the peace of age . . .

This, as I say, was just two years since, though it seems a hundred. They took my tools and type, and drove me out. They gave my house to a lackey of the Archbishop, then afterwards leased it to law students. Others suffered worse, I do not deny it. And a year ago, our banishment was lifted, so that many, like Dr Humery, returned. Now, they wish the rest of us back. They need our arts to make the city prosper. I do not doubt Dr Humery has been leaned on to write me. Still, I choose not to oblige them. If students have had my house, what state must it be in? They will have pissed in corners, kicked holes in the walls, broken my plates and pots. Even were it heaven-clean, I would not return. For the present – perhaps until my death – I will stay here.

My first school was near home, at St Christoph. I have happy memories of it, apart from the time I was bullied. We learned to count and write. We got the Book of Psalms by heart. We charted distant stars. We chanted from our grammar book to the beat of a teacher's cane:

'How many are the parts of speech?'

'Eight. Noun, pronoun, verb, adjective, participle, conjunction, preposition, interjection.'

See, I have it by heart still, tribute to the power of repetition. I confess that as a boy these rotes oppressed me. But children cannot be left to learn for themselves, else knowledge would never come. To copy over and over is the *fount* of wisdom. This rule I apply also in printing.

Arithmetic in that school was taught with arabic numerals. It was only when I had grown the legs for my second school, at the monastery of St Viktor, a three-mile walk from home, that I found what heresy these symbols were. Asked on my first morning to write down one to nine, I put the numbers as my old teacher had shown me – 1, 2, 3, 4, 5, 6, 7, 8, 9 – and felt proud at forming them neatly. But Brother Benedict, the ancient monk appointed my new teacher, whose only hair sprouted from a large brown mole on his left cheek, shook with rage when he saw what I had done.

'What Infidel language is this?' he bawled.

'They are numbers, master.'

'They are the work of Satan.'

It cannot have been the first time he had met the Devil's numbers – other boys before me (my brother Friele among them) had come from St Cristoph to St Viktor. Yet he acted as if I were Lucifer and he appointed by God to stop the Fall. His hands still trembling, he condemned my error and said if I should ever repeat it he would himself *beat* and *whip* me, which from his purple face and basalt eye I did not doubt. Seeing how I trembled myself, he spoke more mildly to me, and having slashed out my offence with angry flourishes of his pen (as though caning the numbers with ink), he tenderly crafted his chaste reply: I, II, III, IV, V, VI, VII, VIII, IX.

'Observe,' he said, 'the pure and beautiful simplicity. With roman numerals, you need master only three signs to write nine numbers.'

Not wishing to anger Brother Benedict afresh, I hid the thought that some roman numerals require several strokes, in the case of VIII as many as four. What was *simple* about that? And why IV and IX – where was the logic? Another matter puzzled me, too:

'May I ask a question, master? How do I make nought?'

'There is no such sign,' he said, freshly displeased. 'As a Christian, you must forget the notion of nought. In God's universe, everything is alive and inhabited, even hell. There is never nothing.'

'But how can I do sums without a nought?'

'I repeat: there is no such number. The closest God allows us to come to nothing is purgatory. But even purgatory, though an in-between, is still a living place, not nought.'

'Then how do you make ten?'

'A ten is written thus: X.'

'And if you wish to multiply a number tenfold, is the same rule followed? When three becomes thirty, is it IIIX?'

'No, thirty is XXX.'

'So eighty is eight crosses rather than an eight and a nought?'

'No, eighty is LXXX – the L standing for fifty.'

'And one hundred, which I write as one and two noughts?'

'One hundred is C, which you can remember, if you wish, as standing for Christ our Lord – whereas nought is the sign of the Devil. What could be clearer? We have spoken enough.'

In Brother Benedict's opinion, boys should not speak but only listen. And he did not consider we were listening to him unless we sat rigid with fear. Fear of himself he implanted but also fear of God, who we thought must have his basalt eye and thunderous temper, if not the moly cheek. We hoped by being well behaved to make Brother Benedict look more kindly on us, and for God in His turn to love us too. But these hopes were swiftly dashed. God, said Brother Benedict, was much displeased with His creatures. Men and women, young and old, high and low – all were doomed. The Reckoning would soon be on us. The light of Revelation was at hand.

'And the sea will rise a hundred feet above the mountains, like a mighty wall. And trees exude a dew of blood. And earthquakes lay men low upon the ground, and buildings fall. And the mountains turn to dust. And the dead walk out of tombs. And the stars fall. And the heavens and earth burn to nothing. And these shall be the signs.'

In such fashion, Brother Benedict filled us with doom. His mole twitching as he spoke, he seemed elated at the prospect of Apocalypse. He did not mention Resurrection, and none of us dared ask.

Each day I woke in terror of Revelation. Each night I slept in terror of Doom.

After a year or two – passed mostly in trembling – with Brother Benedict, I moved into the class of Brother Erhard, a younger monk newly arrived. Though as hot for learning, he had a temper less Apocalyptic. Having supped on new ideas in Paris, he could not care if the numbers we used were roman or arabic so long as they added up. Puzzles of logic were a hobby of his: if three men crossing a river each with his sister (and none trusting her virtue with the others) should have a boat only big enough to carry two, how might all safely reach the other side? He made us also reason and philosophise. Piety towards God was ever his aim, and Doubt must have its limits, but he liked us to debate with him. Since I was eager in all subjects, and had a mouth ready to argue, he was pleased with me.

He loved my hands especially, which he thought, being dexterous, were 'gifts from God'. When we were set some Biblical text to copy, I would take infinite care over the spacing, the angles, the depth of the ascenders and descenders. And at the end, mine would be the paper brandished in class.

'Here, boys, look at the beauty of the script,' Brother Erhard would say. 'Regard the elegance of the strokes. It is more like woven tapestry than parchment. This is a hand guided by God.'

He loved my hand the more because of his, the backs of which were blotched with purple, as if when a child he had been leprous and must forever wear this badge of his disease. His other mark of distinction, he being otherwise fair and in rude health, was his right eye, which bulged more brightly than his left, and looked to have been stolen from a different man, or perhaps from a creature, say a hare. While his left eye swivelled like any other, this right stood fixed in its socket, as though it had stared too hard one day and become frozen there, unable to climb back under its lid. The eye made me feel awkward to be alone with Brother Erhard. In class, during debate, I could look above him or to either side of his head, but alone I did not know which eye to meet. There were also those hands, which during lessons would sometimes rest upon my shoulder or, if commending me, pat my back. Though happy to have my work praised, I feared being touched by purple blotches. I did not in earnest think him leprous, but boys that age are cruel, and once the Leper became his name among us, to distinguish him from the other monks at St Viktor – the Hunchback, the Pig, the Furnace, the Cesspit and the Mole – I could not banish the notion.

To touch is a common habit between men and boys. When some days I look over your work, Anton (though my eyes are too poor to see it clear), do I not place a hand upon your shoulder? It is sweet and gentle human currency, which gives pleasure to us both. But with Brother Erhard that pleasure was mixed with fear. I liked his lessons. I liked his mind and voice. I liked his gentle manner. But his touch made my skin creep, like gooseflesh.

Next time he touches me I shall bite him, I vowed. Though I lacked the courage when next time came, after a fashion I did bite him, as you will see.

_J_

I saw little, in these years, of my brother and sister. Friele went off to study in Erfurt. Else married Claus Vitzthum, and filled out like a fat robin even before she was got with child. My happiest moments were with my stepsister, Patze (daughter of my father's first marriage), who against my mother's wishes would sometimes visit – and be waiting for me with goat's milk and oatcake when I came from school. Having herself been parted from schooling when young – *stripped* and *robbed* of it, as she put it – she had an appetite for study, and sat with me by the hearth. Even the *Donatus*, my Latin grammar book, warmed her interest. *Amo, amas, amat, amabus, amatis, amant*: so we would drone together by log-flame and rushlight. There were other verbs too: it was not only love we made. But love of a sort it was between us. She became less stepsister than stepmother to me, while my true mother hounded the servants or lay in bed. By that fire, we read extracts from such priestly-pious texts as my father owned. But the *Donatus* was our holy book.

Had the monks at St Viktor known of our studying, they would have condemned it, saying that women *contaminate* knowledge ('did not Eve teach Adam evil?'), and that no book should pass between their hands. But I loved those evenings with Patze – the flicker of candle-flame, the glow of logs, the *Donatus* between us – and did not forget them.

I was pressed to think of joining the Church. My mother thought to nourish me at the Virgin's bosom. My father hoped to robe me in a cassock, since he had no place for me in his cloth business. 'The Church would suit you,' they said. Brother Erhard said so too. I could train as a priest. Or be a clerk for the Archbishop of Mainz. Or, if I craved more scholarship, enter a monastery. All this I had explained to me at length.

I had a calling, everyone agreed, and for a time I wanted to believe them. I laboured to perfect my hand. I knelt for matins on cold stone. I bowed my head to the stained-glass Jesus and his blue-robed mother. I sang Gregorian chants with all my heart. When the monks who taught us hymned the glory of times past, mine was the voice at highest pitch.

Life has lost its colour since the time of Noah.
Now youths no longer study.
Wives do not keep faithful.
Priests are in the alehouse.
Birds fly before they are fledged.
Everything is out of joint.
The earth is drawing its last breath.

I loved to sing. So though I hated the meaning of these dirges, and wanted to chant the opposite (that the world had just been born, and needed suckling, and with care would grow), I hid my dissent inside my throat, and meanwhile won praise for my vowels, my tunefulness, my perfect clarity.

This praise did not endear me to my fellow pupils. But since few of them hankered for a future among monks, their persecution of me was mild – stray taunts rather than daily

27

crucifixions. The more Brother Erhard favoured me, the more it was understood: poor Johann would be assumed into the Church. The assumption might come once I left school, or after I had studied at university, but come it would. This stood fixed as the Pole Star. I had been chosen. The book of my life had already been written and bound. I was to be entombed.

Why it grew to seem an entombment I cannot say. But one day came the chance to play heretic – and escape.

Brother Erhard asked would I help him prepare the chapel for vespers. The tasks were few and menial, and merely a pretext – so I sensed – for us to confide in private. We stood together gazing upon the altar.

'When you look at the candles, what do you see, my son?'

'I see the wonder of God shining through the world.'

'Anything else?'

'I see the undimmed purity of the Virgin.'

'Anything else?'

'I see the spirit of their only son Jesus Christ, begotten not made, whose miracles are a beacon for all men.'

Such were the answers he had taught his class to give. Next, I knew, he would ask me about the bread and wine. In the pause before he did, I said:

'And . . .'

'Is there something else, my son?'

'And when I look at the candles on the altar, I notice there are twelve of them.'

'For the twelve apostles. For the twelve months of the year. That is correct.'

'Also I notice that the candle on the far right has burned much lower than the others.'

In the pause of catching my breath to continue, he said, in a kindly tone:

'And you infer a divine meaning in this?'

'No, father. I think that candle may have burned lower because of standing in a draught from the cloister.'

He laughed a little nervously. I plunged on.

'For I also notice that the candles to the right of the altar have all burned lower than those on the left. And though it

28

may be unwise to read too much in this, since it is possible they are merely older candles, having burned for longer than the candles on the left, or else by chance they were shorter to begin with, the likelihood is that all the candles were placed on the altar together and were originally the same length.'

'These are worldly thoughts. I am not sure where they lead.'

'They lead to other speculations, father. For instance: does a candle burn more slowly in an airless place? Also: given the same amount of wax, which burns the faster – a candle twice the length and half the thickness, or one twice the thickness and half the length? Again, I cannot help but notice that the fifth and sixth candles to the left of the altar have by chance been placed closer together than the others, and as a result the altar rail beneath them shines more brightly at that point. This might suggest that if the abbot wishes to command a better view when dispensing the bread and wine, the candles should be otherwise disposed, since the light given out by several candles placed close together is greater than when they are evenly spaced.'

'The candles are firstly symbols. Their use is secondary.'

'But to use them well does not diminish them as symbols. Whereas in this case their arrangement as symbols has diminished their usefulness.'

'These are interesting notions. But I am not sure how they profit us.'

'Profit is exactly my concern. At the altar I see waste and imperfection, which are surely an affront to God.'

'If a man has his mind on the next world, God is not affronted. The affront is when we fall into lowliness. As Johannes says in the Bible: "Love not the world, neither the things that are in the world. If any man love the world, the love of the Father is not in him."'

'But can we not seek to improve the world?'

'The world is not for us to improve, but for God. All change and novelty must come from Him. Think of your Johannes again: "All things were made by Him; and without Him was not any thing made that was made."'

'What about the wheel?' I asked. 'Has not man learned to build houses and make canals and dig wells?'

'Yes, through God man has learned these. But by himself he should innovate nothing, for this is to find fault with the Creator. To be charitable, to relieve the poor, to look after the sick: in this way we can please God and improve the lot of our fellow men. But if we essay more, that is hubris.'

'Do you think I am guilty of hubris?'

'In relation to the candles?'

Brother Erhard smiled, ready to take me back in the fold. 'You are a young man, with passion and ideas. A degree of exuberance is not hubris.'

'But I have other thoughts, father. I think of how the communion plate might be better fashioned, with a deeper curve. I wonder about reducing the thickness of lead in the stained-glass window, to allow more light in. I ponder the texture of vellum in the books we read, and how it might be smoother. My meditations tend always to those adjustments which would make life more comfortable – the preservation of food, the heating of houses, the provision of fresh water, the hastening of transport, the disposal of waste. I cannot banish this habit of thought.'

'In time, perhaps, God will banish it for you.'

'I do not think He wants me to banish it. In any case, I will not let it go.'

Brother Erhard opened his mouth, on the brink of a reply, then shut it tight and suggested we pray. Though his hands were clasped, this did not stop them shaking. He did not again mention our discourse, nor persecute me for it, but I knew from his altered manner, and from the way his bulging hare's eye refused to face me, that our intimacy was at an end. He it was who had encouraged me in disputation. But once I dared to dispute what to him were sacred notions, he reached his limit with me. Though one eye of his dared to stare out, the other was sunk inward, to God, and did not like my practical philosophy. He must have spoken shortly afterwards to my parents, telling them he no longer thought their Johann fit to be a novice, for both took on an air of disappointment with me. Thenceforth, to my relief, my vocation ceased to be a theme at the supper-table.

There is a danger – this as a coda – that in recalling speech from half a century gone one embellishes it. I may be guilty of putting wisdom into the mouth of babes. But some such dialogue between myself and Brother Erhard – pressing on my low practical-mindedness – did occur. Our understanding after that day was at an end. I had unassumed myself. I no longer had a calling. I had rolled away the stone from my own tomb.

I had meant these confessions to keep to the past. When the age of sixty has gone, the present seems scarcely worthy of mention, being a dull litany of pain, gout, itches, infections, failing sight, fallen arches, cracked skin, aching joints, baldness, breathlessness, raised blood vessels and the panic of a weakened heart. If the old harp on their past, who can blame them? Their present is a tuneless melody played on broken strings.

If I were a king, busy ruling still, my present might be worthy of note. Likewise as a pasha visited each night by concubines, I would have matter for the delectation of other men. But having no power and little vigour, I cannot hope to entertain you with accounts of me as I am. Picture me here, by the window, with Anton at my elbow – his pen even now scratching down these words as I speak them, or almost as I speak them, his pace today being a little laggard – and you will understand the meaning of *retreat*. Four walls, two chairs, bed, desk, vase of flowers, pen and paper: my world has shrunk to this. My sister-in-law trundles about downstairs. Frau Beildeck's broom swishes across the yard. The cries of distant children pitter at the window, like a handful of pebbles. But in this room there is only breathing and the scratch of Anton's pen.

Still, though my scales must be tipped towards the past, it is meet on occasion to show you what lies in the other pan.

And I will now break the seal of my past narrative to report an episode of yesterday, Easter Sunday, which prevented dictation for the best of the afternoon and forced me to release Anton early with a promise to pay double if he returned this morning – an unlooked-for prize to him, since as well as the extra gulden it allowed him to go drinking at the fair, which is why he looks so sickly-sluggish today (there, he must be guilty, for he sets down every word). Around three, just as I was settling into my testament, Frau Beildeck knocked at the door to announce a visitor. None was expected, and I was tempted to ask her to dismiss whoever it was, inviting them to come back later. But Frau Beildeck, being a servant of long standing (she first worked for me in Strasbourg thirty years since) and knowing me better than I do myself, must have observed that notion flit across my face, because she added firmly that the visitor had 'come from afar'. Though this, I suspected, was hyperbole (to Frau Beildeck, anything beyond Eltville is afar), I agreed from courtesy to see the man, if only to explain why I could not. He was waiting below, and though I made noise enough clattering down the wooden stairs, did not hear me approach him. Perhaps this was as well. He was standing with his back to me in the garden. And in an instant, seeing the dark figure from behind – the broad shoulders, the powdery hair, the podgy hands clasped behind his back, the alder walking stick leaning against the wooden table – I took him to be Fust. Johann Fust. *Mein Doppelgänger. Mon diable.* My dupe.

I was by the garden wall at the time, and put my hand out to steady myself. I had not seen Fust for several years, nor thought to meet him again. What did he want with me? Had not our battles been concluded? Or was he come to make reparation? Stepping towards him along the path, I already felt discomposed. And when he turned to face me, and smiled, and I saw he was not Fust at all, having neither the furnace mouth nor pig-sweating skin, the shock made me stumble on the grass. Though no younger than I, my visitor bounded to the rescue, hauled me from the turf, and offered an arm and walking stick. I was sorely embarrassed, but my relief that he was not Fust more than consoled me.

We sat together on a wooden bench, my intention to dismiss him abandoned. He was an Italian, a builder and architect, formerly of the mint in Venice, and lately involved in the construction of the monastery at Marienthal, whence he had come (Marienthal is but a stone's throw from here – so much for Frau Beildeck's 'afar'). He is there under Nicholas Jenson, the Frenchman who worked for me in Mainz and with whom I am still in touch. Lately we have been negotiating over the production of books for the monastery, whose brethren have high ambitions and deep coffers. Fired by Nicholas's reminiscences, this Italian – Rimaggio – had resolved to meet me. At last, I thought, a print-pilgrim come to pay homage! But no, he had come for my own benefit. Knowing from Nicholas of the eye trouble I suffer – my difficulty in engraving punches and discerning letters – he wondered had I heard of eye-glasses or spectacles. I have indeed heard of spectacles, and even once tried some, in Cologne, to no avail. He said the art in Germany is still in its infancy but in Italy is fully grown. And since he has briefly to return to Venice next week, he offered to fetch me a pair – or better still, two or three pairs to choose among, since different lenses can correct different forms of eye weakness. I thanked him well, and gave him five gulden – as well as ordering up the usual jug of Rheingauer – as a token of good faith. My readiness to accept was hastened by my earlier error. If I could confuse this pleasant stranger with Fust, then my eyesight must be worse than I thought.

So yesterday's interruption of my dictation promises a happy outcome, once this Rimaggio returns from Venice. Yet I cannot wholly blame myself for the error into which I fell. Though Rimaggio, when we sat drinking together, bore no resemblance to Fust, once he stood to leave (he hoped to reach the inn at Erbach before dark), I saw he had a way of holding himself, and of stroking his chin while weighing decisions, which reminded me of my old partner. Moreover, I do not think it surprising, after what happened between us (which you will learn of in due course), if Fust should sometimes inhabit my mind. As Frau Beildeck said when I told her of it at supper: 'Fust? That man will haunt you to the grave.'

Having disentombed myself from the Church, I hoped my father might find room for me in the family cloth-trade. He had for Friele, after all. But the world was changing fast.

For years Mainz had been ruled by mint-men like my father. Now the power was passing to those who used their hands. New mayors were elected from the guilds. New laws were passed which stripped away our ancient privileges. 'There was respect and justice once,' my father moaned, like a monk at St Viktor, 'now everything is out of joint.' When he came home at night, he sat raw-eyed and sullen by the fire, my mother stroking his neck rather than plaguing him with tribulations of her own. Two or three times we left town in haste to spend weeks and months in Eltville (I was even made to go to school there). These flights were so that my father be spared from paying tax. The why and what of it I did not understand. But I shared his anger at the council 'strangling a man to death', and I read the threatening letters that were slipped under our door, and I knew our settled world had passed.

I felt loyalty to my father. But his class would not admit me to the mint. I admired the work of craftsmen. But the guilds would not admit me either. Thus I waited for a sign of what to do.

How old was I when it came? Fourteen? Sixteen? The year escapes me. But I recall the morning – shadow, hammers on metal, the smell of fish.

I had risen early. Near our house, in the market, peasants

had laid out their flax. They reeked of ancient flower water, and I did not linger, nor at the stalls selling spices from Alexandria or lemons from Castile. The barge traders beyond offered good cloth – cotton from Holland and Burgundy, silks from the Levant. But there I did not linger either, nor at the fish-market, to which my mother sometimes sent me, if the cook was ill, to buy eel or trout, a task I hated because of the slime-scales that would stick to my hands. Further on, by the Eisentor, past goats wandering the alleys, and Jews with round hats and saffron badges, lay the workshops of carpenters and smiths. Since being bullied from it by Matthias and his gang, I had never ventured into this district. But I was older now, and less fearful, and – helpless to resist – found myself drawn inward by the music of the guilds. The pinging of chisels, the clobbing of hammers, the huffing of saws: what sweet cacophony! Some men stood in the shadows of their workshops, others sat outside, but all were hard at labour. They did not stare, or look hostile, at a stranger come among them; indeed they scarcely noticed me. Had I been bolder, I would have liked to ask how this clasp had been shaped or that leather thong knotted or those jewels inlaid. But the men were busy and I moved on. Ahead, the street grew quieter. In one open doorway, where light fell on a dry mud floor, a girl sat sewing a wimple. Grey-smocked and barefoot on a wooden stool, she was my age or less. But her intentness, as she plucked that needle, touched her face with beauty. I hoped my eyes might catch her own, but nothing would prise her from her absorption. In the end, I shuffled my feet to make her look up. She did – and blushed. No longer taut and rapt, her face, despite the pinkness spreading over it, was plainer than I had thought. I walked away, to let her resume, but sneaking back some minutes later was astonished to find her beauty come again. I have seen that beauty many times since, in the strangest places: on scribes, goldsmiths, ferrymen, printers – even, once, on the face of a midwife delivering a tavernkeeper's child. When someone crafts at their highest pitch, thence comes the look – an attention inattentive to the daily world. A priest might say it is the beauty of God shining through creation. I call it the beauty of work.

After the quiet of that sewing room, my walk towards the river was a brutal medley. Porters brushed past lugging sacks and crates. Barrowmen wheeled casks. A ship, I thought, must just have docked – then glimpsed the Rhine beyond the city walls. What strength and majesty after the piss-smelling alleys! What wide horizons! There lay the ship, offshore, riding at anchor. Two giant cranes hoisted its cargo on to the quay. Like Frankfurt, Mainz enforced *Stapelrecht*, the right of staple: all passing ships must unload their goods for sale, so the city burghers could take their pick. It was how Mainz made its wealth – from sitting on the Rhine and getting bargains. My father said we lived at the centre of the world, not because our city was large (Cologne and Lübeck had more inhabitants), but because the wares of every nation passed through. Seeing that ship at dock did not, though, puff me with pride in the place of my birth. Rather, I dreamed of journeying by boat to some imagined elsewhere – as though stowed aboard inside a barrel and unloaded in an alien land. Just minutes since, the girl sewing her wimple had filled me with the beauty of work. Now this ship filled me with a longing to go away.

Distracted, I wandered off and must have walked down-river a mile or more. Logs floated by. Three swans lost their heads in the water. From the current came a murmur. I am not a man for river-sprites or legends of old Father Rhine. But a voice in the tide there seemed to be, and with the hair standing on my neck, I knelt on the bank to catch it. 'Follow the Rhine,' it said. 'To know what is in you, first you must travel elsewhere.' Perhaps the voice was not another's but my own, the river speaking what I wanted to hear. 'Elsewhere' it said, over and over. Hearing it, I lost track of time, and paid for this on my return, with a flogging for being late to school. I took pleasure in the soreness of my flesh. My sin was to have dreamed of leaving.

Later, when I was old enough to go to taverns with him, I used to debate with my brother Friele if it is better to journey or to be rooted. For a Gensfleisch, the latter, he said: being from an old family, we had a duty to stay and keep our place. I disagreed. I was, I told him, restless to be gone. I wanted to live in a new skin. So Friele would berate my disloyalty, and I would berate his indolence, and we would end with getting drunk and singing songs.

But the voice had spoken. To know what was in me, first I must travel elsewhere.

3. Erfurt

The first elsewhere lay not too distant. Nor did it mean breaking with my family. My brother had studied at Erfurt before me. My twin cousins were there now, a year ahead. Had they suspected my eagerness to escape, my father and mother might have felt different about sending me. But for a boy of my class university was expected, so my parents without protest paid the fees.

Fresh-skinned, I enrolled in the name of Johannes Eltville and had my lodgings at a student hostel. The new horizons soon narrowed. As a first-year, I had to keep house for honours students – to wash clothes, scrub floors, and, if the hostel budget was overspent, beg and busk in the street. The fire smoked in the hall. Easterlies blew under the door. During the long dormitory night, I could not sleep for the giggles of boys in bed with each other. I envied them the warmth. Had one climbed in with me, I would have welcomed it. Tiredness overtook me. More than once, during classes, I fell asleep. Round Christmas came an invitation to share lodgings with Frilo and Ruleman – at the house of their friend Nikolaus Fungke, one of a family of coinmakers in the Allerheiligenstrasse. I daresay my parents had a hand in it, word having got back that their Johann was not thriving. Even so, I accepted gladly. To be denied comforts may be an education. But I had learned my lesson by then, and saw no virtue in suffering.

As to my formal education, much was as it had been at St Viktor. Latin and Grammar. An unreasonable amount of Logic. Astronomy *ad infinitum*. Eternal passages of Scripture. The natural philosophy was new – so too the psychology – but I cannot say my mind expanded. Only physics fired my interest, and it proved too paper-theoretical. The lecture-room was a bare hall, with students on wooden benches arrayed before the reader in the pulpit. I had formed the impression, from Brother Erhard, that the older a student became, the more he must debate and question. Not so. The aim for us was to spew back in writing every morsel we had been fed. Our lectures passed in silence. To interrupt would have been to Doubt. What we were told was incontestable.

The one teacher I admired was Professor Hassek (I never knew him by his first name), who had come to Erfurt after being driven from the university of Prague. Fox-faced and ferret-haired, he was not a pretty fellow, the less so for having been born with a tear in his upper mouth – a hare lip – from which he might have died had not his father been a surgeon of the latest knowledge and thus able to stitch it up. It made his speech an oddity, though I ceased noticing that soon enough – after years of being stared at by a hare's eye, what more natural than to be spoken to by a hare's lip? Besides, the wisdom that broken mouthpiece put forth was greater than any I heard from smoother tongues. Professor Hassek cannot have been older than thirty, but seemed a man who had travelled wide, read deep, and thought long. Philosophy and divinity were his subjects, and alone among the teachers he liked to hear our ideas, not have his own spewed back. The topic he kept debating with us, both in and out of class (for he sometimes joined us at the tavern), was the Council of Constance, then lately ended. Had the influence of Rome grown too great? Should the German nation have more control over its churches? Should there be wine as well as bread for laymen at mass? How might God's word be brought to an illiterate population? Which order had most to recommend it – the Benedictines, the Augustinians, the Dominicans or the Franciscan friars? These matters excited us then. When any two or three of us came together, this was our discussion – aside from Frilo and Ruleman, who if they heard debate break forth would declare they must be off to 'hunt a stag'.

Though Professor Hassek dwelt among ideas, he also

embraced the world. 'Modern' to him was what men must strive to be, and he loved to talk machines: water-powered bellows, crushing mills, wood lathes, spinning wheels with flyer pedals, blast furnaces, heavy-wheeled ploughs. He enthused about three-field crop rotation, by which two pastures might be worked while only one lay fallow. He hailed the spread of mechanical clocks, which he said would alter mankind. Medical knowledge stirred him too – how to operate on a hernia, or trepan the brain, or fill with gold-leaf the cavity of a tooth. Through being his favoured pupil, I was present one day at a dissection (the art of it being new and one which many clamoured to see). This dissection, of a young woman who had died of a tumour, was held not for medical students but for some thirty of us reading divinity, in order to determine the seat of the soul. Among the blood and innards and hacking of ribs, the soul was not found. Indeed, to see human flesh being handled as a butcher handles meat made me wonder briefly at man's purpose on earth and where his spirit leaves from when he dies – thoughts that later returned, as you will see. But I was grateful to Professor Hassek for finding me a place at the dissecting table.

I had been taught that to live in piety I must turn from worldly arts and aspirations: 'Who loves the world hates God' was the refrain. Professor Hassek preached a different sermon: that God reveals his truth to labourers in work-shops and fields. He was not a man much liked – some called him a Hussite and a heretic – and within a year of my quitting Erfurt he had himself been hounded from it, stripped of his position and left to die, so it was rumoured, of a broken heart. But if any inspired me, it was him.

Lack of money plagued me in Erfurt. Despite my fees being paid, and having brought funds with me, I was forever overspent. Most of my fellow students suffered the same. If you had asked where our gulden went, we would not have known how to answer. Or rather, we would not have *chosen* to answer, knowing all too well. To offset the wooden benches, the dry Aristotelian logic, the silence demanded of us in lectures, we liked on occasion to carouse: to drink wine and brandy, gamble, ride, and consort with women. I do not say go with women, which would imply a fleshly immodesty when in my case, at that time, there was none. Though some from outside town were familiar with the farmyard act, most of us were not, and simply enjoyed the *company* and *conversation* of women, which could be bought with a glass at most inns. Such pleasure never comes cheap. And it was more than usually dear in Erfurt, which though home to a university, was no large town. Being young, and in need of night's intoxicants, we paid the price. But it was one we could ill afford.

To clear their debts to pleasure, some students found employment in stores and workshops. Others served at the very inns where on other nights they would squander their earnings. I chose a more monastic discipline, such as my schooling at St Viktor had fitted me for. I became a scribe. In the university was a stationer, an ancient, stooping, moulting Parisian called Bouchot, whose task it was to maintain a stock of textbooks – the *Donatus*, Aristotle, St Thomas Aquinas, and so on. At a price sternly fixed by the authorities but whimsically varied by him, these books would then be sold or loaned to students. A loan might mean borrowing a book for a long period of study; or it might mean – as with me – having it just a week to make a copy. To begin with, I made these copies for myself. In time, being quick and accurate of hand, and seeing the profits offered by the trade (Monsieur Bouchot would buy textbooks from departing students in order to sell them to freshmen at three times the price), I took to making two copies. M. Bouchot – having satisfied himself the text was correct – would then buy the spare. I cannot say I warmed to him. He was a man whose face, from being so long submerged in it, had begun to resemble vellum. The skin looked to have been treated with lime, scraped and stretched and left to dry, then rubbed with chalk and pumice stone. The long minutes he spent inspecting my manuscript for faults were an ordeal, since copying was supposed be done in daylight and I worried that traces might be found – a smoke-smudge here, a drop of wax there – of my working by candleglow. But M. Bouchot's praise – 'the delicacy of the line! the evenness of the spacing! such a hand!' – was worth the wait, and at first he paid me well. The books I copied were not whole texts, but pecia – four leaves, or eight pages, written in double column, for which he paid according to the number of words. For most he gave me five pfennigs, then sold them at twelve. But the day came when, having pored over my latest submission, he offered a pfennig less. At first I took it to be an error. I am, by nature, a man who seeks perfection and my copying had steadily improved. But he said I had miscounted the words, pretending they ran higher than they did, and that he needed 'to put this right before the business goes to ruin'. Perhaps other scribes had deceived him in this fashion, but I was not among them. It occurred to me afterwards that diligence had been my downfall: I had created a surplus of stock, and the supply of texts exceeded demand. This lesson in business I stowed carefully in a recess of my brain.

Meanwhile, in disgust with M. Bouchot – for whom, at the lower rate, I did but two more assignments – I removed myself to the Benedictine scriptorium on the Petersberg. Instead of taking pecia home to copy nightly alone under a candle, I worked by day – whenever study allowed – in a team of scribes. The objects of our devotion were bibles, psalters, missals and textbooks, which we copied under the light of three high windows. Payment was no better than M. Bouchot's had been. And I learned the torture of working six hours at a stretch: cramped wrists, swollen elbows, aching back, thumb and fingertips scalded by constant pressure on the quill. (All this on a good day; on a bad, in winter, my nose would drip upon the page and my toes itch madly with chilblains.) But I was taught new disciplines: how to rule a page to perfection; how to pare a quill and slit a nib; how to illuminate in different colours until a text looked to be spiked with gems. The ink was made from oak apples – gall nuts – crushed and soaked in rainwater, then stirred with a fig stick in green vitriol till it turned gummy and black. The quills came from geese (see, I could not wholly un-goose myself), the left wing-pinion curving best to sit in a right hand. It was here too I learned the ways of vellum – how calf-skin rubs smoother than goat, how ink sticks better to the flesh side, and so forth. So though the profit I made in pfennigs was small, for my later ventures I profited greatly. When some months later M. Bouchot appeared, whining at my loss and pleading to have me back, I took pleasure in declining.

There was one great irritant at the scriptorium: noise. Having hitherto scribed alone, I was used to just the scratching of a pen. Here I worked among grunts, belches, farts, moans, songs, whistles and gossip. Each scribe read the words aloud as he wrote them down. I was odd in that way, having always been a silent reader and reproached for it at school:

'I do not hear you reading, Johann.'

'I was reading, sir, but to myself.'

'That is not reading. Unless you speak the words aloud you cannot take them in.'

This I used to refute through parroting back by mouth what my eyes had seen. The teachers, though placated, would tell me henceforth to change my fashion, which I did not. I am odd, I confess it, but cannot see why we should plague our neighbours by saying out the words, which can pass straight from the page to the mind (or vice versa) without the mouth having to join in. Yet scholars and scribes keep this habit still. They call it the voice of the page, and think it more truthful than writing. With the printing of books will it die out? I hope so. In my printshop, I welcome noise as evidence of industry. In the scriptorium, I hated the jabber of those around me. So distracted was I once that in copying out the Ten Commandments, I left out the word 'not', and ordered men to steal, kill, commit adultery and bear false witness. The error was later discovered, and I made to correct it – but not before I was ridiculed and docked several pfennigs from my pay.

The scriptorium on the Petersberg being run by monks, the other noise was that of prayers, which we said three times a day. We also sometimes sang hymns, among them an Ode to All Our Labours, whose rhymes I grew to hate:

> Unless we scribes this book enhance
> By writing in God's hand,
> The words will lack His governance
> And never breathe or stand.
>
> Likewise in vain we undertake to
> Decorate the page
> Which if His brightness shines not through
> Will turn to dust and age.

The dignity of labour when God is master of the guild! With what solemnity we sang of this. But I had seen the obscenities written in margins by scribes, blistered and chilblained, whose endurance had run out. For what is noble in copying? The act is mechanical. If a monkey could be trained to copy the Bible, would its version be less holy than a monk's? I do not think so. And did not think so then.

Our masters in the scriptorium urged us to be neat and self-effacing. But in all my time there I never saw two hands the same. Because they could not put their names or be given credit, the scribes liked to parade themselves in other ways – with flourishes, blots, curlicues, misspellings and other marks of distinction. As a reader, I resent such intrusion. I like the relation with an author to feel private; I think he does too. I hold him in my hands, and he takes me into his confidence, and neither of us wants a third to come between. Print is better that way, because self-effacing. It makes the script undistinctive. It takes all 'character' out of the characters. It is oblivious, as no man's hand can ever be.

Forgive me, Anton. It is not my intention to speak ill of scribes. Even with my poor eyes, I can see how fine your hand is. And with us, since no machine has been invented to translate speech straight to print, there is nothing for it but dictation. But what I learned in the scriptorium is that the scribe is a meddler. And I began to think how to stop his meddling.

Six months before I left Erfurt, my father fell ill. A message was sent through the Brotherhood of St Viktor, one of whose number – a plum-faced priest – had come from Mainz on business and brought with him a letter from my mother, urging me home in haste.

The news was no shock. If illness is in part a state of mind, my father had been ill for years. The losing battle over tax, not to mention the losing battle with my mother, had made him waxy with defeat, and each summer on my return from Erfurt he looked a decade older. This time I returned to his corpse. I was lucky with carts, and reached home before the burial. His coffin lay open in a crypt of St Christoph, our parish church. He looked at rest at last, free of taxation and my mother's nagging. Cold though the crypt felt, a fly – a bluebottle – was crawling over his face. He must indeed be at rest, because he made no attempt to brush it from his cheek. It struck me, peering down, that I had never known him. Fathers, so I had read in ancient books, were expected to instruct their sons in manhood. But my father had scarcely ever talked to me. At the funeral, the parish priest paid tribute: much respected citizen of Mainz, apple of its eye, feather in its cap, and so forth. My judgment was harsher. My father had meant no harm and done no good.

My harshness surprised me. My grief too. Unable to face my mother, who looked to me now that Friele had a business to run and a girl to woo, I returned straight to Erfurt to complete my bachelor degree. I had been diligent. It was understood I would pass with ease, and be asked to study further, and perhaps one day be given a teaching position. Whatever appeal this had held before now fast receded. The memory of that fly returned, crawling on my father's cheek. If all his life had come to was a bluebottle in a crypt, or the worms now consuming him in the ground, how much had it been worth? By his crypt had been an ossuary, a room of bones, which began to haunt me. Though I kept faith with God, I could not keep the Devil from whispering: 'The world is an ossuary, nothing but.' Stalked by grief, eaten by despair, I ceased all study. Where once I drove my mind over hurdles of memory and deduction, now I let the reins slip. Unharnessed, I let go. Wine and beer were my forgetfulness. I passed my days at the inn, and my nights stertorous on the nearest pallet of straw. I discovered too, like Saint Augustine, the sins of the flesh, and once paid a woman to do the deed – a buck and squirt in an alleyway, which cost me what M. Bouchot paid for two pecia. Not that I worked for M. Bouchot now, or at the scriptorium. My hands shook too much, my breath reeked the acid of self-loathing. I was not fit for gentle company.

My funds would have run dry from the liquid habit had I not made the acquaintance of a cellarman called Hans. He was a broad, bear-faced, last-notch-of-the-belt sort of man, who had been a cooper once, putting hoops round casks, but was more eager now to drain a barrel than bolster it. After some hours together at the Ferryman's Haven, he took me back to the wine-cellar he was paid to guard by night. His notion of guarding was unusual, and had his master not been a feather-witted noble who stayed only rarely in town, he would surely have been unmasked. Among the tools of Hans's trade are the *gimlet*, a drill to bore a bung-hole in a wine-cask, and the *Velincher*, or *pipette*, a pipe for drawing out samples. He invited me to assist him in manning the pipette – the thief-tube or monkey-pump as it is known by sailors, whose heavy sampling of barrels during voyages is common through Christendom. A virtue of liquor is that it heats the brain, and makes the body insensible, which was as well, since the cellar-floor we lay on while we sucked was cold as sunrise. From night till dawn we sported there, sucking and snoozing like a pair of babes at teat. I learned through Hans the four phases of inebriation: we were laughing-monkey drunk, roaring-lion drunk, wailing-wolf drunk and pissing-swine drunk by turns. But after a time, I settled into my own form of drunk, which was mute and hopeless. Even Hans, the least demanding of friends, began to tire – and when the inn closed did not invite me back.

I bore the privation as best I could. But my need for his pipette growing urgent, at last one afternoon I went to his cellar. The door stood a little ajar. When no one answered my knocking, I walked through, towards a distant rhythm of wood. There stood Hans with his back to me. Instead of sucking on barrels, he was manhandling a wine-press, which creaked like a boat as he rowed it. I had seen wine-presses before, at the monastery of Eberbach. But it was the one Hans rowed that left its print. I had thought him as sunk in degradation as myself, but now I saw his day-life of labour – his hands sore from pulling the screw, muscles running in his back, beads of sweat frilling his forehead as he turned my way. He looked awkward to see me. I felt the same. He must an hour more heave at the press, he said, if I cared to stay and watch – he would then be free to drink. For a time I did observe him, and took good note. My later printing press was fashioned like a wine-press. *In vino veritas* – perhaps I owe a debt to Hans. But at the time, rather than inspire me with his example of hard work, he crushed my spirits all the more. Without bidding farewell, I slipped away, to the street, to drink alone.

My absence from lectures had not been missed at the university. Though my written work was complete, no degree could be awarded – no robe placed on my shoulders by the rector – until I had faced half a dozen examiners for a spoken test. And this test, given my condition, I was sure to fail. I lodged alone with Nikolaus Fungke then, Frilo and Ruleman having graduated the previous year. Since the onset of my drinking and melancholia, Nikolaus had kept clear of me. Indeed by the time the test was due, I had not spoken to any man or woman alive for several days. One night I heard a violent knocking at the door, which roused me from my wine-slumber. I pulled the bolt back. Professor

Hassek. His eyes, as though a mirror, told me how I looked: unwashed, unrested, unmanned. He parted me from the jug I held, threw water over my face, made me change my clothes, and cooked me a calf's liver he had brought wrapped up in cabbage leaf. Then he made me talk. I had not the tongue at first to convey my thoughts, since they were jumbled up together. But what he teased from me was Doubt. I had lost my faith in living, I said. Why strive to improve ourselves, if all we came to was a bluebottle in a crypt? It felt like heresy. But Professor Hassek did not condemn me.

'Many men before you have questioned their purpose on earth,' he said. 'From expressing this Doubt, their faith has been strengthened.'

'But to pass from the earth as though we had never been here . . .'

'If we do good we live on in the minds of other men.'

'If we do bad, we are remembered more.'

'If we do bad, we have an afterlife in hell. Whereas if we achieve good . . .'

'But our term here is so short – sixty years if we are lucky. We might as well not live at all.'

'You should not fear oblivion, Johann. You can leave something of yourself behind.'

Such was the liquor he made me sup at, in place of the wine I had abused. And into my sluggish brain were piped old enthusiasms I thought had run away into the gutter.

For the next two days, I rose early and studied. I cannot say I was fluent in the oral examination. One of the interrogators bore an unhappy resemblance to Brother Erhard, and stared at me hare-eyed, as if ready to be disappointed. Disappoint him I did, I am certain, and the other examiners as well. Then Professor Hassek spoke. 'For the final theme, would the candidate describe how he might reason with a man who doubted his purpose on earth.' He let me start, then staged an argument, he playing the part of Doubter while I spoke as a priest. It was a game only, thrust and parry, thrust and parry, but we were practised at it. His colleagues watched, listened, leaned back, smiled, conferred, then invited the rector to place the master's gown about my shoulders.

The days of book-learning were behind me. I was ready to join the world.

4. Doves

You are impatient, I can tell. You wish to know not of *studies* or *intellect*, but of an *instance* that led to my invention. Was there a moment when . . .? An experience that gave . . .? A dream, an epiphany, a visionary spark? I see what you are after. Archimedes discovered density while taking a bath. Zeno's paradoxes came from watching athletes. Surely with me too lightning must have struck? I have told of Hans's wine-press. But you find that lowly and demeaning, myself at the time having been drunk. Is there not a nobler episode to recount?

Well then, I will find you something. But first let me say that when men shout 'Eureka!' I mistrust them. I have heard that cry too often round the streets. It proceeds from hunger and mushrooms. Those who bawl it are not scientists, but mystics. To invent a thing, to bring novelty into the world, is nine-tenths practice and labour. An idea is like a child: it does not burst fully formed on the world, but grows slowly from within. And no idea is wholly new: if we see further than our parents, it is by standing on their shoulders, not by virtue of ourselves alone. We learn, observe, borrow, use, pilfer. This is true with me especially, since mine was not a single invention but several. Press, hand-mould, matrix, metal type – no moment's lightning could have given me all this.

Still, I understand the question. When one day, God willing, pilgrims begin to stream here, they will ask it of me too: 'Was there not an instant when the hairs stood on your flesh – when you saw and *knew*?' Already, I have rehearsed the scene. These pilgrims want a story to take home with them to Prague or Padua, something pleasing-simple any infant can grasp. What shall it be if not the wine-press? I could tell them how one day, while idly pressing a ring in a pot of wax (my signet ring with its Gutenberg coat of arms), the thought struck in a gunpowder flash how I might likewise carve letters in wood or stone, and stamp them on paper, and in this way print books. Some such tale might serve. But my listeners, having children at home, want something more magical. So I tell my story of the doves, not sure if they will trust a word of it – or if I do.

It was a summer morning, I say. I had gone out walking from Erfurt, a Sunday it must have been since I was not at study. The houses, the hayfields, the river's brown curve – these I left behind, and entered a forest more silent than a cemetery. Between the trees, I climbed a knotty path. The only sound was that of my own breath. Walled in by bark, with only a glimmer of sky through the pinetops, I began to fear I had left all human company for ever. I was minded to turn back, but the path now led downhill and a hint of light and running water drew me on. Some minutes later, I came out in a glade and spied a cottage by a busy stream, and below the stream the tiniest of churches. Weary from walking, I threw myself down on the grass beside the stream. From behind the cottage came the chatter of birds, blessedly noisy after the eerie silence of the wood. I had thought myself alone, but then an old woman appeared carrying a flask of water and a chunk of bread. She was dressed in peasant black, with apple cheeks and a hairy chin. I thanked her warmly for the fare, and while I busied myself with chewing and swigging she told me something of her circumstances, her husband having been a miller till he died and she now living alone. When I had my supped my fill, she beckoned me to follow her. Behind the cottage was a wooden cage – or aviary – from which a medley of birdsong rose. Drawing from her apron a handful of hazelnuts and beech-kernels, she began to feed the birds inside, all the while making chirruping sounds between her lips. Hedge-sparrows, coal-tits, wagtails, yellowhammers, robins, bull-finches, half the birdlife of Germany was pecking at her finger through the wooden bars. After a while she bid me join her in the task, which I did, liking the touch of feather and beak, but feeling sorrow that these pretty birds should be shut up. Seeing this doubt of mine, the old woman took my arm, and pulled me from the cage and pointed at the roof of the little church. With a nut between her fingers, she held her arm aloft and changed her chirrupings to a throatier sound. At once, from the church eaves, a flock of doves flew down. The throng of them through the air (like a blanket being tossed across the sky) made me fearful at first, but they whirled gently overhead, till in nervous ones and twos, then bolder threes and fours, they flew to the old woman's fingers. The birds clung to her arm, wreathing her in feathers. I expected squawks and battles between them. But either the woman had trained them, or each trusted its turn would come, for there was no squabbling. Nor did the mother birds neglect to feed their young. The woman gestured for me to copy her, which I did, the birds being at first wary of me but soon finding my nuts and grain enough of a lure. Their claws scratching at my wrist, they pecked at what I held, then flew off with food between their beaks. Back and forth to the church they blew, like scattered paper, feeding their young, and a strange peace descended on me, at having been witness to such joy and freedom.

And so we stood there like Saint Christopher, the doves eating from our hands. And that is when I knew.

When I knew what? you may ask. I have asked it myself. Even before I left the place, what happened in the forest seemed like a fairytale. So what ties it to printing books? It is this. As I stood with my hand raised, it was as if the dove that perched there spreading its wings had become an open book. And the dove departing from me was like a book taking flight. And the grain the dove held in its beak was like a kernel of knowledge seeding itself through the world. This was the vision I saw. And against it I set the memory of scribes, and of the earthbound slowness of their labour, and of the books around them shut in cases, kept from the world by lock and key. It was then I saw what I must do in life, to help words fly free as doves. I did not know how, but from that moment I resolved to find a way. This is why – I add for my audience – when I came to print my Bibles I urged those who bought them to illuminate the margins with birds, and also with trees and leaves, in honour of what the forest taught me.

This little lecture of mine still lacks some smoothness, but will polish with the telling. When my listeners return to Prague or Padua, and repeat it there, the faces of their children will fill with wonder. Like a fairground magician, I have learned the usefulness of doves.

5. Idling

Thanks to my father, I was now a man of modest wealth – or would be, when my mother ceased disputing his will (inflamed by a clause leaving some gulden to my stepsister Patze, she had set a team of lawyers on it). I need only appear once a year at the city hall to draw a healthy pension – or have it sent me elsewhere. Here was the chance to travel at last. Why did I not take it? Why for the next few years did I live – once more a Gensfleisch – in Mainz?

Partly it was my mother. She felt lonely. She wanted a man around the house for company – and since my brother Friele was occupied with his fiancée (who shared our sister's name), that man had to be me. In due course, Friele married his Else. We showered sweet peas over the bride – the same bride who, as I tongue this out, sits embroidering her widow's wimple below. Shortly after, my mother and I moved across town, to a new house, so that the true heir, the first son, the new head of the family, could move into the Gutenberghof. To judge by his grin, Friele must have talked her into it. To judge by her sighs, my mother resented it deeply and had agreed out of a sense of martyrdom. 'Your father would have thought it only right,' she said, her eyes filling with tears. A procession of carts arrived at the little high steps to carry away such chattels as she saw fit. Self-sacrificial to the last, she left behind the best (was not Friele the rightful owner now?), and took for herself only items that were crude, worn, chipped and half-broken, the kind usually found at the back of cupboards. As for the house we moved into, it was one a smith would have settled for, and a peasant killed to own, but not what my mother had been used to. Tall and narrow, it was sited at the more sewery end of town, and whenever my mother left it she held a kerchief to her face, too delicate to withstand the assailing smells.

The house had four floors, which meant much clopping up and down stairs, and my mother clopped with eloquence – sometimes rat-a-tat-tat in anger (that a woman such as her should be living in such a place!), sometimes with a slow sad drag of her widowed feet. Our best servants, as well as our best furniture, had been left behind. We had but two now – a cook and a maid – and if one of them fell ill, as happened often (they also being too delicate for the sewery end of town), my mother would have to perform tasks beneath her. She did not stoop so low as to make dinner – if the cook was ill, the maid stood in; and if both were ill, a servant would be loaned from a neighbour. But she was sometimes brought down to shopping in the fish-market. To guard against the shame of being seen there by the servants of former neighbours, she shopped late, when the fish-mongers, all but sold out, were washing the slime and roe from their slabs. Often then she had to buy fish that had been shunned for good reason, on account of lack of freshness or edibility. Though these dubious fish of hers could be part-rescued with herbs and garnishings, there was a general falling off in our diet, and this put my mother yet further out of sorts. When I returned to the house at dusk, I would listen in silence, as my father had, while she bemoaned her lot: the cold, the damp, the servants, the price of everything! To the complaints my father had borne she added one more: the discomfort of living in the new house. The move had been my mother's choice, I reminded her. But the point was not well taken. She would weep into her widow's black-edged handkerchief, and tell me at length that she could not possibly tell me what she felt.

'You would not understand,' she said. 'Every bone aches in my body. But that pain is as nothing next to feeling so *alone* and so *empty*. Do not tell me that will pass. Till I am dead, *nothing* and *no one* can console me. Even my own family, even you Johann, are no comfort now.'

The light of freedom would flit across my face then. If my

staying with her did no good, why not leave? But my mother was quick to see and snuff out the danger. Seizing my hand, she said:

'Promise you will stay here for ever, Johann. Swear on the Bible you will not leave me.'

I swore, of course. There was no choice. Despite the agues she spoke of, my mother looked in perfect health. She was only five and fifty. How long would for ever be?

'I want to work with my hands,' I said, to those who asked, which they laughed at, and took as a confession of idling. Work with your hands! Unthinkable! Every Gensfleisch since Adam had had a 'position', and one must be found for me. Friele, having been pressed to it by mother, offered a place in the family cloth-firm. But since he could use me only as a tabulator, to measure stock and draw up accounts, the offer was refused. Frilo and Ruleman, when I met them at the tavern – Zum Tiergarten and Zum Mombaselier were those we patronised – invited me join them at the mint. But all they meant was some lowly accounting position, and I did not relish having to watch them swagger about their business – all day long the image of what I might have been but for grandpa Werner would be smirking at me like a face on a coin. Nor did I want a living as a priest. I did not want numberwork. I did not want paperwork. I did not want to save the souls of men.

'I want to work with my hands,' I said. As an apprentice with the guilds I could have done so. But the guilds, having grown in power, were now more than ever a family shop, closed to outsiders, especially outsiders of my class. No statute prevented casual labour, though. And when I opened my heart one night to two coinmakers I was drinking with, they said I should come and work for them. It was an offer made in jest, from the effects of beer and brandy, but next morning at eight I was at their door. Bemused, they shook my hand and took me on as an ill-paid helper. My first jobs were too lowly even for apprentices, lighting fires and fetching water and suchlike. But having proved my willingness, I was instructed in various arts – how to strike copper, how to engrave dies, and how to regulate the heat of metals. Thanks to God having given me dexterous fingers, I held my own at most things. I even tried my hand at carpentry. But what I loved best was to work with metal. To make something so black and unyielding express a soft filigree beauty: this was a challenge I never tired of. In time, the coinmakers offered a better position. But feeling the walls close in, I moved on to another workshop. Over the months, I tried several more. It meant I was forever beginning afresh, so that I looked like a wastrel. My wages rose no higher than for the boy of twelve who sweeps the floor. But with money at home to keep me, I could afford to swallow my pride.

The tradesmen of Mainz being small in number and confined to the same part of town, my face – and my habit of poking it first in this workshop, then in that – soon became known. They called me Jo-Jo, and teased me for my flightiness: 'How long will you be with us, then, Jo-Jo?' 'It has been three months now, Jo-Jo, are you not away yet?' The teasing was kindly, if patronising: I had found my niche, as a butterfly. I laughed along with them. Better to be thought a clown than taken in earnest. Better misapprehended than understood. To a degree, I was a spy, acting under cover. But since my final purpose remained a secret even to me, I was not withdrawn or inward. On the contrary, I made merry. All my former selves were shed: the pious schoolboy, the monkish scribe, the grief-stricken, wine-dark son. In place of them came Jo-Jo, eccentric maybe, but also noisy, affable, prankish, gossipy, a lad like any other. I farted with the best. On early-falling winter nights I struck terror in my fellow workers with tales of fiends and ghosts. I was the first to pinch the rump of the wench who fetched us bread and ham at lunch-hour. I never stuck long in one place. But while I was there, I belonged.

The dream of most men, I noticed, was to own a basket of tools. Brace, bit, bow drill, lathe, punch, spanner, the kind varied but the tools must be theirs, not the property of any other man. In my head, I too owned a basket – not of tools but of skills. A basket of skills, I thought to myself, is more easily carried than one of tools. You can take it anywhere. You can use it in all manner of ways. And no man – so I thought – can steal it from you.

Meanwhile I had money to spend – the pfennigs earned in workshops and the gulden from my father's will. Mainz was called the golden city then, *Aurea Moguntia*, with no lack of places to squander the gold. There were the taverns and tap-rooms. There was the gaming-house in the flax-market. Best, there were the bath-houses. The smiths and masons had their bath-house in the Eisentor, and if I felt like larking I would go with them. But for the most part I joined Frilo and Ruleman at Mill Gate, where the bathing-women soaped you more gently and had more grace when they flirted and teased. Whores, my cousins called them. But to me they were like the water-nymphs of the Ancients – fallen angels, maybe, but angels all the same.

Bath-house angels were the only women I came close to then. The daughters of the rich I could not woo because I was *un-minted*. Nor could I approach the daughters of craftsmen: except for Midsummer Eve, when they came to wash for luck in the river, their arms wreathed in mint and sandalwood, they were kept under lock and key. So washerwomen were my comfort. Back-scrubbing was not their only service. For ten pfennigs they would take you in their mouths and for twenty between their thighs. Betrothed but not yet married, Frilo and Ruleman were eager customers and urged me to join them, 'the three of us together'. Feeling no joy at the prospect, I left them to it and stayed with Ute, an Alp of a woman nearly as ancient as my mother who, since she used hard bristles and cold water, never stirred me to seek more than the briskest scrub. But when my cousins began to cast doubt on my manhood, the bath-house angels meanwhile lamenting that without added takings they could not live, I was talked into going with Inge, a woman more my age and amplitude than Ute. It was – I was – a damp squib. Her flesh smelled of sea-coal, and though gooseflesh roasting on coal should be a fine thing, I did not catch fire. But she was kind to me, and though her lips against mine felt like leeches they acted as a cure. Next time, I let myself be creamed by little Marguerite, whose hands were soft as an infant's, whose eyes the colour of columbine, and whose skin was warm as fresh-baked bread. A true angel! Thereafter I always chose her. She told me of the poor hovel she lived in, and the child she had, and her wish for a life of more than scrubbing. Between stroking me, she sang ballads of ruined maids, and when she finished I would ask her 'Sing another', as an excuse to keep her longer and pay double the rate. Though it was only business between us, in time I felt tender to Marguerite – her infant fingers, her shining lips, her copper hair below – and came to think her my own sweet angel.

They say that in German cities the hangman's wages are paid by whores. Some now want to ban the fleshly trade. But the bath-houses are a drain to young men's urges, which without such a conduit would be blocked and fester. For me, they were a tonic to health. And though it is years since I last used them, they are a service any city should be pleased to fund.

'This cannot go on,' said Friele. 'You are become a laughing-stock.'

It was the day of the August carnival, and my mother and I were eating at his house. The day was fine and the meal pleasant enough: lentil purée, roast carp, fava beans, poached pears in syrup. But once the servants had cleared away, and my sister-in-law Else gone to rest (she being heavy with child), Friele began to berate me for my life of jobbing – my 'wastrel clowning in the Eisentor' as he called it. To my mother, the revelation of where I worked came as a shock, since I had let her think my employment more elevated. She wept into her handkerchief while Friele raged.

'To squander your life with smiths demeans the name of Gensfleisch. It shames us all.'

'But I thought these smiths were now your friends,' I sneered back. 'I hear you are cosy with them.'

Friele had close ties with the city council, on which many from the guilds now sat.

'We want to end the city's bankruptcy,' he said.

'By making our class pay heavy taxes. By surrendering the privileges which father fought to keep.'

'The times have changed, Johann. I have a family to think of.'

'Since you are working with the guilds, you cannot mind if I do the same.'

'You only work *for* them – and they laugh behind your back.'

'Let them – what harm is there?'

'Council discussions are at a delicate stage.'

'You think my jobbing will upset them?'

'It is important we reach agreement.'

'Then I have more power than I thought.'

'Your only power is behaving like a child. Unless you mend your ways, I will arrange with the guilds to mend them for you.'

'Please, please, boys,' wept my mother, from her hand-kerchief.

And so for her sake we relented and made ready for the carnival. Friele dressed up like an abbot, myself like a jester, a gulf between us as we stood fixing our clothes in front of the mirror. I knew by his threat he meant to have my jobbing ended. I knew too he would blacken my name with my mother, and make her think of me as a magpie planted in her nest. His cloth business was not prospering. My annuities would be useful. He hoped her money, when she died, would go to him.

Seething under my coldness, I slipped away and joined the crowds down by the Rhine. Since all wore masks, I could not tell who my friends were. It was as though I had no friends – because of Friele, because of the guilds, because of my mother's shopkeeping, all hope of a future in Mainz was closed to me. A harlequin led us towards the cemetery. Musicians played on cymbals and viols. When their tune died, an Adam in a fig-leaf spoke: 'You came from earth and shall to earth return.' The *danse macabre*. Now skeletons came from the charnel-house to claim us. King, priest, mason, miller and prioress, each was danced in turn over the graves and laid out on the turf for dead. A pair of knights followed next – I knew them from their laughs as Frilo and Ruleman. When made away with, they acted like men smitten by the plague, and plunged to earth clutching their throats. Soon I too lay dying in the grass, my face tickled by beetles and ants.

What was due to happen next I knew from other years. After Judgment, Resurrection. A priest commanding us 'Arise!' But before the word was spoken, some shadow passed over me, some downpress of black space, tying my limbs and pegging me to the greensward like a tent. I have never seen the Devil in person – unless his name is Fust – yet at that moment he held me tight. My body shook from fear, but the shaking did not loosen the coils. The Devil had me locked inside his book, and in its pages I read my future – an infinite and senseless endurance on earth. What had prompted this? The feud with Friele? The melancholy air of the viol? The *danse macabre* we had enacted? The memory of my dead father? I could not tell, but was fast in the Devil's press, unable to rise. Those standing around thought I was fooling, or drunk, and laughed to see me in hell and unredeemed. But when still I failed to rise, Frilo and Ruleman kneeled by my face, and pulled my mask off, and slapped me hard across the cheek, to cure me of my seizure. It took four strong men to prise me from the ground and set me upright.

As the troupe revelled back towards the taverns, I was soon forgotten. But to me, this was a vision sent from God – or grown from within, out of the soil of my own fear. That fear was being trapped in Mainz. I could not breathe within its walls. I must find a way to leave, or suffocate.

My mother would wail. My brother would feel guilty. But I would not let my family hold me. Like a fox caught in a trap, gnawing through its own limbs, I must escape.

How quick I would have sprung free I cannot say. But then, as luck would have it, my mother fell downstairs.

To her, of course, it was not luck at all. She blamed the maid, for raising a cloud of dust that hid the top step. She blamed the cook, for having brought upstairs, for her inspection, an eel (just then bought at market) which leaked water on all sixteen wooden steps. She blamed the eel-water for being so slippery that her fall, once begun, could not be halted. She blamed me, for not being at the bottom to catch her. The fall was not calamitous. She suffered no broken bones. A week of hobbling, a month of grimacing, and she was cured. But having never liked stairs – 'too steep, too narrow, too new-fangled, too many' – she now saw them as Alps of inhospitability and refused ever to mount them again.

Her climbing days behind, she moved her bedroom to the parlour. But what she wanted was to move house. Raising a limp hand from her bed, she fixed her baleful eyes on my sister Else. Let me come and live with you, the look said. But with three daughters to raise, and Claus to nurture, and a modest-sized house, Else would not be moved. The other Else, the little sparrow, Friele's wife, my sister-in-law, unschooled in my mother's wiles, was easier cracked, and invited my mother back to the Gutenberghof. Perhaps Else had her own motives: her baby having been stillborn, she was childless still, the house felt big and empty, my mother would be company, she might even bring the luck of a son or daughter. In her artlessness, Else must have supposed that the offer, having been sought, would be accepted. But in this she mistook my mother, who agonised for weeks before deciding, then changing her mind, then changing it back. 'I must do what is right for you, Henne,' she would say when nightly weighing the scales. What was right for me did not, in truth, concern her. But to declare myself frankly – as in 'I will be fine on my own', or 'I will be happy knowing Else is looking after you' or 'For God's sake go, mother' – would have resolved her to stay. So it was a fine line I trod between pushing her out the door and looking griefstruck at the thought of parting.

The uncertainties did not end the day she went. Her limp hand and baleful eye when I called at the Gutenberghof declared that misery had travelled with her: Have me back, the look said. Leaning close, I whispered, as I knew I must, that her room was just as she had left it and she could return whenever she wished. She looked at me conspiratorially, relishing the drama of defection – then brightened and talked of something else.

I did not think she would return. But to risk a change of heart would have been rash. Next day I gathered my belongings and, with a note pushed through her door bidding farewell, at last quit the city of Mainz. I never saw my mother again.

Part two

6. Journeyman

On a cool September morning I set out, imagining every flax-wagon and manure-cart would offer a lift. I was soon rid of the notion. Even when I hailed them cheerily, no driver would stop. A beer-dray with rumbling barrels clopped by without a word. An abbot rode a high grey mare, a little donkey clip-hipping behind – the donkey was riderless, the mare's saddle could have accommodated two, but the abbot stared straight past me. By lunchtime that first day, I was still only ten miles from Mainz. Disconsolate and footsore under a beating sun, I could scarce credit my fortune when a cider-faced pig-farmer slowed his haycart. The good Samaritan! I clambered up beside him, unlaced my boots and let him chatter. His talk was of outlaws haunting the roads ahead – men who would extract a purse by chopping off its owner's hand or steal a maidenhead with a dagger held to the throat. Dressed as I was – with a fine cloak and two leather bags – he feared for my safety and urged me to go by river instead. The next town lay on the Rhine, where a ferry called twice a day. I thanked him for his advice and he set me down there.

So river-roads were how I journeyed thereafter, downstream, towards the sea. First the broad highway of the Rhine – through Koblenz, Bonn, Cologne, Düsseldorf, Duisburg, Wesel – then smaller water-alleys to towns further northward. Each boat I took was different but made the same creaking and slapping as Hans's wine-press – the sound of work and freedom. Gulls called from the air. The sinew in the helmsman's arm was like the current we were running with. It did not take me long to put a nation between me and mother. The Rhine flows four miles in an hour. With a good steering oar, and a captain content to sail past dark, even more sluggish rivers – the Main, the Ill, the Lahn, the Weser – will bear you forty miles a day, further than any horse could gallop. I did not, besides, own a horse. Shoes were my only saddle. And river-roads are kinder to the feet.

From Mainz, I had taken too much baggage. I ditched the bulk of it within the week. (As Christ said: 'Leave everything and follow me.' I heeded the first command if not the second.) Soon enough all I carried were these: a cloak, which served as a blanket by night; a hat, broad-brimmed to keep the sun off my face and the rain from trickling down my neck; strong shoes (I was no barefoot pilgrim); a purse for coins, maps, provisions and samples of my writing; a pair of stones to strike a spark; and a small knife, more for cutting bread and cheese than self-defence, though in Antwerp I pulled it on a drunken soldier when he attacked me for speaking with his betrothed. I had a staff, too, which helped me beat off rabid dogs and kept me upright when fording rapid streams. The gourd hanging at my side was replenished with water from mountain springs and village wells. By asking the way from men I met working in the fields, I did not often lose myself. The further I travelled, the harder it was to understand them. But by rooting out a common tongue, as if through a mouthful of thistles, we found ways to understand each other:

'Wer pist du?' they would ask.

'I yam Johann.'

'Guane comet ger, brothro?'

'Van der hille, da.'

'Yah, but gueliche lande cumen ger?'

'Von Deutschland.'

'Hast a follo guanbe? Adst cher heute? Brot? Käse?'

'Nah. Erro, e guille trenchen ein Bier.'

For a bed and pitcher of wine, I found monasteries the best of hosts. It was their doctrine. Every man who came to them troubled in spirit or sore of feet must be taken under God's roof. I may have been favoured since I knew Latin and could show them samples of my hand. At the more visited monasteries the abbots were grudging, and I heard monks grumble that from doling out stew to pilgrims they, God's servants, were left only with soup. But at most I saw a plenitude that would have made me want to join the order but for such luxury seeming an offence against God. Could it be His divine purpose that while peasants lived off gruel and porridge, here within the cloisters were mutton, bacon, olives, fish, beer, cider and the finest wines? If night was falling, and a hostelry lay two miles off, and a monastery three, I would always walk the further distance. At the Crowns and Stars and Eagles and Black Horses, you had to lie sometimes four together on a mattress stuffed with bracken and fleas. In Brussels one bitter late January night, I shared a bed with sixteen others and was glad of it. As the Bible says, 'If two lie together, they have heat; but how can one be warm *alone*?' But a layer of straw on monastery stone was otherwise preferable. After a night spent at an inn – with the snoring, and the lack of chamberpots, and the hands sneaking after my purse or person (and I never knowing whose hands, since candles were not permitted) – I would resume the road feeling wearier than when I had stopped.

In this fashion, I journeyed several years. Until circumstance wrecked the loom, the pattern was regular as the weave of a cloth. Each winter, from November to April, I would hibernate in some large town (Ghent, Paris, London and Venice were among those I stayed at), taking work to earn gulden. Each spring, however settled I might be, there would come a fit on me to be gone. The sun mounting daily higher, the roads drying out, the river-ice melting, the mountain passes casting off their cloak of snow – these would be my signal to quit. If not on board a barge or ferry, I would sleep in a hayrick or grassy hollow or clover-bed. I bought fruit from markets, or picked it from trees. September was my favourite month. The days were still long, the roads dry, but the burn had gone from the air and the grape-harvests made people merry to be with. If remote from settlement, I lived on wild berries, beech-kernels, hazelnuts and greenstuff. It was the season of ease.

There were times I felt discouraged, and thought of my mother, and worried after her health and wished myself home. There were times I feared for my own life: crossing the Alps by ox-cart, I did not dare open my eyes. But the longer I journeyed, the bigger and harder the core of myself grew, as though flesh and pulp had been usurped by the stone within. My skin darkened. My muscles hardened. The soles thickened on my feet.

Floating down rivers or tramping lanes, I did not lack for company. All Christendom seemed to throng with moving types – vagrants, pilgrims, gypsies, jongleurs, scholars, forever on their way to somewhere else. Six months a year, I joined their tribe, a dusty-foot in search of famous sights. In the library at Chartres, I saw books so precious they were kept on chains. In Padua, I saw (and heard) the astronomical clock. In Rome, Vienna, Seville and Lübeck, I saw, wrapped in a cloth, what was sworn to be the head of John the Baptist. I had not known till then that he had more than one.

I journeyed for pleasure but also as a means of learning. First, I wished to find the differences in men from different parts. Among peasants and even in towns, the wisdom common as onions was that Italians have eyes in the back of the head, that Spanish men boast an extra leg, that the English speak with their noses, that the French (being over-seemly) wash their bodies twice a week, that the Russians grow turnips from their ears, and that the Germans (in every nation but ours I was assured of this) do shit from their mouths. But what chiefly struck me as I roamed was the sameness of men the world over. Their heads sit upon their bodies, and though they kill they do not eat each other's flesh. Nowhere did I see monsters. I think there are none, but in the forests of our own mind.

Second, I travelled to see machines. Cogs, camshafts, levers, pulleys, trip-hammers and screws – wherever I went, whatever their use, I sought them out. Mostly I saw mills: fulling mills, grain mills, tanning mills, beer mills, iron mills, woad mills, saw mills, paper mills, mustard mills and silk mills, whirling like magic apprentice boys. A few were driven by wind, but the rest were built on river-banks and ran off water. I loved the ease they brought to men, and how water too was changed by them, from idling gentle and glassy-still towards their paddle-wheels to coming out (as though itself ground and pestled) in churfing foam. I loved the rhythm they made – *again* and *again* and *again* and *again* – and never tired of hearing it. I loved the different tasks that a single stretch of river could perform: the water rushing by one monastery in France was made to crush olives, sieve flour, trample cloth, heat beer-vats, puff the bellows for the forge, and carry off waste. I have heard this tide of industry called a nuisance – oh, the dinning of forges! the gnawing of cogs! the corrupting of rivers with acid and lime! But the sight and sound of engines never failed to gladden or excite me.

To give an instance. Once, near the Harz mountains, I had been walking bleakly all day through a mizzle of rain. It was desolate country, far from any town, the only noise the breathing of cows. That nothing had stirred there for centuries (the groans of plague victims aside); that men should be so dwarfed under the sky (and our numbers halved since the Black Death); that God should dwell so far from us (and never show Himself) – such thoughts oppressed me, and with dusk looming I felt close to despair. Fear too – if there were wolves within the forest, what hope for me after dark? Then from the distance came the chink of metal on stone. Brightening, I climbed a nearby hillock and gazed down. Below lay a pit, or shallow lake, where men were hacking with picks. It was some seam they had cracked open with kindling logs. Now they were digging it out, and loading their ore on a wooden cart. This cart, when full, was pushed along a wooden rail – sweating work, since the rails sloped upward to where a furnace lay. All this I watched from the hill-brow, before descending to the furnace, the *Stückoffen*, to warm myself near its hearth and talk to the men who worked there, whose tongue was German like my own. The bloomery roaring with fire, the clank of iron bars, smoke smutting the air, flecks of bright dust blowing into the thatch of the furnace-house – how these raised my spirits! When the men left off working, I walked with them to their town, two miles off, where we drank till late, before I resumed my journey next day.

Mills and metal and machines: these – so I came to see – are what build our future. A man might make a tidy sum from them if he knew how.

With craftsmen, who feared machines would one day take their jobs, I kept such thinking to myself. Each winter I would stop in a different city, hire myself out, then swift move on to another workshop and be hired again. 'Whose man are you?' I was asked when seeking work. 'No man's man,' I would reply. By belonging to no one, and staying nowhere, I had found my place. It was how I had behaved before, in Mainz, as Jo-Jo Gensfleisch. But I felt older and more earnest now, and recast myself as Johann Gutenberg, craftsman and traveller, formerly of Erfurt university. I made caskets with tinmen in Amsterdam, forged medals with coinmakers in Augsburg, graved boxes with goldsmiths in Aachen, and in Antwerp fitted silver round precious stones. My hands were still apprentice hands. Trumpets, fish-hooks, sewing-needles, razors, church bells and can-nons were beyond me. Raw and clumsy, I would burn my wrists on forges, slice my knuckles with chisels, and file skin from my fingers and thumbs. Nonetheless, I felt at home. The hissing of hot iron in a trough of water, rust-stains on a leather apron, balls of molten steel running like little globes across a tray: these were a kind of poetry to me, with which the prettiest May-blossom could not compare.

I loved especially the art of moulds. By scooping a hollow

in iron or steel, and pouring hot metal inside, you could bring forth a solid object – a mirror of what had been sunk in. The goldsmiths I worked with cast only trinkets from these moulds. Was there not a better use? Dozing beside the furnace, while the bellows-boy puffed it to full heat, I would daydream back to the scriptorium, and imagine myself carving a page on metal instead of quilling it on vellum, and from that page casting a copy in relief, from which in turn, by rubbing ink on paper ... But to cast a page would be like making a stained-glass window all in one. The only way was to build in pieces – as though each letter were a fragment of glass. This I knew. Or did I? What exactly I knew, or when I knew it, I cannot say. There was no gooseflesh moment, no cry of Eureka. But my mind did run on metal, and on how books and scribes might be spared each other by means of *artificial writing*.

As a child, I had been taught to write letters slowly one by one. Slow, childlike, one at a time – therein would lie my answer. But that came later. For now I was a journeyman, nothing more.

The last city I wintered in was Basel. A council being held there, to debate the reform of the Church (as at Constance before), I came in hope the place would be thronging. So it was, with bishops, diplomats, writers, doctors, lawyers, minstrels, thieves, beggars and whores. But of craftsmen willing to hire me there was none – only a surly knifemaker called Fichet who paid me what he then charged me for board. Knifemaking being dull labour, and Fichet of a temper that made me want to plunge our every product in his back, I quit his employ, and fell back on teaching men to write. Like any other writing master, I paraded myself at markets and fairs, with a sheet of parchment to display the many scripts I was proficient in, and a promise to take no time in passing on my art. Though it was years since my scribing days at Erfurt, I had kept my hand and did not lack for custom. Teaching a palsied wool-merchant his abc was not work to be envied. But from it sprang labour less arduous, as word of my services got round. A delegate at the Council – an ancient priest from Augsburg – sought me out and asked would I take dictation from him. Like many gathered for the Council, he had a duty to report back to his bishop – and being slack of mind or hand wanted a scribe to write these letters for him. Since his fee was generous, I agreed to perform the service. From excess of wine, he sometimes fell asleep while dictating, and left it to me to finish his sentences for him. Yes, Anton, you may smile: I too once sat dutifully at elbow, transcribing the drunken meanderings of an old man.

Soon other delegates employed me, some from as far as Rome. This was how I met Nicholas of Cusa. He said that we had met before: in Cologne, where he had worked as a lawyer, or Erfurt, Koblenz, Heidelberg, Paris – he was sure he knew me from *somewhere*. If so, I had forgotten. He was not, to look at, memorable: middling tall, sallow-cheeked, grey-haired even at thirty. Lawyer, philosopher, politician, diplomat, emissary of God, he was too many things to be one man. In any company he would glide about, gentling and smoothing, neutral as water, like a stream round a stone. But his mind was a lovely thing, not transparent at all, rather subtly coloured, as if a rainbow had dipped its shining bow there. And in his gentle stream ran a strong, cold current. Nicholas liked to ask questions: was I familiar with this, had I read that, what did I think of these? It was not that he needed the answers; as I knew him better, I saw he already had them, and was testing me, or shaping his own ideas. I saw too that his fluency – his in-betweening – was all on the surface. Below, he was a rock in his opinions. The Church must be strengthened or die. The priests must be humbled, the mass and the missal standardised, the monasteries inspected for error, the people given more freedom at worship, the Pope accede to the infallibility of the Council. I feared for his future in the Church if he dogmatised as he did to me when we were in our cups. That way lay excommunication or even death.

But Nicholas was wiser than I thought. In his smiling public mask, he spoke for many in the Council, and that winter the Pope gave way and agreed to the notion of reform. Nicholas was then writing his *Catholic Concordance*, and though most was done in his own hand, portions of it I wrote down for him. Often he would break off from dictation to talk of books. Some years before, he had discovered in a German monastery rare manuscripts of the Ancients, and endeared himself to the Vatican by transporting them to Rome. Eastern methods in bookmaking drew him too. Friends of his in the papacy had travelled the Silk Road and been given blockbooks to bring home. He showed me one with symbols on it consisting (so he said) of thoughts from Confucius. These symbols had been rubbed there off a block, not handwritten. Later, for the Pope (whom by then he had fallen in with), Nicholas went to Constantinople, and brought back books made by Tartars and Muslims. Through him I learned that the arts of bookmaking are as old as earth itself.

Though I valued Nicholas's friendship, I did not stay in Basel beyond that winter. Restless again, in May I journeyed south to Rome and Naples. There I hoped the wisdom of the Ancients might linger in the air still and breathe itself inside me. But finding the climate too hot for inspiration, I sat instead beside the sea. I had seen the sea before, while crossing to England, and understood it to be an abyss of darkness, a chasm of terror, a watery pit of sea monsters. But in the south of Italy it does not look so, and a few who live there worship it, and plunge without their clothes into its brine. This offended me at first, but later I too went naked in the waves, and in the hot day found the sensation pleasing cool, and afterwards let my skin be pressed and dyed by the sun. Though the Italians who dwell down there are barbarous to look at, yet they mean no harm. It is a soft and slow and gentle way of living for a summer. You too should one day try it, Anton. It does no harm for a season for a German to go south and melt the cold iron in his soul.

In late October, I went back north, meaning to winter

somewhere before journeying again. And came to Strasbourg. And stayed there. And heard sad news about my mother. And met the woman I planned to wed.

7. Ennelina

Ennelina: how to bring her before your eyes? No painter could do the work, no printer either. Even a moving picture, if that were possible, would not catch her. A beauty like Ennelina's is elusive. It eluded even me, when I first met her.

For five days after coming to Strasbourg I had searched in vain for lodgings. As a last resort, I went to one Frau Stimm, a distant relation of my mother, whose house lay in Stadelgasse. An axe-faced widow in black, she did not look pleased to see me. Having peered suspiciously at the papers I carried – a degree roll and suchlike – she handed them down to the girl kneeling at her feet (the widow had perhaps never learned to read, but was too ashamed to say so). This girl – Ennelina – lived next door, and had been prevailed on by her mother to call daily on Frau Stimm to ease her gout. The easing came from an ointment bought at market, which Ennelina was just then rubbing on Frau Stimm's swollen ankles and toes. So I discovered later. At the time, I noticed only a girl of fifteen or so (she was in fact twenty), whose chief mark was irritation, my arrival threatening to detain her when she wished only to have rubbed sufficient and be gone. Standing up, she took my papers by one corner (her hands being smeared with unguent), perused them quickly, then with a vouching nod – 'He seems genuine' – handed them back to the grim widow and knelt again to her task. Smiling through a rack of missing teeth, Frau Stimm asked me to sit awhile. This I did, having need of lodgings, though the sight before me, of feet purpled with pus and yellowing with corns, made me wish myself elsewhere. I remember thinking that to have my weary feet rubbed by a girl – as Christ had his anointed by Mary Magdalen – would be a comfort. But I do not recall Ennelina making an *impression* on me. How could she, with her head bowed in abasement and an old woman's bunions in her hands?

But I was grateful she had vouched for me. And having once moved into Frau Stimm's attic room (rented to me at no family rate), I called on Ennelina to render thanks. It was a Sunday. The maid showed me up to the parlour. Ennelina had just returned from church and was letting down her hair from under a wimple. I scarcely recognised her – and wondered if she did me.

'Johann Gutenberg,' I said, holding out my hand. 'When we met before . . .'

'. . . You were in search of a room.'

'And you giving balm to Frau Stimm's feet.'

'She is an old neighbour of ours.'

'Your neighbourliness goes beyond duty.'

'It is a thankless task, true enough.'

'But she does thank you, I trust.'

'I fear I am rather taken for granted.'

'That is shameful. Many would envy her your ministrations.'

'Rubbing feet? There is no great art to it. I could instruct you, if you like. She may expect it of you soon enough, being family.'

'I would sooner embalm her corpse.'

'That art I cannot teach. But how to rid hair of nits . . .'

'Does Frau Stimm also require delousing?'

'Or how with one's hands to soothe the living . . .'

'I fear my hands lack the softness of yours.'

'With practice softness will come.'

'When do my lessons begin?'

'What lessons are these?'

This last came from an older woman then entering the room, who I knew from Ennelina's blush must be her mother. Younger than Frau Stimm, but widow-weeded too and as grim of visage, this woman introduced herself as Ellewibel, and asked my business. I told her it, and Ennelina described our previous meeting. She – the mother – did not seem taken with me, perhaps on account of my appearance, which was that of a lowly craftsman or wandering scholar. Since university my dress had been peasant-humble – woollen jacket, linen britches down to my knees, long stockings, laced wooden clogs – because those clothes were best for working. But with the lady and daughter arrayed for church, and their house a good one, with fine things in it, I must have looked ill-kempt. To judge from her scowl, the mother would have been pleased had I left at once, but Ennelina out of courtesy asked would I have a little Alsace, which the maid brought. My throat was dry – I took a generous swig. 'Speak to us of yourself,' sighed Ellewibel, with a look that said she expected little and hoped I would be quickly done. Speak I did. But the talk did not come freely. I was too much distracted by Ennelina's transformation. How had I just days before thought her a girl? She was fresh-cheeked and her body slender. But a woman for all that.

Let us change places a moment. Let me go who knows where outside, while you my reader stand in the room with her. Observe her eyes (two sapphires set in daisy-white). Regard the gentle curve of her hips and bosom (like those upper and lower 'o's I liked to illuminate in books). See how her hair unloosed from church pours gold upon her shoulders. Watch closely as she tilts her head back in laughter (the wren-dart of her tongue, her shining flock of teeth). Look all you can: your eyes are surely clearer than mine. But looking is not enough. You will have to hear her speak (that finch-light voice). You will have to touch her skin (the peach-soft cheeks, the silky fennel of her wrist). You will have to taste the wine she offers (and sip the glass where her fingers held it). You will have to inhale the honeysuckle of her breath. And once you come as close as this, I will not remain outside a moment longer. I will enter the room in a jealous rage. I will take you by the throat. I will draw my knife. I will ... I will ...

I will not. But see how simulating her stimulates me, brings it all back. It does me no good, at my age. I worry for my heart. Fetch some wine, Anton. I need to halt a moment.

There, I am recovered, and the page can run on without a pause. (This, I find, is how it is with writing: the manner in which the author passes his time – whether speeding or idling or struck dumb – does not show itself, unless, as now, he makes a point of alluding to it. I might leave off one sentence to walk an hour by the Rhine before beginning the next. Yet in the space between full stop and capital it will seem only an instant has passed. And this is a kind of wizardry the author has, that to the reader he will seem to be present, and fully occupied in the narration, even if he is not. Who would know but for my telling it that I have just now drunk half a jug, and have been listening to Anton speak of his family – not least his splendid *noisy* mother – and of the farm-work he does when absent from here? With time Anton might speak also of some girl he holds dear in his affection – his Ennelina! – but is as yet too shy. See, he blushes and would have us return to our labours, which but for my insisting on it would show none of our pleasing interludes in this little room.)

Where was I? Ah yes, Ellewibel had bid me speak. Speak I did, as though my life hung on it. The words at first stuck in my throat, which at the sight of Ennelina had dried like summer earth. But the wine (just as now) seemed to irrigate me. I quickened like a spring. I poured forth.

Ennelina being the object of my desire, it was to her I directed my talk, with tales of the places I had visited, the men I had studied with, the adventures along river and road. Her eyes shone a brighter sapphire on hearing these. But Ellewibel meanwhile looked stony, and gazed accusing at my dusty shoes, as though I were a poor scholar or vagabond. I saw my talk must be better channelled, since what seduced the daughter was hardening the mother against me. So with the aim of seeming more solid-dependable to her, I spoke of how I had come to Strasbourg with the aim of 'setting up in business'. This was not altogether a lie, since it had struck me while idling in southern Italy that I might soon put an end to my casual labours, and become a partner to a goldsmith, say, or polisher of stones. Now as I spoke to Ellewibel, this passing fancy began to sound, even to me, like a scheme in earnest.

'So this business would be in what?' asked Ellewibel.

'In an art of some kind,' I said.

'And you would have men working for you?'

'Yes, smiths or engravers or stone-cutters. It depends what materials I can find here in Strasbourg.'

'Surely gold is what makes most profit,' she said.

'The covetous love gold best,' I said, a little vexed with her, 'but iron is more needful. It is the shield against enemies, the share ploughing the field, the tie holding the house.'

She stared doubtfully at me, so I added, which was an error:

'I have worked with several kinds of metal.'

Ellewibel looked at my hands, as though their shape and roughness confirmed me as some jobber who would never have a business of his own. Then she asked, with a glance at my dusty shoes:

'But have you the means to set up?'

I was close to anger now, so I told her of my origins as a Gensfleisch, and how my late father was one of the mint in Mainz, and how my mother's mother had been married to a Fürstenberg, and how my uncles and cousins were all wealthy. I had never during my travels spoken of my family, in part so that the guilds in other towns would not make difficulties for me (as had happened in Mainz), in part because I wished to present myself as though a man fully sprung from his own loins, whose parentage was himself. But now, out of enchantment with Ennelina, and irritation with her mother, I let it all flood out. The effect was more instant than I could have presaged. The mother smiled. She attended. She fawned. I became in her eyes a different man, as the dirt on my shoes turned the shade of gold-dust and blue blood coursed through my veins. More wine was pressed on me. It having been established that no other party was expecting me for lunch, the maid set a third place at table. I sat down with mother and daughter to eat.

I have had many a fine meal during my life, but none as memorable as that. I speak not of the food, of which I recall little except that it was far from lavish and made me think the household poorer than at first appeared. (To judge by other occasions I ate there, the lunch would have been eggs seethed in hot water, poached bream spiced with saffron and cumin, then jellies or baked tart: Ellewibel offered little else.) Nor do I mean I was fully content, for I regretted the outpouring of my origins – also the talk of setting up in business, since I had been in Strasbourg but a week and felt loth to tie myself to one place. Then too there was the warmth of Ellewibel's more than motherly gaze, which lifted years from her and made me think she might have intentions on me for herself. Still, none of these currents could dampen the pleasure of sitting there, nor keep me from babbling of my travels, nor cool my ardour for Ennelina.

'In every place,' I said, 'I have met both the worst of men and the best – some drunk, idle, boastful and lecherous, but others diligent, kind, and loyal to God. In a hundred years, I am sure I should find these vices and virtues mixed the same.'

'So men are the same the world over?' said Ennelina.

'I could have told you they were,' said Ellewibel.

'No, but men and women both?' the daughter persisted.

'Between them is the same difference the world over,' I said.

'But are there no differences in people,' asked Ennelina, 'according to climate?'

'Yes,' I said, 'where the air is damp, as in England, they are buttoned and cloaked up, except when ale is drunk. In Venice, where it is hot, few clothes are worn, which brings licentiousness.'

'They say Venice is a beautiful city,' said Ennelina.

'Indeed – if beauty is to go into a pastry-shop and be solicited by half-dressed waifs with painted cheeks.'

'Are the girls there so immodest?' asked Ennelina.

'The boys too. That is the way of Venice.'

'It is no different in Frankfurt,' said Ellewibel. 'And of

course, you with your family being such a catch, Herr Gensfleisch . . .'

'Gutenberg,' I corrected her.

'But you saw none of the monsters we hear of?' asked Ennelina.

'Nothing stranger than my own cousins, Frilo and Ruleman, who are twins impossible to tell apart.'

'Poor them,' said Ellewibel. 'Twins live half as long as other men.'

'That is silly rumour, mother.'

'I have heard it on good authority.'

'Doctor Kraus is no authority, except on the bath-house.'

'Do not insult Doctor Kraus, Ennelina, after he strove so hard to save your father.'

'The only monstrosity,' I said, breaking in to stop mother and daughter scratting at each other, 'is what men are reduced to by their rulers. Poverty, hunger, insanitation – it is shameful we have them still.'

'You at least are not poor, Johann,' said Ellewibel.

'What reforms would you make?' said Ennelina, ignoring her.

'I would preach the laws of science,' I said.

'Not the word of God?'

'Indeed. I think of them as one and the same.'

Thereafter I sermonised awhile, as men are wont. On my travels across its breadth, I had (I said) come to conceive of Christendom as a body, with the Rhine, Rhône, Seine and Danube its arteries, and the canals, dykes and smaller rivers its veins. Yet the body was diseased. The only way to cure its festering sores was to spread the healing knowledge that most men lacked – of God and science and themselves. If only this knowledge could flow forth . . . And every man and woman be taught to read . . . And books be made faster and cheaper . . . Until ignorance was vanquished, and wars were at an end, and the sweet current of truth ran through all the world . . .

So I ran on. Even to me it seemed dull stuff. I was too distracted to do myself justice. Nothing Ennelina said, nor any look she gave, revealed what feelings she had for me.

And yet I knew. I gleaned it from her impatience with her mother, who turned the discourse a dozen times or more back to Mainz, and to my standing there, and present wealth, which at last provoked Ennelina to a snappish 'Oh mother, leave him alone and let him eat'. This emboldened me to leap off on some river-tale from my past – an episode on the Loire when a frothing medicine-pedlar (maybe rabid) had set upon a scabby carpenter, and might have killed him but for those of us sitting nearby first yanking his knife from him then throwing him from the boat into the river, in which he sank as plumb and true as any witch. I added some fabricating detail to this tale, to lighten it for the table, indeed to spice it wholly with humour so that its dark conclusion (a death by drowning) might be skipped past. My telling made Ennelina smirk and giggle behind her hand, till at last she could not contain herself, and choked and laughed out loud. As she did a tiny morsel of food – a chip of almond, perhaps, or flake of bream – flew from her mouth and landed on my wrist. With any other person, I would have wiped it off, as though it bore disease. But because Ennelina had achooed it, I let it rest there like a precious stone or (since it felt light and soft and damp against my wrist) like a seed from which love might grow.

I had made her laugh. She had sneezed this jewel at me. For a glorious moment, the mother was quite forgotten. We had landed arrows in each other's heart. We had tumbled into love.

*

As it began that day, so it went on. Every Sunday I called at her house. We would walk past the cathedral and its half-built spire, which seemed to grow (like our intimacy) week by week. We would pass beneath the storks nesting on roofs. And we would take the steep path down to the river. This was the Ill, which made an island of the city. The Rhine lay further off, though in summer we walked there too.

At first during our courtship we were chaperoned. Ennelina coming from a respectable family (her father had been an architect till he died when she was eight), it was improper we be left alone. And since she was an only child, with no sister to do the work, her mother was obliged to accompany us. This Ellewibel did with zest, sometimes linking arms with me, and at all times seeking to impress on me her youth and likeness to her daughter ('Tell me honest, Johann,' she once said, 'could you not take us for sisters?'). But though in their names there sounded some faint echo of each other, otherwise there was none, and my eyes were only for the daughter. Ellewibel must at last have seen this, for in time she grew tired of chaperoning, and a succession of cousins, aunts, grandmothers, neighbours, spinsters, cooks, maidservants and fishwives were appointed to accompany us in her stead. Then the day came when all chaperoning stopped, and we were left to ourselves.

I see it now as from a great distance. Let me try to picture it close. High summer. Wheat coppering the meadow. Swallows skimming the Ill. Along the river-bank walks Ennelina, a ray of sunlight gracing her head. Beside, in her shadowfall, not bold enough to take her hand, walks young Gutenberg (since he seems so distant, as though another not myself, let me third-person him too). By a moored boat they stop a moment, she to wonder if they dare untie the vessel and venture in it somewhere, he to examine the actions of the rope, which rises and falls, tautens and releases, as the river tugs the boat this way and that. In a moment they move on. Soon, as ever, they are talking. The talk is of the food they like, or which he does, since she, so he has noticed and is now chiding her for, rarely takes more than a morsel from her plate.

'You should eat more,' he says.

'You do not like a woman to look slender?'

'Of course. But a man needs food in order to live.'

'With women it is different.'

'You prefer to starve?'

'We try to keep our minds clear. Fasting is a kind of

medicine to the soul. If the body waxes fat, the spirit grows thin.'

'You cannot live off air.'

'I have heard of saints living for years from sips of water. And of nuns eating only linden-flowers.'

'You believe such stories?'

'I believe one needs little: water, meat-broth, fish-stock, oat-gruel, fruit, almond milk. These are enough.'

'But without spit-roasted hare or pork crackling or pumpkin soup or beer, what pleasure is left?'

'There is pleasure in denial. Eve took only a bite of the apple then gave the rest to Adam.'

'That was her sin.'

'The sin was his, in not refusing.'

'Is your philosophy all refusal? Must all appetite be denied?'

'Not every appetite. But when the heart is full, the stomach is content to be empty.'

Here Gutenberg takes Ennelina's arm a moment, to steer her round a puddle. He would like to take her wrist, to touch flesh not cloth, but is too shy. His own wrist still burns from the stain of her achoo on it. That was weeks ago. Such closeness since. Does she love him yet as he loves her? He hopes so, but dare not trust it. Now her hand is clutching him: she has spotted a heron up to its pins in the river ahead, head fixed on the water as if in prayer, and they pause to watch it. In a whisper he tells her of strange river-birds he has seen in other countries, and her eyes grow wide, as they always do when he speaks of travel. He suspects that look comes less from love than envy: his travels have freed him from his mother, as she is not free of hers. The heron splashes up into the air, a fish in its beak. Its cranking stiffness makes him think of a pump – and soon his mind is running on machines. He has lately, as promised, set up in business, hiring a man called Andreas Dritzehn to polish stones with him. It is work they do by hand, but since the stones – no diamonds – are more tumbled than they are polished he is sure some device could make it easier. Something water-driven? With cogs? And could the work of setting the stones in metal – gold, silver – be hastened by casting? In his distraction, he strides on, leaving Ennelina behind. She calls ahead, wondering should they turn back, but he has hurried on too far and does not hear. Here is an emblem of how he is, this Johann Gutenberg: a young man in a rush, careless of what he most loves.

'Shall we turn home now?' she calls again, her voice skimming off the river and stirring him from his fit.

Guilty, flustered, he runs back.

'I am sorry,' he says. 'I was imagining my future.'

'What does it look like?'

'All mills and presses and foundries.'

'Poor you. Machines are noisy and dirty.'

'But they lighten men's load.'

'Women's too?'

'That will come.'

'How? Machines will never peel turnips or scrub floors.'

'Already they can heat water and grind corn. One day perhaps they will drive carts or fire cannons.'

'And what will be left for men to do?'

'Cultivate their minds.'

'But you love working with your hands, Johann.'

'So I do. But I will put them to new uses.'

Now this man I scarcely think of as me slips both hands in Ennelina's – the first time ever! – and begins to stroke her palms and wrists. They stand and face each other, peering hard. Together in the dusk, they pool their eyes. If we could leap into their heads, we might see them inventing a life together. Now an arm of his slips round her waist, to draw her closer, mooring Ennelina to his heart. Delight is just a breath away. And now they find it, their talk ceasing, their mouths seeking new uses.

Sunset. The river nuzzling the shore. And these two in their innocence. Let them enjoy it while they can.

How long a stretch of Sundays did I walk out with Ennelina? Six months? A year? At first, as I have said, a third walked with us. But when this chaperoning ceased, there seemed nothing sinister in it, only the thought we could be 'trusted'. If by trust was meant a contract not to fornicate, then indeed, at that time, we could be trusted. But I see now that by walking with Ennelina unsupervised, I had entered into a different contract. This was not with her but with her mother, who, having given up any hopes on her own part, had decided Ennelina and I must wed.

How she arrived at this I cannot say, since, though I loved Ennelina from my heart, marriage was a word unuttered between us. My family name was commendation enough, perhaps. Or my setting up in business. Or Ennelina's dangerously advancing age (she would be twenty-two next birthday). Or else they had talked, mother to daughter, and agreed upon marriage between them. I confess to feeling cornered when first the notion was aired. 'Air' is not the word: by then, the notion was so deeply *earthed* and *rooted* in her mother's breast, nothing could dislodge it.

Anything I say of this today will be spiced with bitterness – the bile of failure and the sap of guilt. Ellewibel zur Yserin Tür (to give the woman's name in full) had been taught how to scheme by her architect husband, and since his death had been fully occupied drawing up plans. She had three schemes, reducible, like the Trinity, to one: to get her daughter married; to get her daughter married to a man of wealth; to get her daughter married to a man of wealth and for that wealth to devolve to the mother. (I set aside for now the fourth plan, which had little prospect: that is, of finding a husband for herself.) If I had had my wits about me, I would the sooner have seen Ellewibel's wiles as those of a procuress. I would have seen too why one as beauteous as Ennelina should pass twenty and yet be unmarried – not through lack of suitors but from the mother in her eagerness driving them off. But none of this struck me then. My eyes were locked on Ennelina. And what I saw was a woman in no rush to settle down.

'I would like,' she said once beside the Ill, 'to do some good in the world.'

'As you do with Frau Stimm?' I asked.

'There are others I could help more.'

'Whose feet are worse than hers?'

'I mean women with no money or too many children or some sickness.'

'Here in Strasbourg?'

'I might also journey abroad.'

'With whom?'

'With no one.'

'It is too dangerous for a woman to go alone.'

'Some women can look after themselves.'

'But they are safer in the company of husbands.'

'There are husbands more dangerous to their wives than any stranger would be.'

'I would never,' I said, 'be such a husband.'

At this she blushed, and changed her theme, as though talk of husbands discomfited her. No, Ennelina could never have schemed marriage with her mother – I exempt her from all blame. If in time she thought of me as a husband, it was from love arriving, not from having planned it all along.

No, the marriage suit was never hers. A snake, a weasel, a vixen dreamt it up. And that can only have been the mother.

It was after my own mother died that I first felt *pressed*. She had fallen again, and from the effect of a broken hipbone became feverish and did not recover. My sister's letter came to the house of Frau Stimm, whose copious tears wept for this unmet cousin relieved me of obligations in public grief – though in private, I confess, I sobbed to think of not seeing her again and at my sudden going from her and all my childhood having fled.

There seemed no purpose in returning home, my mother being under the ground by then. The will, I knew from Else, was as my mother had first written it. I was not punished for my defection. The estate would be divided between the three of us, with Friele, as the elder son, taking the lion's share. As well as the annuities from my father, I now stood to inherit a large sum. This news I naturally passed to Ennelina, and she in turn naturally passed it to her mother. Less naturally – indeed with icy calculation – Ellewibel pinned me down when next I saw her: how many gulden exactly? payable when and at how much interest? to be invested in what – and *whom*? I felt like a salmon in the claws of a bear. As if a dowry rather than a will was under discussion. As if the money was not my own to spend.

I had not settled how to use the money, but did not intend to settle it on Ellewibel. My mother had set me free at last: why spend my capital on another mother? I could buy a house. I could invest in a larger enterprise. I could do something in life. It was not that I did not love Ennelina. But the thought of her mother as my book-keeper was more than I could bear. I do not say I dillied with Ellewibel, let alone that I dallied with her daughter. We were well matched in age – I was thirty-five, Ennelina twenty-two – and I loved her as I loved no other. But since I felt no haste to surround myself with mewling infants, and Ennelina had some years of childbearing left, I lacked her mother's urgency. All in good time.

Ellewibel saw it differently, and over the months adopted every fashion with me: first gentle as a dove, then stealthy as a fox, then needling me like a hedgehog. Sundays became a trial. If I could have arranged it so, I would have met Ennelina in town, in the market-place or church square. But since custom required I come to Stadelgasse, my only recourse was to quit it again as soon as possible, with Ennelina looped on my arm. To prise her away could take upward of an hour: a full and frank account of my current finances must first be given the mother. And to prise myself away after depositing her at dusk could take even longer, since supper would be offered, and much talk ensue of mutual acquaintance in Strasbourg, touching especially on pending marriages. By the time I left, evening bells would be tolling from the city churches. I did not ask for whom.

One Sunday in March, above the mating-calls of storks from nearby roofs, the mother put her case more bluntly. It would soon be spring, she said, a proposition with which I happily concurred. Her daughter was not getting any younger: agreed. We made a lovely couple (with this I half-agreed, since Ennelina was certainly lovely). She had always taken it my intentions were honourable (they were). But surely no gentleman plays with the heartstring of his beloved like a cat with the tail of a mouse (no indeed). In certain quarters of Strasbourg (which?), rumour had it that such accusation was now being made (against me). These rumours were most distressing (to Ellewibel, who wiped a tear from her eye as she spoke). Was it any way to treat one's betrothed (betrothed? had I ever spoken of betrothal?), let alone her poor widowed mother. Did I not consider Ennelina sufficiently good (well born) for me? Had it struck me that by toying with her affections I was treating her little better than a whore? Let me deny if I could that I had always been made welcome at Stadelgasse, but I should know that if I could not soon make plain my good will and respect by naming a day, and by setting aside a goodly sum (to be agreed) for the nuptials, then my presence forthwith would no longer be welcome.

Thus the courtship: not mine of Ennelina, but her mother's of me.

It was in part out of cussedness with Ellewibel that I had the city clerk of Mainz thrown into gaol. The weather being cold and the mother hot, we had cut short our usual Sunday stroll. A kiss from Ennelina at the door as I left might have raised my spirits. But her mother must have forbidden it, because the kiss was not bestowed. Intimacy with Ennelina was now to be rationed, until a proposal from myself was forthcoming. I left in angry gloom.

There were other reasons for it. For some months, I had been been waiting on my annuities, which in the past had reached me promptly, no matter where I was living. Since the council of Mainz was now run by the guilds, who resented such legacies, I suspected the payment was being obstructed – and began to fear it would never arrive. There was also the capital owing from my mother's estate: until I received it, I could not fully establish myself in business, let alone think of getting wed. In all, I was owed over three hundred gulden – enough to buy a large house, lay in a good wine-cellar, and double my business plans. The injustice of it gnawed at me like the March wind: what hope had I of making something of myself in Strasbourg, with Mainz ruining me? I wondered if my brother Friele was conspiring with the council against me. Was my sister part of it too? And Frilo and Ruleman? Once I had had friends in Mainz. Where were they now to protect my interests?

Such were my thoughts when I turned the corner at Stadelgasse and walked into Niklaus von Wörstadt. I knew Niklaus from schooldays at St Viktor, and we shook hands. He had come to Strasbourg on an important assignment, he said – a delicate business negotiation. Relations between the two cities were to be improved. And he, as City Clerk (he blushed with pride at stating his position), was entrusted with the task of 'acting' for Mainz. Having known Niklaus as a snivelling schoolboy of small intelligence, I could not take seriously the notion of him acting as anything; his only playing at school, in the part of Joseph during a mystery cycle, had been a miserable performance. But as he preened and squawked, a fancy took hold, which since the next street housed the debtors' prison I was able to carry through. As we passed the prison door, I invited Niklaus in, on the pretext of introducing him to 'one of the most important men in Strasbourg'. This was the gaoler, Gunther, whose son ran errands for me. The men shook hands, a look of puzzlement passing over Niklaus's face. Then I told Gunther that I was serving a writ on Niklaus, and explained the circumstances, and while he detained him went home to fetch my papers. A judge was meanwhile summoned, and my petition set down in writing while Niklaus was locked up. To pass the time, I asked Gunther what tortures he had lately meted out to prisoners: which did he find the more effective – rack, wheel, bed of nails, whip or burning wax? Niklaus looked at me imploringly between the bars. I felt nothing personal against him, but in business sentiment is a weakness. The judge, arriving, could not but approve the writ. But Niklaus being an envoy from another city, and on a trade mission, and having come with expectation of more spacious lodging, the judge thought it prudent we consult the mayor. While the mayor was fetched, Gunther said how busy the rats were in the cells now it was nesting-time and they in need of tasty morsels for their young. Niklaus was sick into a pail. The mayor arrived within the hour, a man I knew from the tin trade. I had feared he would be angry at my lack of tact and throw me into gaol instead. But my stratagem delighted him – by humbling the man from Mainz, I had helped Strasbourg in their pending business. He shook the hand of Niklaus between the bars and told him he could see no prospect of release until the money owed was paid me. A week or more in the cells awaited the prisoner – unless I, Johann Gensfleisch, also known as Gutenberg, agreed out of the goodness of my heart to show clemency. All eyes fixed on mine: Judge, Gaoler, Mayor and Prisoner. Of pity or compassion I felt none, but I could see the virtue in offering an olive branch, if a written promise was given me first. Very well, I said, since the mayor and council of Strasbourg wished me to show leniency, and since the prisoner was an old acquaintance, I would as a favour consent to his release. But the debt must be repaid with interest forthwith, and the prisoner set his seal to this. The Mayor beamed approval. The Judge composed the writ. The Gaoler unlocked the prison door. The Prisoner, relieved, stepped free.

Niklaus's hand, as I pushed the writ in it, was shaking. He had forgotten, I think, what mettle I am made of. He would not forget again. Nor would the cities of Mainz and Strasbourg.

I had served notice. Johann Gutenberg would not stand to be shoved.

My belligerence served me well. Three hundred and ten gulden, special delivery, arrived within the month. I was a rich man.

I moved from Frau Stimm's attic, rented a large house with workshop, and hired a husband and wife to be my servants. I could not have chosen better. Housekeeper, handyman, messenger, cellarer, paragon of trust and loyalty: Lorenz Beildeck stayed with me till he died. Lotte Beildeck, cook and cleaner, matched him in industry and outran him in the race of life: here she is still, belowstairs, nearly thirty years on, bustling and haggling on my behalf – a formidable woman, easily riled when she thinks I am not accorded due respect, as Anton here found on his first day, when he referred to me in her presence as 'Herr Doktor', and was sorely scolded, it being a rule of Frau Beildeck (who blames doctors for the death of her husband) that all refer to me as 'Master'. Master I was, after my legacy, not only of her and Lorenz, but of men like Andreas Dritzehn, a nervous, green-faced beanpod of a man (and father of two) who was learning the ways of metal and stone. For years I had sat at the feet of others receiving instruction in the secrets of their art. Now men like Andreas came to sit at mine, and I dispersed those secrets for profit. The Devil of all Arts, they called me. I exulted in the vengeance of it. The guilds had refused to let me in. Why then, I would let their secrets out.

But I also harboured secrets of my own. I had a plan, an enterprise, which required both a fellow investor (I could not risk my own money entire) and a workman I could trust. The workman was soon found. For all his nerves, Andreas Dritzehn took so quickly to stone-tumbling and metal-cutting that, rather than let him practise the art elsewhere, I invited him to join me. The investor took longer. Then I met Hans Riffe, a city official, high-placed, but eager to add to his council salary with some speculation. He was to have one-third of the profits, and I the rest, with Andreas paid by piecework. But when Andreas heard of this plan, he asked to put in eighty gulden of his own. And since there was room for another worker, we were joined by a second Andreas, Andreas Heilmann, hearty fat beetroot to the other's trembling beanstalk, who was admitted on the same terms. The two Andreases would each take an eighth of the profit, Hans a quarter, and me one half.

A fair apportionment. Indeed, since the notion for the enterprise had been mine, a little generous of me.

It is true I did not apprise my partners of a second enterprise to which their money would also be put. But what concern of theirs was that? Their only motive was profit. I sincerely wished to profit, too. How the profit came need not be dwelt on. We were yoked in a common cause.

Our enterprise was to make mirrors. I did not speak of making books.

8. Mirrors

Mirrors? Our race has an affection for them. On every wall they hang neck-high, like a gallows. Or else they stand at tilt on tables, inviting entrance to their magic rooms. What a *danse macabre* they join us in, men saluting them, women seducing them, children breathing mist till they disappear. A face peers in, a face peers back, and this, so philosophers say, proves the truth of our existence: if our reflection is there, then so must we be. But why are we so weak that we need forever to be confirming our substance in glass? And can we trust what we find there? Is it us? Or the ghosts of us? Or our best selves, who live in another world? And if another world, where God lives, might He reveal himself in mirrors or is He ever invisible, as here?

Forgive these abstractions. I have had no use for mirrors since my eyes faded. The only glass I crave, aside from one brimming with wine, is the sort I was lately promised by that Italian: a lens to restore my shrinking vision. If he brings me one from Venice, I may see the world freshly printed again. The Rhine, the garden, the apple orchard: I shall rejoice to look on these. But mirrors I will shun. They tell me only what I already know – that I am going downward, towards the earth.

Yes, I am sombre, and worm-eaten with age. But at the time of which I speak I had hope, pride, joy, soaring ambition. The mirrors of my enterprise had a noble cause. I did not make them to indulge men's vanity. They were for pilgrims to carry to Aachen, to catch the soul of God. This property of mirrors is one to which the Pope attests – and who am I to dispute it? If a holy relic is displayed, and you capture its image in a mirror, then God's spirit will abide with you thereafter. At Aachen the mystery moves like this. Every seven years, a bishop stands on a balcony and parades the robes of the Blessed Virgin. He exhibits other relics, too: Christ's swaddling bands and loincloth, the blanket that wrapped the head of John the Baptist. These relics give out the light of the Lord above – and pilgrims come to Aachen in hope of capturing it. Tens of thousands make the journey, crowding every square and alley, and holding high their mirrors to catch God's holy rays. Those who succeed in the abduction – and I have never heard of any who failed – then bind their mirrors in cloth and carry them home. Once safely back, the mirrors are kept covered in drawers, so when occasion calls – with an injured child, or ailing cow – the holy light can be unwrapped, let out and used as medicine in the cure.

I see you smile, Anton. You too, my unknown reader. You are men of science, and wonder at me: did I truly believe that mirrors could heal? But my beliefs are neither here nor there. A man must earn his living somehow. My job was to give the faithful what they craved.

As a child, I had seen holy mirrors in Mainz. As a man, I saw them in the towns I journeyed through. Always they were made the same. At the centre was the glass, a small circle held in place by metal tongues. Above it a larger circle, with the face – in metal relief – of the crucified Christ. And below it, in another circle, an engraving of the Madonna and Child. The mirrors were hammered out in workshops, then sold about the streets or at vestry doors. It was from knowing I could mint them faster and sell them cheaper that I set up my business. By the time of the next Aachen pilgrimage, I hoped to press out tens of thousands. Our alloy was of lead and tin. In the early days, we worked with a soapstone mould. But I am happier in the art of coinmaking, and found a means to modify it. From engraving a die in hard metal, castings could be taken in a softer. Better still, we built a coining press, from which to stamp them. Was it that which gave me the notion of a printing press? No, I had it from the wine-press. But the carving, the heating, the stamping, the cooling, the cleaning, the *pressing out*: these skills were carried on to the making of books.

And we were copying. It was like standing between a pair of mirrors and seeing your image multiply over and over. Thousands upon thousands from the one source, and each matching the next as close as Frilo resembled Ruleman. A goldsmith could engrave such mirrors as we sold, and the detail in his latticework would be finer. But he would take half a day to make one. Whereas we in the same time could make twenty scarcely inferior, and sell them at half his price. I had calculated hard before setting up. If we could sell eighty thousand mirrors – and the pilgrims numbered many thousands more – that would yield twenty thousand gulden: 2,500 for each worker, 5,000 for the investor, and 10,000 for the inventor of the idea. I would be a rich man.

The next pilgrimage, I knew, lay three years off, and this date we worked towards. But then it came out in a talk with Nicholas of Cusa – whom I met again when he passed through Strasbourg – that the plague had lately struck in Aachen and from this the pilgrimage had been put back. I was dumbstruck, and my heart beat like a hammer for fear my enterprise would be undone. To Nicholas, this was no tragedy, since he disapproved of my mirrors as 'preying on the weak and credulous', and urged I put my hand to a nobler art. But it was news unpleasing to break to my partners. Half the mirrors were already made by then, and our capital sunk in them – and now I was telling them all profit would be deferred at least a year. Hans shouted black oaths and demanded I repay him. Even the Andreases, who had always followed me like sheep, baahed angrily. What could I offer to placate them?

There was no choice. I told them my secret. The work of the books.

I had intended to tell no one but Ennelina, whom I knew I could trust as myself. I had indeed already told her. We were walking by the Ill again, and I sketched it out as best I could – letters carved in reverse on metal, built up in lines to make a page, then inked over and squashed on paper. She, though, saw no virtue in it. Talk of presses and furnaces made her fret. She loathed things 'all stamped the same'. Besides, she had a fondness for scribes.

'When I read a book,' she said, 'I like to know a living man has written it.'

'Most scribes are barely living,' I said. 'They do their work by rote. A bloodless instrument can do it better.'

'But a machine pressing out words over and over the same – I hate the idea. It will seed a contempt for nature. It will blind us to the wonder of Creation.'

'Has my copying thousands of mirrors' – here I touched her face – 'blinded me to the wonders of you?'

'You can flatter and kiss me,' she said. 'But I do not like your scheme.'

That she did not like my scheme was easy, when our lips met, to forgive. Besides, I knew she would keep it secret. Others were harder to trust. As I had planned it, men would make this thing for me, or do that task, but only I would command the whole. In the Krämergasse, I had set the chestmaker Konrad Saspach to construct me a press. The full purpose of it was not disclosed – he need only follow my designs. Likewise, the goldsmith Hans Dünne was engraving me punches: though it was letters I made him carve on them, he did not ask questions as to my plans, and I paid him well to speak nothing to others. At home, with his punches, I began experiments. To sink a punch in a bar of copper was simple enough. But how from molten metal to get a smooth-faced letter, and then align it with other letters, so that once inked (supposing ink could be made to stick), and then pressed on paper whose texture was neither too brittle nor too greasy . . . After a year of my burning the candle at home, the work was little advanced. But at least it was secret. Once I hired workers, that secret would be harder to keep. The trick was to keep it long enough so none could outstrip me. For if my secret was stolen at the start, if my magic should be out too soon, then I would risk losing the race . . .

I see you smile, Anton. What vulgar talk is this of ownership and competition, of *stealing* and *racing*? Art, science, mechanics, the march of progress: are these not a common endeavour? So they are. But I was young then, and hot with an idea, and unwilling to give it out. My fearfulness was proved right, as you will see. With men, races are inevitable. If a man could leap on to the moon, there would always be a second man straining to leap further – or a third, claiming he leapt there first. A race among equals makes fine sport, as the Romans knew. But if a runner is lamed by his rivals, or tripped while lapping them, or in some other way robbed of victory, that is no race. Likewise, if a man conceives an idea, and another man steals it. Yes, what matters is how inventions are used, not who made them. But inventors deserve a mark at least, a signature, a colophon, a footnote. As to stealing, I cannot deny some of my own flowers were picked from other men's gardens. But the full, glorious bloom of them – that was mine alone.

You will grasp, then, why I found it hard to tell Hans, and the two Andreases, of my larger enterprise. Could I trust them not to betray me? Would they be discreet? But the delayed Aachen pilgrimage gave me no choice. And in truth they must have already had some inkling, since they came to my home, and pleaded with me to speak of the enterprise I housed there, and to 'hide nothing'. I showed them my metal pieces and half-built press, then sat them down over a jug of Rheingauer, and made sketches and did sums, and spoke of making books in common use (a Latin grammar for schools, say), and excited them so much they were soon pleading to join me. It would take time, I warned, and would be costly of materials. Hans had not the assets to contribute more, but agreed to leave in his money, in expectation of greater rewards. The two Andreases, seeing more capital was needed, agreed to find it – from loans, legacies, by mortgaging their houses, somehow. To the eighty gulden each had put in for the mirrrors, I bid them add a further 250, of which a hundred was to be paid at once.

It was agreed. I drew up a contract, and each put his hand to it. We were in business.

The agreement was amicable. I did not dream where it would one day land me.

9. The Trap

It was Ellewibel who landed me first. Not as a husband to her daughter, but on a charge of breach of promise. In court. I blame the mother for the monstrous injustice of it. But I also blame myself. The signs had been there. But so busy was I six days a week, and so deeply in love on Sundays, I did not read them.

After the time I had thrown the city clerk of Mainz in gaol (word of which must have reached Ellewibel), she became, for a time, more pleasant, and bullied me no further in marriage. Because my standing in Strasbourg had risen, she did not wish to vex me – that may have been the cause. More likely, Ennelina prevailed on her to stop, she being content at our walking out and no more urgent for marriage than I was. I prefer to think this than to believe a *tactic* had been agreed between them. For as her mother's ardour for a ceremony abated, so Ennelina's passion for me increased. Our priests teach us that woman is capable of many stratagems, that her words and looks and sighs cannot be trusted. But surely she cannot fake the heat of her body, or its juice. Ennelina affect her passion? No, she was honest, and loved in truth, and this was what moved me. Each time I held her, my heart was a squirming nest of wren-chicks. Leap off, let go, fly out, brave the air: so said the flutterings within. My education had taught me to deny. My work bid me harden and be cold steel. But my body felt like molten metal. And desire said to seize this chance to love.

Candour compels me to enter a box long shut from view. I am in a confessional; you are the priest; writing is the screen that separates us. The modest reader might like to leap to the end of this chapter. You, Anton, I advise to write this, if possible, with your eyes averted. Concentrate on shaping the letters, and do not dwell overmuch on meaning. You young think that we old were never young; we old, grown restrained, collude. But it is time to burst that bubble of deceit.

One Sunday, walking outside town, Ennelina and I happened on a ruined farmhouse, no doubt left empty (like so many others) since the great plague of the last century had stolen its tenants. In this farmhouse, safe from view, by a discreet unrobing, Ennelina began to show herself to me. Each Sunday, a different part of her – as if her body were a set of holy relics, and I the dazzled spectator trying to capture its rays. How it began I cannot recall. Perhaps, in my fervour, I dared her. Soon it became a ritual. And though maidenly shyness required that she be coaxed, there was nothing spontaneous in these self-displays. The pattern – an ascending, or descending, immodesty – we schemed ahead. While Ennelina bared a knee for me, or a thigh, I would sit on a hay bale sucking straw, like a farmer at auction weighing up tups and ewes. Yet I did not feel to be at market. If I had thought these shows were part of a marriage bargain, or suspected the mother of making her lay out her goods so as to hook me, they would have chilled me. Instead, I felt excitement – and saw it in the eyes of Ennelina as she discovered her power to command me. Each week she became more daring. Since female dress revealed a little of the body already, and since Ennelina well knew that certain parts would stir me less (a man can only stare so long at an armpit), the end of her Book of Revelation soon approached. I marvelled at her. How could so soft a creature make me so hard? The squishy pouch under my belt had stiffened to a rib. Eve, the Bible says, came from a rib. And woman, ever since, has had this power to turn men to bone.

I can see, Anton – forgive me, but these things cannot be hidden – you too have become excited. So let me not further stretch it out. How far – how completely – Ennelina would have gone in showing herself I cannot say. Nor will I tell how far she did go, except to say I fell short of seeing her naked. But one week, by chance, our pattern changed. We were by the river, just approaching the farm when we saw, in a flurry of white feathers and strange grace, a pair of swans mating. It was a beauteous sight, not lowly or animal at all, and perhaps the thought struck Ennelina, as it did me, that if even God's humbler creatures could be touched by loveliness from the act of congress, then surely we, as men and women, being His chosen, would be moved and ennobled by it even more. What the priests teach against fornication seemed, in that moment, a cruel and empty edict – and was, besides, no stay against desire. I turned to Ennelina on the river-bank and pulled her close. My rod and staff discomfited me. We had never kissed as deep as this before, not even after her shows in the farmhouse, which for all that I have said were strangely innocent. Now we held each other hard, and let our mouths try out new tongues and hands roam wide in our own country. Her body was a book on which I wrote my needs, till a pink flush illuminated her neck and throat. Longing stirred between us, below our laps. Since we were pressed together, my desire could not be hidden from her. But nothing would abate our ardour.

We broke off an instant to stare into each other's eyes – then walked straight to our trysting place. Mouldy walls, earth floor, an open roof: the place was empty as the grave. No one would witness us. We might not have minded if they had. This was a fit that possessed us both. Without disrobing, we laid ourselves on a scatter of hay, nuzzled and crawled over each other like new-born pups, and – to my delight and later dismay – fornicated.

It shames me to use the word. Not fornication – dismay. Why dismay that Ennelina, whom I loved, should become my lover? Had it not been what I desired? Was the experience not estatic? Did I hesitate that Sunday, or the next and next? To feel her slender in my arms but the waters so turbulent beneath us – no passion could have gladdened me more. It was like rushing over the rapids at Bingen: heartlift and nervethrill and surrender of flesh. And yet each time the act was over, in the shallows, coming to, what dark clouds sat on me! As if it would have been better to have died. As if rinsed of all feeling. The toads of despair and disgust squatting inside.

I did my best to hide this from Ennelina, but the condition did not improve. The higher the pitch of our communings, the lower, afterwards, I fell. It did not help, perhaps, that consummation came without rather than within. To be plain – at the risk of making the modest-minded gag – what I knew of fornication I knew only from whores, who insist on a man being parted from the hub of his pleasure before he spend. To withdraw from the friction *in situ* so as to spend *in vacuo* is to be robbed of a vital portion of joy. It is to feel the chill wind of winter in the midst of summer heat. The burn of pleasure should carry all before it, but no, one's mind is forced to be elsewhere, then one's member is, then the issue stares up like cold mercury from stomach or thigh. Nor did Ennelina like me wrenching myself from her. I at least had spent myself; she, I think, fell short.

I had reason to withdraw, aside from habit. If not, I would get Ennelina with child. There were arts for avoiding this – rennet of hare and suchlike potions. But we were not worldly enough to procure them. And without them, it was this or else abstain. There was no choice. My week at work would pass in a fever of longing. I would call to mind what we had performed and re-enact the pleasure, with myself. Spending would recall my dismay to me, and I would tell myself I must, come Sunday, resist. But contrary sensations would soon rise up again. Then Sunday would arrive, and desire vanquish reason, and we two powerless lie down. I speak of this as repetition but it was not: no act of love is ever a copy of another. Nor did we remain still, in any sense. Our passion grew. We became more fluent. And when each time I felt the moment come to remove myself, Ennelina would flinch, and pull me tighter to her, while I fiercely struggled to be free.

I do not think she wished to be with child, as a ruse to entrap me. She trusted that we would marry when I had become a man of greater substance and she a woman of broader horizons. Lying together was a bud, not a blight, to our flowering future. There was no sin in it, so pure did our love seem. Yet puddles of doubt had seeped into my mind. It was not that I loved her any less. But with this love was mixed – dismay. Her passion, her cries, the flow from her body: were these *respectable*? My class had taught me to look for certain qualities in a wife. These daily virtues Ennelina had: calm, loyalty, good sense. More important, she had spirit – would never be one of those big-eyed dogs that wag for their master no matter how hard he thrashes and beats. She was, I mean to say, her own woman, not one wedded to the spindle. She had ambition, and talked of going out into the world, perhaps as a Beguine. All this was to the good. But what of her nakedness, her haytime sighs, her barn noises? Sometimes, in her simple enthusiasm, she reminded me of peasant girls I had kissed in hill villages. At other times, in certain artful movements she had, she reminded me of a bath-house angel. I did not doubt she would be faithful. True, she had given herself to me before marriage, and a sterner man might have wished her more abashed at that, more blushing and eye-lowering and fearful of condemnation. But the thought I might one day become a cuckold – this did not enter in. She would make an honest, wimpled wife. But what of the unwifely other self of hers I had lain with? What would happen to it? Would it stay or go? And how could I marry the two? In my muddle and fever, I could not answer these. The Church had instructed me to think of fleshly pleasure as ugly: this was all I knew.

I also wondered: would I make a good husband? It is better to marry than to burn, St Paul says. But was it better in God's eyes to keep myself for work (as monks do) than to marry? And what if I should marry and (my desire unabated) burn as well? Marriage, so the Church teaches and I observed with my own parents, has nothing to do with pleasure. Yet if I married Ennelina, and shared a bed with her, pleasure would be plentiful and on tap, to be drawn on nightly, like those wine-barrels I had sucked at with Hans. I would want to lie with Ennelina all the time. The Church forbade this. The act was legitimate for conception, nothing more. It was forbidden on feast days and fast days, during the time of bleeding, during pregnancy, during breastfeeding, and on Sundays. It was also proscribed in all but one posture, and we had already ventured several more. Being unmarried, we were spared the worst of penances. But the sins we laughed at in our joy (to be among the damned for having chosen Sunday as our tryst-day!) could not be joked of once we were wed. Nor did I greatly savour the image of Ennelina as a mother, run to fat and with children like piglets at her teat. If she became that sow, I might be free of my ache. I had seen this happen with other men, who once their wives became cooking ovens – their hourglasses going pear-shaped, their runnels of pleasure become caverns – began to despise them. But to will this to happen, to choose to share Ennelina's body with a houseful of brats so as to stop myself from burning for her ... Any home we had would be passionate and troubled, or else passionless and calm. I did not relish either prospect.

Though mired in confusion, I did not unburden myself to a priest. Whether Ennelina did I cannot say, but I doubt it, since any priest would have damned her with such hellfire she could not have risked the act again. Both of us well knew how women who fornicate with men not their husbands are regarded by the Church. Their bodies, rotten with worms and putrefaction, must be purged by the fires of hell. Such images I tried to banish as I clove to Ennelina's body, which had such warmth and sweetness. Yet when I touched it after spending – in my desert of dismay – it turned a sickly ash, as though lice were crawling in her hair and rats had gnawed each chasm ... All this was a torment to me. I loved Ennelina yet hated my desire for her. I burned too much yet dreaded to extinguish the flame.

Our mouths saved for kissing, we spoke less freely to each other than before. I began to keep things back. I did not even tell her of the house in the suburb of St Argobast (big enough to lodge workers and run a printshop), which I was then making swift to buy. But Ellewibel, the evil weevil, got to hear of it. And taxed me again as to my intentions. And when I did not give due answer set her trap.

Evil weevil, wolf-bitch, mother dragon: is it just to call Ellewibel such names? Am I too hard on her? Perhaps. But I am hard on myself too. Hardness is a habit with me. It has been my life: hard graft, hard metal, hard bargaining. Ennelina was the only softness. Her pillow breast, the velvet of her thighs, the wet silk between them every Sunday for a season. I did not know then what I possessed. What I would give for such softness now.

A man's longing is supposed to die with age. Mine grows daily more alive. When I was young, my longing made me fearful and guilty. I wanted to beat it out of me with presses, punches, furnaces – to fight fire with fire. I was a man in haste, afraid that passion would slow my work. I would not give it time then. Now I cannot act on it, I have all day.

Ellewibel asked would I take some shoes to be mended. She would do it herself but had been lamed by them – and could not trust a servant, nor let Ennelina roam abroad in the lower, *cobbling* end of town. She limped across the room to make proof of her lameness, and handed me a pair of boots, their leather withered as a toad. Piteous-eyed and dragging herself like a three-legged cat, she had never seemed so like my own mother. I did not believe the hobble. I did not doubt she was using me. But if running the errand would placate her, how could I say no?

The shoemaker she sent me to – she was particular I use no other – was named Klaus Schott. I found him stooped over a last, a row of tacks ranging along the width of his mouth. (Like a line of type, it occurs to me now, but as I have said before no blinding flash began my notion of printing, and by then, besides, the experiment was under way.) He took the boots from me, looked inside them, turned the soles over like a gambler inspecting his playing cards, and asked me to return on the morrow. Knowing the ways of shoemakers, I left it three days, to be sure. But the shoes were still not ready when I called and he asked me to sit with him while he did the work. For a man with nails between his teeth, he spoke a good discourse, and over the stim-stam of his hammer we parleyed of this and that. I have noticed that men often speak in a language pertaining to their craft – the foundryman as if life were all fire, the sailor as if it were all water. With Klaus Schott it was all feet:

'And how is she getting along, Frau Ellewibel?'

'She is middling well, I think, her limp aside.'

'And the Fräulein? Still treading the paths of righteousness, I hope?'

'She too is flourishing.'

'I hear you have been walking out with her.'

'It is true.'

'And have swept her off her feet.'

'That I cannot say.'

'And have now taken the next step.'

'I am sorry?'

'You have promised to marry her.'

'I . . .'

'And have given her tokens.'

'I . . .'

'And have set a day.'

'I . . .'

'For Whitsuntide.'

'I . . .'

'That is excellent news. I congratulate you. There: well and truly nailed. That will be five pfennigs.'

I left in a fluster. I had neither asked Ennelina to wed me, nor set a day. As to the tokens, these were only metal trinkets brought from work – a hairpin, a coin I had struck, one of my Aachen mirrors, the letter E in metal type – to impress on her my workmanship but with no proposal attached. What had misled the shoemaker, then? Who had told him of an impending ceremony? It could only be Ellewibel, but she spoke nothing of it on my delivery of the shoes, and for myself I did not broach the matter. That Sunday Ennelina was allowed an hour longer abroad with me than the custom. We made hay of it at the empty farm. 'Your hands – I love your hands,' she said.

The writ was served the following week: a suit for breach of promise, on behalf of the daughter, issued by the mother. No doubt Ellewibel supposed it would spur me to act – that faced with court I would promptly *pay up* and wed. What Ennelina supposed I could not guess. She had sometimes berated me for working too hard: why could I not on summer nights walk with her by the river instead? why only these Sunday afternoons? 'If ever we marry,' she said, 'you will have to change.' But she had never pressed it. Nor do I think my wealth allured her. Of late, she had sighed again of doing good in the world, as a Beguine. This I could not credit since at the instant she said it I was manning her. But it spoke true of her uncovetous nature. Why then had she changed course? Did her mother force her? Or was it a stew cooked equally between them?

Had my temper been less hot, I would have asked her. Inflamed, I assumed the worst. That she was conspiring with the she-wolf to snare me. That she wished to bring me to book for our pleasure. The vision I had in the graveyard at Mainz came back. But now the Devil who held fast my arms, and who would suck me underground, wore the face of Ellewibel. So be it: I had not succumbed before, and would again fight free, this time in court. Judges put the fear of God in some men. Not me. The only judge I fear is God Himself.

The writ having been served, I ceased to call on Sundays. My body burned for Ennelina, but I put the heat to fuel my work. My mind milled with memories, but I used the flour to bake a future without her. There was no logic to it, only this: she had been my lover and therefore could not be my wife.

The day came for the case. I had no witness to call, only myself, but I had standing in Strasbourg, and knew that breach of promise suits were rarely won by the plaintiff. My only fear was the cost in compensation if our carnal relations became known.

When it fell to my turn, I answered truly.

'Is the plaintiff Ennelina known to you?'

'Yes.'

'You have been walking out together for some time?'

'Yes.'

'Was ever the notion of marriage raised?'

'In private, to myself, I entertained it, and often contemplated it. But it was not discussed between us, let alone resolved.'

'Did you never promise to marry her?'

'No.'

'And your position is . . . ?'

'I cannot marry her for now.'

It was easier for me to speak this since Ennelina was absent from court. Had she been present, a single tear would have melted my resolve and she might be sitting with me now. But without her daughter's tempering spirit, Ellewibel put the case against me instead, swearing that in her company I had discoursed on wedding plans, and had often addressed Ennelina as my 'sweet bride and everlasting wife to be'. Such impostures I had foreseen: they did not nettle me in the least. But nothing had prepared me for Schott the shoemaker, who rehearsed our conversation together and transformed my denials of intended marriage into gleeful proclamations of it.

'You say Herr Gutenberg mentioned Ennelina in your presence, Herr Schott?'

'He boasted of giving her love-tokens, your honour.'

'And did he speak of marriage?'

'Yes, when I asked him had they fixed the day, he answered "Aye, for Whitsuntide".'

Such malice I could not abide in silence.

'Do not believe him,' I shouted, staring nails across the

111

court. 'He is a miserable wretch who lives by cheating and lying.'

A few of my words may have been stronger, since Schott at once issued his own suit against me, for defamation, and the Judge, having heard his complaint, and wishing to be rid of it before coming to judgment in the principal case, ordered me to pay the cobbler fifteen gulden. I had no choice but to hand it over, dreaming meanwhile of hammering Schott's ribs on my anvil, and in my furnaces melting him to ash.

With Schott consuming my rage, I no longer felt hatred for Ellewibel. She was malice-deep and grasping, but deserved more pity than scorn. Since she said nothing of my fornicating with her daughter, Ennelina cannot have told her, for had she known she would have used it against me. I should have seen from this that Ennelina intended to protect me, and to keep open the channel of our love. But I assumed it was only shame that had stopped her mouth. And this shame then spread to me, who regretted what had passed between us, and tore up the seed that we had planted so it could not grow.

As I stood before the Judge, waiting his verdict, I grasped that it could be of no consequence. By contesting the case, I had made my choice. Win, I would lose Ennelina. Lose, I would lose her also.

It pains me now to rehearse that day. I was young and stubborn, and the relief I felt on leaving the court – less at the verdict falling my way than at the case having been concluded – would not allow me to admit my error. There was work to be done. I got on with life. Never look back. Now I am old and do nothing else. I should have married Ennelina. The world would have been different had it happened. But so, for the better, would I.

10. The Founding of Type

Since I could not quench the fire that burned for Ennelina, I used it as a tinder for my work. It lit up new ideas. It kept candles burning long at night. It warmed the founding of type.

Forgive me readers, you too Anton, but now I must become mechanical and deliver a short lecture on my art. I will spare you, if I can, jets and friskets, rounces and coffins, winters and platens and cheeks. But unless you have the look of the thing, and touch the metal, and grasp the lever, and feel the weight, you can have no concept of how I spent those years.

To say it as simply as I can. What I planned was to make books (Latin grammars, prayer books, dictionaries, I had no care at first for which) and to do this by means of a metal impression rather than with a pen. This use of a metal impression I call printing. Printing, unlike writing, is a subtle art. To do the work requires a pentangle of skills.

First you must copy out the *character* you wish to make, tracing it on thin paper from a manuscript. The draughting of types should never be less than perfect. There is no ancient authority for the shape of letters, but a principle must be kept of lines and circles and arches. A true placing of fats and leans, with them sweetly driving into one another, will give the letters decorum. It is a kind of architecture. If any letter is not to scale the whole edifice will crumble.

Second, from this paper copy of a letter, on to the head of a length of metal held in a vice, you engrave a *punch*. This punch must be forged in steel that has been well curried in blood-red heat. To sculpt it, you use small chisels kept sharpened on an oil stone, filing and chipping with them till the character is perfectly fashioned.

Third, with a single blow, you drive this punch into a bar of soft copper, to make the shape of the character in a well, or *matrix*.

Fourth, having fixed it in a hand-mould, you fill this well with molten lead, which – once cooled, hardened and extracted – gives the character (wrong way round) in relief, which protuberance we call the *type*.

Fifth and last, from the type being inked and pressed on paper, there comes the character or *impression* on a page.

To lay its trail, then, printing requires five arts (character, punch, matrix, type, impression). How cumbersome, you say. With a pen, one copies the character straight on a page, and it is over. Ah yes, but a pen is slow and can never do the same page twice, whereas a *galley* of print, once made, leaves its impress in an instant and will copy a page over and over. This then was my scheme: to make type regular and movable, and from it to produce books a hundred times faster than could a scribe.

No notion could have been clearer. But to give it substance, many further tasks within this general framework had first to be performed. To take the characters, the sum of which we call the *fount*. The Latin alphabet has twenty-six letters, fifty-two with the capitals. Was it enough, then, to have fifty-two letters engraved? It was not. For the Bible, my fount ran to 260. There were abbreviations and ligatures to be made, for the scribes use them and our text must look just like a scribe's. What is more, for a line of type to be evenly spaced, and for a page to have straight margins, each letter must come in different widths, so that instead of

a a a a a a a a a a

ad infinitum, to vary the width and enhance the look, we had

a a a a a a a a a and a

each a little fatter than the last. Types should be set with a deep face, and their hollows be proportionate to their widths. If not deep, they will entertain picks – skin-flakes of ink which choke up the face and which can be got out only with a needle. Some letters lose their appearance from being more generally used – such as a, t, ſ and t – and more of these should be cast at the outset to save later recasting.

Our next task was to yield lead type from the copper matrix. Since molten metal is needed, so is a furnace, which might suggest a blacksmith at his forge hammering out hooves, but that type is *tiny* and that each portion of it – not just the character on the face, but the shank, the shoulder, the nick, the bevel, the base line, the feet – must be perfectly shaped. How to do this with accuracy? Feel these samples of type I have here, Anton, and how small they are in every particular, like minnows in your hand. How did we do it? In the end, after tribulation, with a *hand-mould*. Forgive me, I cannot help but rush at you with terms, but the hand-mould I count the best of my inventions, more important even than the press. A mechanical clock is crude by comparison. How to describe it? It is like male and female coming together in congress: a pair of brass Ls that lock on to each other, clad in wood for handling, a loop or spring of steel to steady them. Inside lies a casting void into which the heated glob of lead is ladled. You hold the ladle in your right hand, and as you tilt in the fluid move the mould forward with your left to receive it. The casting void being always the same, each type, whatever the letter on its face, should have the same body and depth, so that the printing come out even. With a skilled typefounder – it took me time to find one but I did – we could cast in the end a type a minute: 600 in a day. But to bring the hand-mould to perfection was work of long and heavy travail.

Now I have taken you past the types and hand-mould, you must think your lesson is done. But has a page been printed yet? Has even a line been set? No, you must follow me further through the printshop, away from the heat, to my *compositor*. Let him sit quiet if he can, since his task is that nearest to a scribe, and the Devil likes nothing more than to distract him. In his left hand he holds a stick or ruler of fixed length. With his right, he delves into his *cases* – a flat box made of seasoned oak with a hundred or more shallow compartments, where the letters are kept. The cases are divided between upper (for capitals) and lower, and are best filled always in the same order – that is, to each compartment a particular letter should be attributed so the compositor knows his way. Also, these cases must rest level with his breast, for though this height tires the arm more, a lower siting will make him hunched and round-shouldered and give pain to his back. From the cases, he plucks out the letters, in time without looking at them, and places them on his stick, in a row. When the line is full, he transfers it to his *galley*, a metal plate. And when the galley is full – that is, the page ready in metal – and the type locked up, he ties it with twine and moves it to the *bed* or *coffin* of the press, where it is held in a metal *chase* by strips of wood or *furniture*.

I can see you wish us heartily at the end of this. It is in sight, at least. We have reached the *press*. You recall how it came to me in Erfurt, seeing Hans row on his wine-press. Its beauty is that it needs but a single action to make a page. With blockbooks, copies are made by rubbing over and over, which is slow work and tiring to the wrist. With the press, though heavy, the labour is simpler – you swing the lever with both arms to bring down the *platen* on the bed, then in the same movement swing it back up. The press has two side columns, and a crosspiece, and a mighty screw or spindle running down the middle. It looks like an instrument of torture, a cross between the gallows and the rack. One of my pressmen called it the Devil's dungeon. He was a drystone-waller by profession, but the raising and lowering of that lever all day, so he swore, was more infernal than building any wall. The work being strenuous is why the pressman must be sturdy as a horse. For firmness, the press should stand flat on solid ground, so that its feet need no wedges, which can cause damage and are apt to come out. It must also be fastened with braces overhead and at the sides, since its action is of such force it might shake the angels out of heaven.

The pressman's other task is lighter: to pluck the printed paper from the press, and hang it up to dry, like washing pegged to a line.

Last, I promise you, comes my printer or inkman (my *beater* as I call him, where the pressman is a *puller*). In his hands he holds a pair of puffballs, like giant mushrooms, two dabbers stuffed with horsehair and covered with skin of dog. Dipping them in ink on a stone table, he works the dabbers sideways on each other in a contrary motion till the ink is spread across. When he then rolls those balls over the type, he must take care to touch the face firmly yet lightly, and not to choke the cavities. For a common page, he should go twice upwards and downwards, but for the first proof four or five times. Once the type is evenly wet from his rolling, he steps back and lets the pressman bring the lever down. It will not work unless he has fixed the sheet of paper firmly in the frame. And since the paper is printed on both sides – another innovation of mine: with blockbooks, so tarnished is the page from rubbing, the reverse cannot be written on – the fixing must be perfect. So too the paper must be dampened to the right degree.

There, you have it – a tour and lecture through the art of printing, as conceived by Johann Gutenberg in Strasbourg and brought to perfection in Mainz.

I see it clear now, from being engaged in the art so long. But in Strasbourg I knew little, being stuck in the foothills with no view of the peak. The printshop we had then was a bare room, not the later humming factory I have shown. A forge, a slop-pail, a carpet of reeds spread over the dirt floor – these were our only comforts. As for the workforce, they were but four: Konrad Saspach, who built the press according to my drawings; Hans Dünne, who engraved and made dies, which work, since it was delicate, I often shared; Andreas Heilmann, who being big of brawn would operate the lever of the press; and Andreas Dritzehn, my green-faced printer. This was my chosen team, or would have been but for a mishap I shall shortly disclose.

In the meantime there were obstacles enough to our

making a book together. The press would not stand firm or bed down flat. The type kept breaking off. The hand-mould would not fit tight. The characters we made were blurred or twisted, and impossible to align. The ink ran like a stream or stuck like mud. The paper creased and tore. Some tasks we solved through trial and error. But others could not be mended.

I began to despair . . .

Then Andreas Dritzehn died.

I had thought a death might buck him up. But the boy is sleeping sound, his head slumped on the wood. I have slipped the pen and paper away, and for this page the scribe is me. I imagined my eyes would not allow it, but with a quill between my fingers I need only feel, not see. After those years in school and scriptorium, maybe the act will come of itself, like artificial writing. My hand is shaky, I fear. If illegible, there is no point in it, so I will stay brief. But as long as Anton snores . . .

I cannot say I blame him. To do his own work is tiring enough, but to be forced to listen to mine. If a press were here now, I could show its workings. But to show in words rather than actions is not easily done. I should have laid more stress on the purpose, which was to raise scribes like Anton from their servitude: thanks to my press, books can be swiftly printed, not slavishly written out. But he would have his answer for me: am I not now using him *as a scribe? What labour does the press spare* him*? It is true. If a press could be invented to turn a man's speech to metal type! Or a machine made to print words straight on to paper as we think them! But till such dreams come to pass, no scribe will be short of a hiring.*

Look at him there: the tilted neck, the side-on face, the gold filings of hair along his naked arms, the hands crossed under his chin as if in sainthood. How I envy the young their power to sleep! To lie unroused five hours a night is the most I now aspire to – and an hour at a stretch is rare, without me starting at some knock or rustle or having to test the chamberpot. It is an old man's problem, they say. But I have had it since Strasbourg, when by day I would make experiments then at night lie awake making them anew. It is why I rarely dream: my dreams are all by day. As to visions, which we distinguish from dreams in that they stem not from the brain but come to visit and inspire us, I am too worldly for them. What does Anton dream? To judge by that smooth brow, those lashes lying like wheat, and that smiling bow they call the mouth, it is a happy dream. If any look of mine, or word I have spoken, has added to his happiness, I am content. Is taking my dictation a drudge for him? Or does he find pleasure in my company, as I did with Nicholas of Cusa? I hope the latter, but cannot tell. Perhaps on waking he will read these words, and with a look or utterance confirm what he feels. I would be grateful for that. No business in my latter years has been as intimate as this. It is like reaching a hand between my ribs to extract my heart. If no trust or affection rest between us, that heart will surely wither from grief.

I see the pen runs away with me. Writing makes me less guarded than speaking. It is like some underground art, that tunnels to unknown places – that digs within. Further than that, even – within the in. Thanks to the quill I hold, I seem to see more clearly – in myself, and to my past. Hidden memories seep out like ink. Anton asleep has transported me back to Peter Schoeffer – apprentice, protégé, trusted friend. He too, after long labouring, would sometimes slumber at his workbench. And such was the love that others in the printshop felt for him – most of them being men of my age, and a few having sons as old as he – we would shush and tiptoe round him till he woke refreshed. You have not yet met Peter, but his time will come. On those occasions when he slept, if no one was watching, I sometimes reached to stroke his neck – as I am tempted to do with Anton now. There, I just did it, without waking him, for see it is I myself who still writes.

Touching has not changed him, but me it has. The pen

*feels softer. My heart beats faster. Stroking the hairs on the
back of his neck makes those on my own neck stand. I do not
mind him knowing – as he will, when he reads this – that I
touched him while he slept. There is no harm in it, no harm
in me. Every* erastes *needs his* eromenos, *the boy offering
gifts of beauty, strength and quickness in exchange for the
old man's wisdom. Unwise though I am, some such barter is
there between us. I also pay him well for his work. When I
first hired him, it was for his talent with the quill (which no
other boy round here can match), not because he reminded
me of Peter. And if affection has grown, no sin sullies it,
nothing a priest would ask penance for. He is a child still.
Though his pen bleeds out my ancient wounds, he does not
seem to notice when I am tearful or angry, merely sets one
word next to another, as though they were bricks. Such
innocence as he sleeps there! I do not forget he is but a cygnet
to my cob.*

*But look, a fly has landed and woken him. I must end my
scribing. I must cease this talk of Peter. Let me speak of
other matters in my heart.*

I do not happily call to mind the months after my break
with Ennelina. If this book is penance, it is chiefly for that
portion of my life. At night I would hear whimperings
outside my window, not knowing if they were hers or a
phantasm of my own guilt. From Ellewibel came notes
pushed under my door – threats to set two burly nephews
from Cologne on me, promises to ruin my business. My
hands stared up at me like dead limbs, from the loss of the
flesh they had once touched. My body ached for the body it
had been one with. The thrumming head, the blistered
tongue, the rumbles from my belly – these told me I could
not live without her balm. I took no heed. I would not admit
the chasm in me. I was no man's man – no woman's man,
either. I lost myself in work. I deadened my heart.

Worse, I *coarsened* myself. Perhaps a man, to achieve

greatness in this world, must needs become coarse, since finer sensibilities will not allow him to prosper. Coarseness drove me harder at my work. It helped me raise money from men who should have known better than to lend. It also bid me swyve and drink. The latter is said to mar the former, but I did not find it. Without wine and beer, I should have lacked the courage for the act, which until Ennelina I had been a novice in. Now, without the conscience of a sentimental tie, I could indulge myself. I began to call at the bath-house, in search of angels. Though there were none as sweet as Marguerite, this suited me – attachment to one angel was not my aim. The need to enter women became ever stronger, like a text I wished to copy every night. Though the act was each time different, the celestial triumph felt always the same – Christ coming to Jerusalem, comets raining down, the soul being received in heaven. If Eve had sown the seed of evil in man, I was now returning that seed, with a vengeance.

It is a wonder no little Gensfleisch sprang from these acts of union. Though some women I went with had wiles and contraptions for inhibiting that mischance, most were more peasant-innocent. Yet none came with bundles to my door. Nor did I hear rumour of one I had lain with drowning a bastard in the Rhine. Nor do I think one will now appear, though the fancy has sometimes struck me of a young man in my employ (even you, Anton!) happening to hum a song which I had heard a bath-house angel sing many years since and through our discourse it falling out she was his mother and I his long-lost sire. This, should it happen, I would delight in, not regret. Even then, despite the lawsuit, I had fond fancies of Ennelina in secret bearing my child. But I knew this could not be, or her mother would surely have been after me for gulden. Perhaps, I conceived at last, I might not have the seed in me for children. The thought of this depressed my spirits and also my desire. Soon I called no longer at the bath-house and contented myself in drinking at home (with the Beildecks and my workers to help drain the barrels, the wine-bill was for five litres a day).

If I could not give her children, Ennelina was better without me.

Since I refused to brag in taverns of robbing her virginity, she had at least been saved from public shame. But I knew she was pious, and to her mind our acts might be no less a sin for going unconfessed. And with the humiliation of the court case as well, she was sure to be sore afflicted. Such were my broodings. I could not, hard as I tried, lose the impress of Ennelina. Each time I slew my heart by roughly cutting off its tendrils, others would grow back in their place. But nor could I bring myself to visit her – to brave the dragon's lair and own my feelings. I feared the world would think me foolish for having triumphed in court then surrendered to the enemy outside. So though I yearned for Ennelina, I would not shift my ground to suit her mother. And this – more than swyving with other women – was my sin. From hatred for the oyster who had made it, I threw away a precious pearl.

Without Ennelina's truth and passion, I was thrown back wholly on inventing. Into the hollow she had left, I poured hot metal; into the silence, words. I should be thankful. In empty hours, I was consoled to think how losing her had led me to the founding of type. But neither work, nor art, nor *coarsening* could rid me of my guilt. Even now, years later, it gnaws at me. There is no justifying how I treated her. But this book is a kind of penance, a confession of perfect sorrow, and by it I hope to save my soul.

11. Plague

Andreas Dritzehn died. It was Christmas, and he a father of young children, just the worst time. We feared it was coming, from his face growing greener each week. He first complained of belly-fullness, yet these were hard times, for him who had borrowed especially, and he could not have been overeating. A pallor sat on him for days – like white froth on cold bean soup. After came chills and fevers, and swellings under each arm. Later still, dark blisters on his skin. The plague, then. Konrad Saspach said once that while they were working together at the press a big black moth flew from Andreas's mouth – as though grown fat with eating off putrefied lungs – and he knew Andreas was doomed.

It was the other Andreas who brought the tidings. In those early days of our enterprise, we worked in two places: Hans Dünne and I engraved punches and made type at my house; the others dabbled with the press, which was kept in a shed at Andreas Dritzehn's. My first thought at the death was for poor Andreas's family: without him, and with loans to repay, what means had they to survive? My second thought was whether the materials of my art were now plague-ridden and full of contagion and thus a danger to us. My third thought, a moment later, was for the press. Andreas had been told to keep it under lock and key. But now his goods were to be passed on or pawned, the family would be poking in every cranny. If the secret should get out, our enterprise would be ruined. I feared especially Andreas's brothers Jörg and Claus, who had nagged at him to show them our materials and to explain the nature of our work. He, being loyal to me, had fended them off, but by doing so he had *offended* them. Now he was dead they would want knowledge and satisfaction.

Where was the key to the shed? I asked Andreas Heilmann. It was here in his pocket, he answered, putting it on the table. Having been sick for a week before he died, the other Andreas had given it him, so he could freely enter and carry on the work. I was pleased he had the key, since it was needful we now destroy the press to keep our secret – and asked him if for this purpose he would go to the shed with Konrad Saspach the following day. He said they could not for two more days, since the next they would be at Andreas's burial, as he trusted I would also. Indeed I would, I said, but asked to borrow the key in the meanwhile, so I could inspect the work one last time. We had lately experimented with printing an alphabet book, and the paper and type still lay there which, so I said, I would like to see. On his departing, I summoned Lorenz, my servant, and told him what secret task to perform. While Andreas Dritzehn was being buried, and we mourners were fully occupied, he must go to the shed, recover any notebooks of mine, remove all the type, take apart the press, load it on a cart, and bring the whole back here.

This Lorenz did without discovery, before giving me back the key, which I returned to Andreas Heilmann. When I then asked Lorenz to break up and make a bonfire of the press, he was surprised, and demanded why, the work having cost us dear in time and gulden. I told him the press had served its purpose, which was true, and that from my notebooks I was drawing up plans to build another. More than that I did not say, except to swear him to secrecy.

It was as well I made haste, for the next day Jörg and Claus came, demanding to discuss the future of the enterprise now that their brother had passed on. I affected surprise at their haste – was their house not in mourning still? – and asked them to return in a day or two, with any papers relating to our contract. In the meantime, I said, since our enterprise must be kept hidden from outsiders, they should destroy the press kept in their brother's shed, and melt down any forms lying in the bottom of it, and also recover certain notebooks belonging to me. I said that Andreas Heilmann held the key, and that he and Konrad Saspach would assist them. Next day all four of them opened the shed, and found the press already gone, and began to accuse one another. No doubt Andreas suspected my hand, but having little fondness for Jörg and Claus he made no mention of this. Ours was a partnership and he stayed loyal to me. In those days I chose my colleagues well.

Though the brothers' noses were thus kept out, the business was far from over. When Jörg and Claus came round next evening, they were angry with me about the thefts from Andreas's shed, until I became angry with them: who was *I* to be accused? Were they not *my* belongings that had gone? We calmed down. I poured them wine and Frau Beildeck brought plum tart. They had a proposal for me, they said. Now poor Andreas was gone, the gulden he had invested must naturally be returned to his heirs. But since from what they understood of my circumstances I might lack the means to pay them this sum (the impudence!), they were pleased to offer an alternative: that the gulden stay in the partnership and they as brothers take Andreas's place. I smiled and poured another glass. I had half-expected this and would by no means be coerced. Claus was the most cack-handed goldsmith in Strasbourg. Jörg's idleness was legendary. Of themselves they were nothing, but their brother's death had given them an opening to plunder his virtue. Here they were, the worms not yet at him, dancing a jig on his coffin. But I would stop their merry tune.

'Did you find the contract he drew up with me?'

'We have all his papers.'

'Have you studied it?'

'Not in detail.'

'I will read from my copy, then. Clause 3: "In the event of the demise of one of the aforementioned partners before the contract expires, then his investment, all things finished or unfinished, all forms and equipment and materials, shall pass to the surviving partners, and his heirs shall be entitled only to one hundred gulden in settlement, to be rendered to them five years after the date of this contract, nothing excepted."'

'What does that mean?'

'It means that three years from now – two having gone by since the contract was made – Andreas's heirs (his children, I take it, not his brothers) will be entitled to one hundred gulden, nothing more.'

'But he invested thousands.'

'He still owed me money.'

'The contract is a fraud.'

'It was witnessed and sealed.'

'You cheated him.'

'He signed it. Andreas Heilmann signed it. We all signed it. Had it been I who died, your brother would have benefited more, since I put in the higher amount.'

'It is still a cheat,' said Jörg, banging his fist on the table, as I knew he would sooner or later, a violent temper being the only exception to his general sloth.

'It is a binding legal document,' I said.

'We will see about that, in court.'

Hot-headed though he was, I did not think Jörg would proceed. In this I misjudged his love of lawsuits. First he took his brother Claus to court, then a neighbour called Agnes Stosser, accusing them of stealing valuables from Andreas's corpse (jewels, money, gold rings and silver buttons). Not content, Jörg then had a summons issued against me. His hope was that the threat of it hanging there would scare me to admit him and Claus as partners, or to pay back what Andreas had put in. But the prospect of the law court held no fear for Johann Gutenberg. I had fought and won before. I would fight and win again.

With Ellewibel I had won because no agreement had been put in writing. Here I would win because one had. How far Andreas grasped what he had signed did not concern me. In his eagerness to profit, he may have missed the smaller clauses. But when he fell ill, we discussed the contract anew, and I saw from his sad eyes he understood. I thanked the Lord for giving me the foresight to insert the clause. Also the friendship of Nicholas of Cusa, who with his lawyer's training always advised me to set down each last detail. But the clause was nothing unusual. We were four men over thirty-five. As such, odds were that one would die within five years. So it proved. I had gambled on a life being lost, and won. Forgive me, Andreas, but I did not know who it would be.

A year passed before the case was heard. By then, Jörg had gathered a *crusade* of witnesses against me. A shopkeeper, a broker, a woodcutter, a priest, two goldsmiths, a midwife, several neighbours and cousins, a little girl who had once seen me accept a bottle from Andreas – twenty-three in all were dragged into the fray. They made a tattered army, and the reek from some, even in the winter cold of court, forced the Judge to hold his nose, for fear their plaguey breath might carry him off. Bilberry-faced and with ears like red cabbages, Jörg was hot for justice. He even harangued my servant Lorenz, to make him reveal how he had spirited away the press and type. 'You villain,' he shouted, 'I will wring the truth from your mouth even if I have to climb up on the gallows with you.' Lorenz would not join the enemy camp. But one after another, Jörg's foot-soldiers testified against me. It was alleged that Andreas had borrowed heavily from several sources (which was true), given me a basket of pears and half an *Ohm* of wine (which was also true), and put in five hundred gulden to the business (which was not). Had the witnesses been less addled and stuttering, they might have swung the Judge against me. But the only one who stood firm was the shopkeeper, Bärbel von Zabern, who sobbed to recall Andreas telling her that he had pawned all his property and inheritance.

'How did you feel when he told you this?' the lawyer asked.

'I was greatly shocked,' she said between gulps.

'And what did you say to him?'

'I cried out "Holy suffering!" and asked him: "If your business does not succeed, what then?"'

'And what did he say?'

'He replied: "Before the year is out, we shall have our capital again and all will be happy, unless God wishes to torment us." But now' – here Bärbel wept loudly, and pointed an angry finger in my direction – 'Andreas lies in the ground, not from God tormenting him but because that wicked man there did.'

The witness was led to her seat. Jörg's lawyer smiled smugly. The Judge looked stern. But I need not have feared. On my side fought an army half the size but thrice the mettle of Jörg's – Lorenz, Hans Dünne, Konrad Saspach, Hans Riffe, Andreas Heilmann and his brother Anton among them. Before it fell to me to speak, it had been proved, many times over, that Andreas's investment was eighty gulden towards the mirrors and only forty towards the books. When my turn came, I gleamed a fresh and honest face at the court, like a new-minted coin, and talked as if it pained me to plead my case – to *press* myself – against a man, not yet a year dead, whom I had plucked from poverty, then loved, nourished and instructed in my arts. I rehearsed the matter of the contract, and the care I had taken in it, and how I had begged Andreas to consider it well, and how he had long pondered it, and how at his bidding we had revised the death-clause, as I called it, which was done so that, if any one among us should die, his heirs would be stopped from learning the secrets of the enter-prise, and instead receive a hundred gulden. As to the brandy-wine and basket of pears given me, I, I, I – here for a moment my voice dried and halted, as if my throat were choked by the sweetness of Andreas's generosity being mingled with the sour breath of his brothers – I would never wish to squabble over such things, any more than Andreas would have, our relations having been so easeful and trusting. But if a bill of lading was to be presented, if *blood-monies* were to be extracted, if all the debts I had cancelled out of precious friendship should now be made an issue, why then, did his brothers wish me to debit them for all the times Andreas had eaten, drunk and slept at my house? If this was their notion of doing him respect, then my housekeeper, Frau Beildeck, could provide a full account, with every *Fuder* and *Ohm* of wine, every *hank* of meat, every *incontinent* laundry item noted down. But – so I went on – I would appeal to the Judge for the memory of Andreas not to be thus despoiled. Though the sum he owed me, at a guess, ran to ten times what I owed him, I would be happy to *wipe the slate clean* in order not to demean him. Here I paused a moment to brush a tear away before continuing. With the anniversary of Andreas's death fast approaching, I said, I and my colleagues had thought of commissioning some bust or statue in his memory. Pray God it not be sullied with brandy-wine and pears.

Wiping my eyes again, I stepped down from the witness stand, this little oration at an end. When the Judge ruled in my favour, and made known in writing the grounds for his verdict, he did no more than his due. A more pernickety judge might have insisted Andreas's heirs be repaid the full one hundred gulden, as in the contract. But since Andreas was in breach of that contract, being eighty-five gulden behind in his contributions, that amount was deducted, and all I owed the family was fifteen gulden, payable two years hence.

Lavish to a fault, not wishing to rub Jörg's nose in his defeat or to make life hard for Andreas's children, I waived the two-year deferral, and paid them the fifteen gulden there and then.

The court case had wasted a fortnight of work. At last I could get on again. Business as before.

12. Burghers

Invitations came. The City fathers took me to their bosom. My growing business interests, my diplomacy in *unimprisoning* the clerk from Mainz, the defeat of the grasping Dritzehn brothers: from these I became known as a man of mettle. As a man of substance too – with a house in the suburbs, three pigs, two servants, a goat, a flock of geese and a broad hedge to dry laundry on. Brokers sought me out for financial advice. Smiths and toolmakers asked me to show them how to write business contracts. The wives of councillors requested I sit next to them at banquets, since it was known I had a 'princely grace'. With Lorenz to assist (no prince should walk abroad without a servant), I had new clothes measured for me at the best tailors in town: it was meet I own a wardrobe at last, rather than appear in modest garments. So busy was my nightly round, Frau Beildeck must forever have been laundering, to bleach the spots of wine and boar-blood from my clothes. I had thought the breach of promise suit might impede my acceptance, but on the contrary. The gossips down the dinner table let it be known Ellewibel was a cantankerous old widow and Ennelina – who word had it now intended 'becoming a nun' – a silly child. It was assumed, being close to forty, I would take myself a *proper* wife. At festivals and dances, I held the hand of many a young lady. None was quite for me. But the eagerness of their eye told me I need not fret at my unmarried state.

By day, I proceeded with my enterprise. In place of Andreas Dritzehn I hired a smith called Martin Brechter, not as a partner (we wished to keep a tight rein on the profits) but as a jobber at a weekly wage. He was cheerful, quick to learn, and easily bossed – a man who would not say boo to a goose. Our metal business had been branching out. We made caskets, bracelets, trinkets. With the Aachen pilgrimage due, we also made more mirrors, adding to those in store. Meanwhile Konrad Saspach built a second press and I chose our first book to copy, the *Donatus*, the Latin grammar I had fondly studied with my stepsister Patze, which being popular in schools yet modest in size (only twenty-eight pages), seemed the right beginning – a source of lifelong income too. The type still troubled us greatly, on account of the letters twisting and bending rather than breaking clean like glass. But this we improved through experiments in alloys. And with Andreas Heilmann having taken a share in a paper mill, we had a good and cheap source of paper. In keeping with my ascent to a man beloved by aldermen, I did less handwork than in former years, and more supervision and draughting. Why my business prospered was hard to say, since little had yet come of it. But the rumour round town had it that Gutenberg was 'the coming man'. At no time in my life have I been more looked to. If I had glanced into one of my mirrors, a smile would surely have beamed back.

Why then do I sigh, calling back that time? Why, in my bed, was it a frown and furrowed brow I slept with?

To start, I was a man more feared than liked, who found it hard to raise money and was already living beyond his means. To keep the work of the books going, I needed investors. But this work being secret, 'engraving and stone-cutting' was my known business. When I spoke to burghers at supper, enticing them with rhapsodies of metalwork ('the rose-glow of iron in the furnace, fierce as the eye of a forest wolf'), their interest was keen. But see these same men by day, put the matter in writing, lay out the sums and workings for them, and panic would scurry about their faces. They wanted my company and good will, but not to join me in business. I was known to be *hard*. A man making a bargain with me could expect to come off worst. Nor were my debts quickly repaid. That was the word round Strasbourg.

Then too there was the slowness of our print-work. We had a half-working press. We had a hand-mould casting three legible letters out of every ten. We had a hiveful of difficulties – making the lines even, holding a galley together, finding the right texture of paper and ink – buzzing at us like angry bees. When setting our contract at five years, I had hoped to master the art in three. But with months only left to run, the end was as distant as ever. And the work, with these delays, turned more and more costly. There were paper and vellum to buy, as well as lead, tin and antimony, and prices had risen. There was Martin Brechter's jobbing wage to pay. The city of Mainz was rumoured to be bankrupt, and my annuities were again held up. As to the legacy from my mother, this was spent by now, on the house and business, and on wine and clothes.

To depress me further, there was Ennelina, whom I could not banish from my mind and body no matter how many tables I supped at or other women I held. In work, a man can forget himself, be free from fretting and I-Me-Mine. But in play he has more time to brood. And what played with me in bed and tavern was the image of sweet Ennelina.

I looked to the Aachen pilgrimage, its time having come round, to ease my mind and fill my purse. Some of the mirrors we kept in Mainz, to sell to pilgrims passing through. But the bulk of them were to be sent to Aachen. The plan was that I go myself to oversee the selling, but, our typesetting being at a delicate stage, in the end I sent Andreas Heilmann in my place. For some weeks we heard nothing. Then word came by letter that the trade was poorer than we hoped. Six assignments of mirrors had gone ahead of Andreas, but one of these went missing and another arrived too late, when an overloaded ox-cart broke its axle. No shop in Aachen would stock our work for fear of angering the local guilds. The street-hawkers we used demanded too high a cut. Rivals who had stolen our method were selling their mirrors cheaper. Many pilgrims arrived without money, having been fleeced along the way. Then there was Andreas himself, who seemed to think his journey to Aachen a romp or feast – each night (from what I heard) he ate and drank our funds away, then next day slept too long abed. Aachen was not the ruin of me, but profits were far below our hopes. When Andreas and Hans Riffe took their share, little remained to put into the work of the books.

Where to find funds? There were cousins I could write to, but that would take too long. There were the Strasbourg Jews – but I would not do them the honour of letting them lend to me. No, the only remedy was to woo the City fathers, in the hope they might give loans. To chance on them out at supper was not enough. They must be brought to my house, where I could entangle them. To do this, I must reveal my printing notion. More even than that, I must show them *proofs* that it could work.

With the few rough pages we had triumphed in turning out, I set about my task. A pair or more of burghers were plucked at a time. Fine roasts of goose were laid on by Frau Beildeck – with hashed leeks, braised turnips and black-grape sauce. The best wines were called up from my cellar. A fire blazed in the hearth. Once the men had been warmed up, and their bellies filled, and their heads fuzzed with Alsace, then I could weave my web.

I recall the night Friedel von Seckingen came with Werner Smalriem – two businessmen who had spoken against me in the Dritzehn case, which made the prospect of taking money off them all the sweeter. As we sat over the stones of a cherry tart, I swung the talk to windmills, von Seckingen (I knew) having a stake in them.

'An invention that helps with grinding corn cannot fail to make a profit,' I said. 'The world will never have too much bread.'

'It is true,' said von Seckingen.

'Yet man does not live by bread alone,' I said.

'Yes, the spirit must also be nourished,' said Smalriem.

'Which is the purpose of my own invention.'

'What invention is that?' they asked together.

'It is a secret,' I said.

'Then let us hear of it.'

'I have spoken too much already.'

'Surely you can trust us.'

'In business it is best to trust no one.'

'But among friends . . .'

'To expect friends to keep secrets – is that not asking too much?'

'Not at all. Nothing you tell us tonight will pass beyond these walls.'

I shook my head at their entreaties, but when pressed a tenth time leant forward, glanced nervously to left and right (as if to ensure no spy was concealed in the dark) and with a 'Can I trust your discretion?' began.

'Have you ever seen a scribe at work?' I asked.

Indeed they had, and sighed, ready to be disappointed.

'And have you any notion of how long it takes a scribe to write ten pages? Two hours? Ten?'

'Something in between, perhaps.'

'What would you say then if I told you I can make one hundred pages in an hour?'

'I would not believe you,' laughed von Seckingen.

'I would think you had supped too much from your own cellar,' scoffed Smalriem.

'We have heard you are quick-fingered, Johann, but no hand could write that fast,' they mocked together.

'Yes, yes, but suppose,' I went on, 'the hand were that of a machine. You have seen a wine-press? Well, imagine a wine-press being used to make words. Imagine a line of metal squeezing out letters on paper. Imagine the method that stamped this mirror' – here I brandished one of the mirrors made for the Aachen pilgrimage – 'being used to stamp books.'

By now their interest was caught at last. But the word 'book' worried them, since a book suggests the Bible, and the Bible says it is easier for a camel to pass through the eye of a needle than for rich men such as them to enter heaven.

'What kind of book?' von Seckingen asked, suspicious.

'Oh, a book of ballads. A book of cooking recipes. A Latin primer for schools. A popular work, produced at pace, strictly for profit.'

'But one hundred pages in an hour, Johann? How is that possible?'

At which point, casually, as if by chance recalling I had a few about me, the rest being all *out back*, I reached under the table and plucked out half a dozen sheets.

'Perhaps I underestimate. These few were printed in a single minute.'

The men handed them round, murmured among themselves, glanced shyly up as though to test I was no magician and this some trick.

'They are a little rough,' I added, which indeed they were. But to these men, in the gloom, their glasses filled up again (Lorenz, having listened at the door, happening as instructed to come in just then with a new jug), their eyes in the candle-flame bedazzled by mechanical mysteries, the scraps of paper were miracles of smoothness. So that when I spoke of having perhaps to abandon the work since I lacked the funds and knew nothing of finance, they forgot the common notion of me as a businessman and saw another Gutenberg – unworldly, foolish, an inventor to be picked and gulled.

'What interest would you be willing to pay on a loan?' von Seckingen asked.

'Whatever the common rate is. Nay, more if need be: I am, I confess, in urgent need.'

'How does ten per cent sound?' asked Smalriem.

Twice the common rate was how it sounded, but I seized at it and said:

'Perfect.'

On which hands were shaken, and invitations offered me to visit these men at home next day. And when we parted at the door, they smiled the knife-smile of deceivers, but the smile was all in me.

Several times this happened with the burghers of Strasbourg. And if a few thought the better of it by the time I called for my loan, still most would have the contract ready – and the gulden.

In this way, a year or more, I kept going on the work of

the books, and stocked my wine-cellar, and lived beyond my means.

🙠

It is not yet your home-time, Anton, so why lay aside the pen? You disapprove of my conduct, perhaps. It seems to you un-Christian. I am – let me frame it as sternly as your eyes do – a knave, a huckster, a fraud. But you are wrong. Was it I who planned to cheat these men, or they who planned to cheat me? With some, the loans were fully repaid, if not at interest. Having my good name to think of, I was not so brazen as to rob every Strasbourg burgher outright. The rest do not trouble my conscience. A fool is swiftly sundered from his purse, and the men I took loans from were the worst kind of fools, those who cared only for profit. It was their own greed trapped them. Does not Christ say, 'Lend, hoping for nothing, and your reward shall be great'? But these men lent hoping for great reward – for which their reward was justly nothing or less. Yes, the City fathers took me to their bosom. But since they meant to smother me there, I did right to be a viper – to bite them and slip away.

Let me plead something more in defence. I was seduced by my own oratory. The press would be, I truly thought, a marvellous invention, and I felt *justified* in stealing money to make it work. Doubtful means, but honest ends. I bow to God, who will judge me harshly for this, but cannot bow to the censure of men. I believed in my work. I knew it would do good in the world. How many others can say as much?

Though he would have condemned my ways of money-raising had he known of them, I also had the backing of Nicholas of Cusa, who often passed through Strasbourg in his journeyings to and from Rome. In the old days we had drunk in taverns. Now he dined at my house. Our supper talk would turn as always to the Church. He was active for Rome now, and against the German Church becoming strong, having fallen in (too deep, I thought) with the Pope. But he feared and hated corruption nonetheless.

'No man can know God,' he said, 'and our faith in Him must always rest on ignorance. But to foster ignorance, and spread it like pig-muck, as the priests do – that is sinful.'

'You mean their way with indulgences and relics.'

'Also the texts they use – the prayer books, missals and Bibles. All are badly copied and full of error, some of them by design to invent new penances that will swell the priests' own coffers.'

'My press could make corrected texts. Perhaps I should do you one, a missal, say, after my *Donatus*.'

'Indeed – and I will use my influence, so the Pope himself is made to authorise it, and every church and monastery between here and Rome is forced to buy one.'

'And then after that I will make the Bible.'

'Is that possible – a text so large?'

'I do not know.'

And I did not. So many pages might be beyond me. And being The First Book, God's Book, the Book of Books, rather than any other, might bring me unholy trouble. Nor, since we had supped well, could I tell if Nicholas was in earnest, or if his influence would stretch so far. But at the root of me I was minded to do it.

It was years before I did. But the seed had been planted. Though my days were spent with inky fingers, and my nights on plucking money from fools, I never forgot the Book.

Do not, then, stare severe at me. There are many ways for a man to serve his God.

With the rush of other men's money at me, the *Donatus* under way, and the Bible glimpsed over the horizon, I was – to use printing talk – *set up*. But inventions, as I have said, are not thunderbolts. For every lightning-strike of inspiration come months when ice sits on the trough. You try this thing, and you try that thing, and when at last they work you try another thing, which if it fails leaves you back where you began. Trial and error: my history has been little else. To begin and begin again, because the mind lacks the wit, or the hand does, or the materials do. How else explain why my printing took so long to flower? How else account for the twenty years? Twenty years! What lightning is that? What white-hot crucible of creation? And yet I do not mourn the time I spent. Inventions can be quickly made. Perfecting them takes an age.

Such battles with lead and iron! Such unceasing metal fight! The matrices were sunk too deep or else too shallow. The jets from the overspill of the casting had to be planed or filed or chipped, the devil of a task. The letters – the soldiers of lead – would not march in line together. The ascenders ascended too high, the descenders descended too low. A type fell out and lay side-on across the galley. The hand-mould would not cleave together tight. The platen would not kiss the bed straight, so half the page was dark, the other light. The press rumbled and shook, and ceiling plaster fell in. The paper shrank or shrivelled or caught fire. The ink was too runny, too sticky, too clotted with lumps. The margins were fixed too wide or else too narrow. Some problems we solved with brainwork, some with handwork, some with brutishness – the texture of the ink, a mix of soot and varnish and linseed oil, was improved by pissing in it. But others could not be solved at all.

Once more I began to lose money, and to despair. I was all men ever in a hole – Jonah in the whale, Daniel in the lions' den, Lazarus buried in earth. That winter was the coldest in years – some mornings at work the metal was so cold it stuck to our fingertips and tore the flesh away. I felt like giving up. Then the spring came – and with it a commission that promised to pay off my debts. A printing assignment. The second begun on Konrad Saspach's press, but the first to reach the light of day.

It came through Nicholas of Cusa, who was in town again, eager to see my progress. Having some sheets of paper about me, from parading to some businessmen the night before, I showed him them. But he being a friend, I did not (as I had with them) conceal the flaws.

'So you are not ready for missals and Bibles yet?' he said, having studied the crooked typeface and smudged ink.

'We are not ready even for the *Donatus*. We can produce pages, but not to the standard of scribes.'

'But a rough and ready pamphlet, topical in nature ...'

'We could do.'

'A work in the vernacular.'

'Our alphabet is Latin. We would have to improvise.'

'But it could be done?'

'If appearance is not everything, yes.'

'I have a notion for you.'

He had a notion for me. There is in German a poem on the Last Judgment, written at the time of King Frederick II. In a portion of it, a Sibyl prophesies to King Solomon the coming of an Emperor called Frederick, who will convert the Jews and crush the Infidel: 'When Kaiser Friedrich hangeth his shield on a withered beam, then will the prophecy be fulfilled in heaven and here below.' Now one of that same name had been elected to the German throne: Frederick III. Nicholas, who had met him, spoke warmly of his intellect, his desire for reform, and his struggle to repel the Turks. Could not the *Sibyl* poem be used to rally men round the king? If I could print it, however roughly, as a pamphlet to be sold about the streets, I would render the nation honest service – and be sure to profit myself.

Nicholas had great hopes of my invention. The pamphlet, I knew, was a test of me, which if I passed might lead to prayer books and missals. It meant breaking off from the *Donatus*. It meant long hours by candlelight. But I agreed to it. From Cologne some days later, through an envoy of Nicholas, came a manuscript of the *Sibyl* poem. Martin Brechter and I set it up in the typeface made for the *Donatus*, running ragged as prose, 27 lines to a page, 500-odd lines, 28 pages in all, with no name attached. Since each pamphlet would cost less than a couple of beetroots, we used the cheapest paper. Andreas Heilmann, atoning at the press for his idleness in Aachen, laboured like a hero, as though Samson, Goliath and Sisyphus rolled into one. Within weeks it was done and stitched together and dispatched for Nicholas to use.

I could take little pride in the appearance (which was smudged and uneven) or in the purpose. Words should be for the glory of God, not earthly kings. But I had kept my promise to Nicholas – and from his showing the pamphlet in high places, I hoped to prove myself to the whole world.

13. Flight

For some months, Nicholas fell silent. Since he travelled widely, this was not unusual, and I assumed him to be on papal business abroad. In the meantime, those poor fools, the Armagnac mercenaries, had rampaged through France, and were now laying siege to Basel – the Pope and our own Frederick having cooked this up together with the King of France. We too in Strasbourg took precautions to defend ourselves. The richest men in town were obliged by the city to supply a horse. Those judged a little less rich, like myself, half of one. Half a horse! They are not easily found, so we were asked to give gulden instead. I had none to give but what was borrowed, and little enough remained of that. Still, I did my duty. The Armagnacs were dangerous men, driven by hunger and a greed for gold, and – with my business promising to flourish at last – I did not want them breaching the city walls.

Then a letter came from Nicholas, asking that I desist from my work. He had been in Basel, where King Frederick was now much hated for having incited the Armagnacs to attack – and had seen copies of the *Sibyl* being burned in protest. 'No more pamphlets,' he said. The order was easily complied with – I had already turned my efforts back to the *Donatus*. But though we printed no more pamphlets, there were copies circulating in Strasbourg, and as the Armagnacs plundered the country beyond, and King Frederick grew daily more detested, here too were burnings in the street. I feared it could not be long before this anger turned on me, as the heretic, nay the Devil, who had printed it. To most, the very notion of printing was devilish enough. And despite my efforts at secrecy, the word was round town of a satanic instrument I had devised that could write better than a human hand. Now this Beelzebub had put forth a poem in praise of a rotten king.

If I had thought the City fathers might protect me against rumour and libel, I was wrong. My princely reputation was soon lost. The invitations to banquets ceased to arrive. Instead, creditors knocked at my door. The Dritzehn brothers were suddenly pitied for their mistreatment at my hands. If what I had printed had been a thing to be proud of, I might have withstood the snubs. But the pamphlet was no ornament. And after anger against it followed something worse: ridicule. It was known the work had come from my press. It was thought this the best my press could do. It was felt I must be a dunce. I had promised magic, beauty, a miracle in bookmaking – and out came this ugly slop. Men nudged each other in the street as I passed, and smiled derision, and whispered mockingly so I could hear: 'There goes the Print Master. Long live our scribes!'

For the first time in Strasbourg – where I had dwelt now nearly ten years – I felt alone. My mind turned back to my first days in the city, when I had met Ennelina and felt a joy now absent from my heart. Ennelina! The sapphire eyes. The finch-light voice. The walks we shared. Her silk against my gooseflesh. Much time had passed since the lawsuit. She would be – what? – nearly thirty by now. Despite all, I had gone on thinking our breach need not be final, that once I was settled and prosperous there would be nothing to stop me knocking at her door again, to offer marriage – which she would smilingly accept. Since I was still far from settled and prosperous, and since for all I knew she hated me, it was foolish to give lodging to such thoughts. And yet I did. In part it was chance that let them in. When I came one day to the City Hall to pay my wine tax, I saw in the register, several lines above mine, an entry for 'Ennelina Gutenberg'. Since no others in Strasbourg bore our names, I suspected this as a jest at my expense by one who knew (as many did) of the breach of promise suit. But to see her name like that entwined with mine . . . How had it felt for her to be denied by me, betrayed, scorned, abandoned, ruined? Could she find it in her to forgive? It was not, it seemed, too late to seek her out. The tax register listed her – if Ennelina it was – as living in town and 'affiliated to no order', which meant she had not left to be a Beguine.

Thinking how to meet her without entering the lair of the dragon mother (whose stubborn anger no doubt kept her living still), I fell into the habit of passing down Ennelina's street. For weeks this went on without conclusion, and I began to think of writing a letter, or daring to knock on her door. Then one evening, leaving the workshop, as if by miracle, I saw her walk towards me. For an instant it flashed on me that she had come to seek me out, with similar design, to see if we could resolve our differences. As she came nearer, I said her name aloud, and she raised her head from the cobbles, and met my eyes, but then at once lowered them, and when I reached to grab her arm stepped aside and around me and tried to pass. When I grabbed again, and this time took hold, she yanked her arm free as if the Devil had it in his vice, then spat at me, and shook herself off. In her wild eye as she pulled free I saw tears – tears not of love but hatred, a hatred welling from the pit of her heart. How stupid of me to think it could be otherwise. Yet I had not foreseen it, and in my shock did not pursue her. The shock was more than being shuffled off and spat at, but came from how she looked. Her flesh was now skin cleaving to bone. Her bloom had gone. A rash had spread across her face. I wondered was the plague on her (it had been about town), or was she living on nothing but lime-flowers. But no, these were the ravages of grief, a grief she owed to me.

So Ennelina despised me as a devil. And was no longer the young beauty I had known. For any level man, that should have been an end. But the rebuff made me only more fervent. Being myself sunk in spirit at that time, because my work was going badly, I felt her more than ever a kindred soul, and imagined promising full atonement till she softened and recovered and we were wed. Such a marriage would strengthen me, and mend my prospects in

Strasbourg, and we two could then be happy, and become Master and Mistress Print, and have children, and together conquer the world. Pride held me back a week, but at last I wrote, begging Ennelina to forgive me, setting down my proposal, and delivering this under her door at dead of night. No reply came next day or the following. After a week, I took again to walking up and down her street, and this time was more fortunate, since I saw Frau Stimm (whom I had not thought to call on, assuming her long dead) standing hunched and shrivelled at her door. Between catchings of breath, she told me that Ellewibel was living but unwell. And that her illness stemmed in part from her daughter having just left to join a convent. I walked away to sit silent in the abyss of my heart. Perhaps Ennelina had long planned to go. Perhaps she had left before my letter. Or perhaps the letter made her leave, she despising its contents and fearing I would hound her to the grave. Whichever way, she was now lost. I must see that, and set aside my idle fancies.

So I told myself. And though the heart is not easily ruled, mine through constant pressing fell into line.

𝒮

My time in Strasbourg moved fast to its conclusion. I had no choice. Ennelina was only part of it. So much had gone wrong in so short a time. My inheritance was spent. I owed money to half the City fathers. The secret of my art had trickled forth and made a mockery of me. I was denounced as a devil and ridiculed as a monkey and despised as a shark. There was no end to my own bestiary.

All this I might have fought off but for fear of the Armagnacs at our gates. Having been turned back from Basel, they were now plundering the country round Strasbourg. Already I had furnished the city with the price of half a horse, ten gulden, no easy sum for me to find. And now I was enlisted to offer armed defence. My companions were men 'without full standing in the guild' – painters, saddlers, smiths and harness-makers who, though the City would not take them to its bosom, were now asked to save that bosom from harm. To find myself thus classed, after the wealth and power I owned but a year or two before, was blow enough to my esteem. But there was, besides – I blush to make this confession – the fear of bearing arms. I hope the reader will not consider me a coward. In mental fight, I give no quarter. In service of God, none can match my ardour. But to pledge my body to a city I did not love, and which did not love me. To use my hands not on ink and paper but on spilling blood. To lay down my life before I had done what was in me to do. All this seemed a fearful prospect. The Armagnacs were a rag-tag army, for whom war brought bread after the hunger of peace. I pitied them, yet knew they would not shrink from striking me dead. For a cause I held worthless, I would not face the danger.

It was time to take my leave of Strasbourg. Our contracts having come to an end, I looked hard at my business, to reckon the cost of winding up. Hans Dünne was no longer part, having quit to do his own engraving. Konrad Saspach had gone too. Martin Brechter was waged by the week, and if I paid him for seven more days than he had worked would not complain. That left Andreas Heilmann, who for all his faults had been a loyal partner. His share I would repay by selling my house, and encourage him to put the sum towards his own business. This would as like be polishing stones – despite his paper mill, he had no special feeling for bookmaking, and would not persist without me.

There remained the press and type. Should I destroy them? My mind heaved to and fro. The typeface was close to looking handsome at last. The *Donatus* was half set. Yet I was tempted to have done with print, and to revert to a life of *Wanderlust*. Which should it be? In search of an answer, I had been out all night walking the streets when, one dawn, the matter was settled for me. Coming home, I had taken the long way round, for fear of meeting creditors. My feet were sloppy with swine-muck, my hands blue with cold as well as ink. I unbolted the printshop door. Silence. Darkness. Perhaps Martin and Andreas felt the same gloom as I did, for neither had arrived before me. But from the far side, under the east window, came a glow like silver. I walked towards it and found the source – a heap of type shimmering from a compositor's case. The shine was unearthly, more glittering than metal is by nature, as though alive. Each letter was like a tiny netted fish, wriggling before my eyes. I thought of the fishermen on the Sea of Galilee, and the miracle of them *casting* on the other side. Was this not a sign from God, that by casting in different water I too might gather a shoal of riches? Behind me the door swung open, and Andreas cried good-day. By then, my mind had been decided. Though my invention was still raw, and no book had come forth from it in Strasbourg, I would keep faith – with my Maker, with my art, and with myself.

I therefore spared the hand-moulds and some of the type, and made secret plans to secure them, so wherever I next went (which place only Nicholas knew) they too would go. As for the rest of my work in Strasbourg, with the help of Lorenz Beildeck I made a bonfire of it: the press, my old notebooks, our early experiments with the *Donatus*, the few copies of the *Sibyl* pamphlet that had not been burned. A fine pyre it made, the smoke above the city making an oblivion of me.

I had intended to go in secret and alone. But once the bonfire was lit, and my house sold to the highest bidder (this in haste, and at a loss), I could not hide my leaving from Lorenz and Lotte. Distraught, they begged to come. Here I was, without a home, a business, a legacy, a future, and still they wished to stay with me. Touched at their loyalty, I agreed.

While the fire burned, and the Beildecks packed their few belongings, a summons came, over the matter of a dozen unpaid loans. The burghers to whom I owed money, having at last found how many they numbered, had begun to lay plans against me – if I went near the court, they would have me thrown in gaol. It was time to be gone. In hours, we boarded a boat together under cover of darkness. Wood creaked on water – the sound of freedom again! Behind us, in the hills above the city, my pyre was smoking. I imagined my enemies coming and raking the ashes, in hopes of finding something to retrieve, if only my bones.

Nothing would be left them. The fire was my oblivion. Johann Gutenberg, also called Gensfleisch, Mirror-Maker and Printman, lately of Strasbourg, might never have been.

♪

Those bonfires: they disquiet you, I can see. You are a scribe, Anton, and revere the work of books. To you vellum is skin, and ink our life-blood, and a man who destroys them violates himself. For words to come to ash, for men to burn the *Sibyl* poem, for myself to make a pyre of my apprentice-work – it appals you, does it not? You nod and jerk as if goaded by a horse-fly. I love your indignation. Many times I too have wished for some record of those years – rough sheets with blurred characters to check against my memory, or to show to my print-pilgrims should ever they come. But none is left. I have no journal, either. I was content to work. And contentment never held a quill.

So, yes, reproach me for my bonfire. But paper crumbles, inking fades. For every book that burns, a hundred more are lost to damp. Mildew, spiders, bookworms, weevils, the nibbling of mice – they are the enemies of perpetuity. The burning of a book is like a murder or suicide, denying the rightful span of life. But sooner or later mortality must come. A page is torn by accident. A careless reader spills a glass of wine. The text comes unstuck from the binding. A sudden gust under the library window and papers are loosed like doves. If I speak of posterity, Anton, I do not delude myself that one book can furnish it. New versions must forever be copied. My invention was made to ease that labour. But even so the work is never done. If my health holds out till you and I have made an end of this, then I will die happy. But your manuscript, though the source, is only a rapid dictation. Another scribe must correct it and make a fair copy, then a compositor set it in type. And though some books may be printed in large numbers (I do not expect this to be one!), most of those copies in time will perish. This cannot be helped. But nor need it be mourned. If a single copy is preserved, the book, the original, the *Urtext* is still alive.

So I cannot pretend the burning of books distresses me. Since I myself consigned to Vulcan the safekeeping of my papers, why blame others for doing the same? Though such fires are often angry and rash, is it not some tribute to the power of written language that men be moved thus to behave? A book is like a friend we laugh with or an enemy we fight against. When we read, it is not only our mind that reads, but our whole body – the lips that move, the hands that turn, the nerves that tremble, the heart leaping in its cage. Since we are stirred so bodily, it can be no wonder if books provoke us to extremes – so that we try to stifle their blabbing or set them alight like martyrs. But a book is only dead matter. Its martyrdom is painless. Unlike Joan of Arc at the stake in Rouen, it cannot feel the flames.

It is dark now, the church bells have just tolled six: time today to make an end. But take this moral home with you across the fields. Every man and woman is unique. When they die, we mourn their loss, no matter that they have gone to God. With books it is different. A book can be reborn. When one version of it dies through rotting or burning, another – just the same – rises in its place. That was my insight. Buildings fall, statues crumble, canvases tear, music is gone in an instant. But once an impression has been made in metal, a book need never die. I am no alchemist, no necromancer, no Lucifer. Eternity to man was never a promise of mine. Only God can promise that. But eternity for a book: that I could arrange.

Part three

14. The Monastery

Early morning at the monastery. Sheepdogs barking across the valley. Roosters stirring lonely farmsteads. Magpies chammering among the vines.

The magpies called like that whenever they saw a fox. To other birds it was a warning, and to the fox a taunt. Hearing it one sunrise, I leant from my high window and combed the earth. At length, I saw him, a slither of russet among the vines. First the head. Then the body. Then the tail, so long and flowing it was like a copy of the body. Along he crept, slinking through the canes and up the hill. I called to mind the Bible: 'Take us the foxes, the little foxes, that spoil the vines.' But he did not spoil the vines. His mind lay up ahead, among the geese and ducklings in the monastery pens.

I had thought till then that foxes hunted by night, but this was dawn. Had he hopes the monks would not be risen yet? But they had been an hour already at matins, praying to God to send the day. And coming from chapel, they heard the magpies and knew. Two among them had been appointed poultry-keepers. The first took grain and water to the pens, while the other with a dog went in among the vines. The dog was a mongrel pup, untrained and jelly-limbed. But its wayward barking saved the day. From my window I saw the fox trot off, discouraged but undaunted, ready to return next day.

Those magpies made me think of my enemies, men I had crossed or was in debt to, who any day might slink up this hill in search of me. The thought did not strike fear. I was a fox myself, and having tricked them before would do so again. Besides, the monastery offered protection, and the monks had become my friends. Still, I had no fondness for hiding out. I intended my stay to be a short one. I looked forward to re-entering the world.

I had come direct from Strasbourg, as arranged. The notion had been Nicholas's, who despite the *Sibyl* pamphlet wanted me to work more closely with the Church. Had I thought of finding a more secluded workshop, he wondered? The walls of cities have ears, but he knew of country places with walls so thick a man might be immured for years and no one know. If such a place would interest me, he had friends and would make enquiries. When the heat was on in Strasbourg, I wrote and yeahed him in the matter, urging him to plead my cause. His answer came back quick, with the name of a refuge and directions how to get there. When Lorenz and I boxed up the type and hand-moulds, it was to this place we had them shipped and drayed ahead. Of our departure under cover of night I have already told you. This monastery I will not name, since my residing there was secret. But if I say I disembarked near Oestrich, it will give you bearings. Nor was it sited far from Eberbach, whose abbot, knowing me of old as a man who had ordered many *Fuder* of wine there, may have spoken for me no less than Nicholas did and thereby helped secure my lodging.

As a workplace it could not have been better. We had the smithy and half the stable-block. Where in Strasbourg the roof had leaked, here all was dry, cool, perfect for mixing ink and storing paper. I had thought a monastery might be all monks, but here were other men in abundance – cooks, goatherds, cellarers, gardeners and grooms. Lorenz lodged with the other servants while Lotte kept house for a doctor in the village below (they were free to meet on Sundays, and, being glad of the living, did not baulk at the fleshly privation). Two local men, Heinrich Keffer and Berthold Ruppel, were hired to assist me with typefounding and with building a new press. I also had monks to help with vellum and ink, these monks being scribes and therefore curious in the work. Twice a week, to earn my keep, I would instruct novices in the scriptorium, Tutor in Writing being my designation. My past as a scribe had gone ahead of me. I was made welcome with a warmth which no written directive from Nicholas could have inspired. The abbot, Brother Konrad, podgy and wet-eyed, seemed to share Nicholas's enthusiasm for my project. And his monks at all times treated me with respect.

One day a snake or fox might enter and make a hell for me. One day I must go out again into the world. But in the meantime, the printer's devil sheltered under the roof of God.

The monastery was heaven – too much so. My brief stay stretched to nearly three years. I could cite you good reasons. We were slow reconstructing the press. New hand-moulds had to be made, the old having been damaged in the journey. Ordering materials was troublesome: though I met the cost myself (with funds from the sale of my house), all metal had to be ordered through the Church, and with Nicholas often away on business, and his clerks slow to act, there were delays. His hope was that I might make a prayer book. But first we went back to the *Donatus*, and struggled much as before. All got away from us. It was like painting on water. The type melted, the ink ran, the paper tore, nothing would stay. Though Heinrich was willing, and Berthold nimble-handed, both were still learning the art. Where I had expected us to hare forward yard upon yard, we tortoised an inch at a time.

Yet it was not the work alone that detained me. Some change occurred, by which in cloistered calm I shed my former restlessness. Several hours a day I spent not in the workshop but in the monastery library. To begin with, I went there in search of scripts that we might copy – something with dignity, in the hand of an ancient scribe, so that no one could accuse our printed books (if ever we achieved them) of looking strange and new. The librarian, Brother Christopher, was at first suspicious of me. His shelves were well furnished, but the choicest books were kept on chains, and the rest could be borrowed only with his permission. In time, he grew used to me and was obliging. But when one day I asked to borrow Saint Augustine's *Confessions*, he stared at me – his eyes blue like flames under a cooking pot – and said I would be wasting my time.

'The monk who wrote it had the ugliest of hands,' he said.

'But I want to read it,' I protested.

'Not to copy the hand?'

'No.'

'Then you can have it,' he smiled, 'though you should approach it with caution. Augustine thinks that by admitting his sins he will inspire the rest of us to do better. I beg to differ.'

It was a novelty to read again. Compositors can set a text and absorb not a single word. Proofreaders can correct a page yet ignore its meaning. Illiterates can typecast without difficulty, provided they learn when a letter is upside down. The work of the books, I mean to say, had not required me to be a reader. Now I became one. Saint Augustine first (I did not agree with Brother Christopher. The *Confessions* are uplifting. And by being honest in small things – as I too have tried to be here – Augustine makes us believe him in large). Then after him, Cicero, Plautus, Terence, Catullus, Horace, Juvenal, Martial, Persius, Seneca and Virgil. Also Petrarch. Also Dante (whose Italian proved a struggle). But my deepest study was of the Bible. It seemed to me the brightest book of life – that if a man could bring its words into his bosom he need never fear to die.

But the Bible also gave me pause. If my work slowed, it was the word of God silting my veins. My blood had run too fast, I had stretched myself too thin, and now He wished to thicken me into knowledge. My past filled me with disgust. When I asked myself who he had been, this Johann Gutenberg, the gentleman born in Mainz and removed to Strasbourg, I could find no answer. He was nothing. I was nothing. And how, if I was nothing, could I bequeath something to the world? In my bed, I slept badly. No dream of hell seared me, but a vision of emptiness and dark. The pulse of my heart beat in my ear as though all was a hollow boum-boum-boum. What had I done of use to man and God? The pilgrim mirrors, the cheap jewellery, the badly printed paean to a feeble king – were such trinkets what my life amounted to? I could not repent having done battle with those spiders who would have sucked me dry – the Dritzehn brothers, Ellewibel, my creditors. But I mourned Ennelina, to whom I had caused deep pain by my shallowness. And mourned myself, who had left Mainz high-hoped and principled, yet come to this.

The night-sweats turned to daily brooding. When I saw the monks at prayer in the chapel, I envied them their cleansings. In the smithy, it was my own soul melting with the type. I barely spoke to those in my employ. To allow a man under me to work alone, without my hovering at his shoulder, had never come easy. I must always be there, showing him how, spurring him on. Now my eyes turned inward, to the apprenticeship of the soul, and I ceased to be a master of men. Heinrich and Berthold hammered and chipped busily enough. Being new to me, they did not notice my metamorphosis. But Lorenz saw, and asked was I feeling tired and wrought, as one might a man sickening with the plague. 'Perhaps the lead in the alloy is poisoning your blood,' he said. It was true that I felt sluggish and my arms were stiff. But my malady was more of the spirit than the flesh. Several afternoons I left the workshop and took myself off to bed.

Thinking to ease my mind, I sought the abbot out, Brother Konrad, in his cell. He was affable, as always, and listened intently. But his shoulders seemed to sag from my burdens, and his eyes were wet, as if streaming with the griefs of all the world. You may sag, his body said, but I sag with you. You may suffer, his eyes said, but I suffer more on your behalf. I felt guilty to pain him so. I felt guilty too at sitting an hour when I ought to have been upright in the smithy. What could be done? I asked. He quoted scripture at me. He advised daily confession. He said the brotherhood would pray for my soul. We shook hands and I left feeling no better. I was grateful to Brother Konrad for giving me refuge. But how to serve God and yet live in the world; how to rediscover the worth of my enterprise; how to do what was in me – with these he could not help. My pain was like the wetness in his eyes – too damp to be blinked away.

That night after visiting him, I tossed sleeplessly on the sea of my own despair. At dawn came the noise of magpies, which dragged me from my bed to the window, in hopes of spying the fox. What I saw instead was a figure down the valley climbing towards me. The figure was dressed in black and rode a horse. The horse's hooves raised dust from the track, and so trampled was I by dreams I felt as though that dust was me. The figure rode ever closer. My enemy come to arrest me, I thought. Or Death, staking his claim at last. Whoever, I was glad of him. I felt tired. I had lost the will to fight. I would embrace him.

♪

It was Nicholas. He waved from the courtyard, and bid me hurry down. I had no hurry left, except towards death. Even the sight of a good friend could not quicken me. Still, I dressed with such small haste as I could summon, and met him at breakfast below. He brought news. First, that he hoped shortly to be made Bishop of Brixen, and would be less free to help me than before. Second, that a new abbot had been appointed in place of Brother Konrad and would arrive the following week. Dark as I felt already, these tidings plunged me in new gloom. Neither circumstance should threaten my project, Nicholas said. But this came as little comfort, since in my mind it was already at an end.

We ate a breakfast of porridge before going together to the foundry. It had been some months since Nicholas had seen our work, and I wondered how far we had advanced. I should have known, but in my late distractedness had lost all track. Fearing the worst, I paused by the foundry door, as if the memory of some undone errand had struck me, and asked Nicholas to go on alone – I would join him in a minute, I said. He looked quizzical, as he had at breakfast when I failed to laugh with him as of old. But in he went, while I skulked in the stables awhile, then took a tour of the monastery outbuildings, pausing by the chicken run to see if that fox had yet been in, which I was glad to discover it had not. Returning, I entered the foundry. Nicholas, with his back to me, was standing by the press, while Heinrich showed him the bed of type and Berthold unpegged sheets of paper from the ceiling.

'It is handsome work,' said Nicholas, turning to me.

Relieved, I began to explain the setting difficulties, before he cut me off. 'But you are nearly finished.'

It was true. Heinrich and Berthold had been advancing without me, and through trial and error, and with the methods I instructed them in, had set and printed the first four pages. Nicholas handed me an example. The spacing was uneven. ℙs were mixed up with qs, and bs with ds. Even when all twenty-eight pages were printed, the *Donatus*es would still have to be sold, and the buyers, mostly schools, would make demands (some would want the pages loose, some sewn up, some already wrapped in boards). But as their grins told me they knew, Heinrich and Berthold had carried the thing forward in bounds. I wrote a brain-note to myself to raise their wages and hereafter give my workers more liberty to act alone. Morning light shone over the floor, and, like the sun burning off fog, Nicholas's warmth helped shed my gloom. What had looked to me grey lead these past weeks now shone a glittering silver. I thought again of Christ's fishermen in the Sea of Galilee, trawling with empty nets until they cast on the other side.

'So,' said Nicholas, 'a prayer book next? Or will you make a Bible?'

When he was gone again down the valley, I resumed the work, and threw myself at it with new vigour, like a man rising from the sickbed of his soul. Within a month, we had set and printed two hundred copies of the *Donatus*, and began to send out word of it to schools. In the midst of this came a letter from my brother-in-law Claus, inviting me to Mainz. Some years since, he had moved with Else into our old family house, while my brother Friele removed to

Eltville. Now, Else having lately departed this life, their daughters married off and Claus working in Frankfurt, the house stood empty. Even should he return, the house was large, and he would be glad of the company. I was fond of Claus. Yet – not from sloth, nor from grief at my sister's death, but from sweating over hot metal – the letter lay unanswered in my room. Nor did I find leisure to share a meal with the new abbot, Brother Ruprecht, in the refectory, or to offer more than curt greeting when he passed the foundry. There were more *pressing* matters to attend to.

To put it in another fashion: I was happy again. Those Ancients I read at the monastery had taught me much. But knowledge like this comes at a cost. Reading, so I find, lowers the spirit, since when an author writes true of men he brings to mind the darkness we abide in – our deceit, vanity and avarice, our disappointed hopes, and the tragic brevity of our time on earth. Such truths oppress us more when we sit and brood on them, as reading forces us to do. To work with one's hands is the other Pole, at least for me. In fingering metal, and dabbing with ink, and rushing about the room there is a pleasure which reading can never furnish. So though the knowledge derived from books is needed, the world being laden with ignorance, yet to me it always brings gloom and sadness. For this reason, though much of my life was spent on books, I am glad to have been a blue-nail – staining my fingers like any dyer or weaver – rather than a scholar at stool.

Thus I climbed from the pit of sloth to walk again on sunny hillsides. But many a snake and abyss lay ahead.

Brother Ruprecht sent word he wished to see me. Since we were deep then in printing our *Donatus*, I asked his servant could it wait. He did not think so, he said, and asked me to go with him directly, which I did, hoping to keep it brief. Brother Ruprecht was no successor to Brother Konrad in looks. His lean face was pink-eyed and hairless, like a baby rat. His smile had a barb of malice in it. His silences waited to catch you with their little teeth. Having set me off to converse on Nicholas of Cusa, and my regard for him, he sat back and watched, as if to set his trap.

'I am sorry we have not talked till now,' he said at last.

'I too am sorry,' I answered.

'I am sorry because our first conversation could then have been more pleasant.'

'Is this unpleasant? Forgive me if I have said anything amiss. I did not intend it.'

'I mean that my task is unpleasant. This *machine* of yours in the foundry . . .'

'It is a press,' I said, 'to make books.'

'What kind of books?'

'Our first is the *Donatus*.'

'A grammar-book. Not a work of God.'

'A work to help children with Latin, so they can then read the Bible.'

'But your press does not directly serve the Church, despite our giving it a home?'

I relaxed, thinking to allay his doubts with the plans I had discussed in secret with Nicholas.

'After the *Donatus*, we shall make prayer books, missals, psalters . . .'

'This is work already done by scribes.'

'A press could do it more quickly.'

'But not with such beauty. When a monk writes, the hand of God writes for him.'

'And yet errors creep in.'

'Errors are easily made and simply corrected. Since only priests see them, no harm is done. Or do you intend the word of God to be read by anyone who pleases?'

It was not a question but a reproach. I stared at him a moment while gathering myself. Those eyes stream with Christ's blood, I thought. That hair refuses to grow because the God he serves instructed it not to.

'To help men and women be literate, to give them knowledge, to make books so cheap even a peasant might afford them: that is my hope, yes.'

'Is there not a more selfish motive – the making of profit?'

'In Strasbourg, I made losses many times over.'

'And here?'

'My outlay has been modest. I pay two men wages. I am allowed to use the smithy. I receive food and lodging in return for tuition. Any profit I might one day make will be put back into the business.'

'But there is still enrichment – an offence against God.'

'The enrichment would come from spreading His word.'

'The word of God needs to be interpreted by priests, not spread about like dung.'

'I do not wish to despoil the Word.'

'But it will happen. To hand it about to all and sundry is dangerous. Would you have ploughmen and weavers debating the Gospel in taverns?'

'If that is what they want to do . . .'

'But what of the dangers? It would be like giving a candle to infants.'

'Such copies we make of the Bible would first be for monasteries and churches.'

'The Bible! You plan to make the Bible as well?'

'I have considered it.'

'The Bible, to have authority, must be written by monks, not by some heretic machine.'

'With my press, it will look as though a monk has written it.'

'But it will be counterfeit, the work of an engine. And God does not inhabit an *engine*.'

He pronounced the word as though speaking of a war engine laying siege to forts. Perhaps he was right to do so, for at that moment, more than ever before, I thought of my invention as a weapon against the useless past, in whose citadels men like him were vainly hiding. I looked into his eyes, which were pinker than ever. Whose blood was that streaming there? His own? Christ's? Some heretic he had tortured?

'Once you see our finished *Donatus* . . .' I said.

'I asked you here because your contract as tutor has come

to an end. I am told you have taught with much success. Indeed, the work of one of your students is now so advanced we have invited him to take your place.'

'But my work at the press . . .?'

'We have need of the foundry for new enterprises.'

'If I offered to pay rent . . .'

'We are a monastery, not a commercial enterprise. *Radix malorum est cupiditas*. Your presence here is awkward for us.'

'If I worked wholly for the Church . . .'

'Please understand this is not my decision, but from higher up, the *curia*. You must gather your belongings. We expect you to be gone within the week.'

I stood up. He did not offer to shake my hand.

Naturally, I brooded on the injustice. Had Brother Ruprecht had more wit, he would have kept me as his man (and I might today be printing for his monks). Instead, he censured me for thinking to make profits. Meanwhile the Church was growing heavy-coffered from its tithes, taxes and sales of indulgences, yet any word spoken against it was denounced as heresy. Something of this I was tempted to say. But being no priest or monk, I knew I could not *justify* myself to Brother Ruprecht. The only justification lay in my art. And that I must perfect elsewhere.

No appeal could be heard. My term at the monastery was over.

In my room I gathered my clothes and thought of Ovid, banished from Rome. Could I now call myself an exile? Perhaps not. To be exiled is to be banished from home, whereas it was *to* home, as you will see, that I now went. Besides, I was already versed in leaving places. For years before Strasbourg, I had been a butterfly, refusing to settle on any one flower. Yet to *choose* to leave a place is not like being driven from it. Three times in my life I have been forced out: from Strasbourg, by creditors; from Mainz, just three years since, by the Archbishop; and in between from the monastery, by a rat-eyed abbot. This middle exile was the mildest, the least peremptory. Yet I had liked the monastery and come to think the Church a home. So to be banished by the abbot caused me hurt. I felt as you might feel, Anton, if I should tell you (which is unthinkable) you must no longer come here as my scribe. Or as Ennelina must have felt when I preferred to fight her mother than be wed. Brother Ruprecht was sending me bleeding into the world.

I gazed from my window one last time. No fox among the vines. No enemy creeping up the hill. But a monastery rat had bitten me in the neck, and like a man wounded I must go.

15. Fust

'A Herr Faust to see you.'

'Sorry, Lorenz?'

'A Herr Faust is at the door, asking to speak with you.'

'Faust? The name means nothing. Does he seem respectable?'

'Yes, master.'

'Then ask him up.'

It was a Sunday evening, some months after my homecoming. The old house felt a little forlorn now, with my parents dead, my sister Else too, and no young children banging about. But Claus, back from Frankfurt, had made me welcome. I had leaned on him also to admit the Beildecks, who worked as servants to us both, and whose attic bedroom lay directly over my own (mine, though, being larger, and leading to a further room used for study). On the ground floor – from which Lorenz and my visitor were presently clumping their way upward – I had sited the press. At night, Heinrich and Berthold bedded down next to it, they, as free men, having come with me. Dismantling the press had not been easy, but we had managed, and shipped it here, along with the cases of type, and were now making a new *Donatus*. Though Claus had invested no money in the enterprise, I think the noise of our work from below brought more pleasure to him than nuisance. Being widowed and forlorn, with no work of his own in Mainz, he liked to see me prosper. In this, he shone white against the blackness of my brother Friele, who when I had called on him in Eltville – he too being now retired – sneered at my business and refused to lend me money for it, supposing me feckless and doomed to fail. Better the brother-in-law than the brother, I say: there is no rivalry, and there may be love of the same woman. With Claus at any rate I felt content. In inviting me to share his house, he had given me back my hope and childhood.

Naturally, I had feared returning. All those years of trying to leave, and here was Jo-Jo Gensfleisch home again. The Return of the Prodigal. I thought I might be mocked, but no, the change in me must be visible, I saw it in men's eyes as they shook my hand – the boy had shed his skin, seen the world, become a man, remade himself as Johann Gutenberg, returned. A pity he had no wife or children. A pity his family were all dead or living elsewhere, and that he and his brother could not mend their differences (and never would, for Friele was dead within the year). Still, he was back in the Gutenberghof, and running a business there, some secret art in metal, and the city having changed in his absence there was more room in it for men like him . . . So the talk ran round Mainz. I sensed no malice in it, no daggers at my back. If any knew what had passed in Strasbourg, and of my debts there, they did not say or could not care. I was a Mainzer now. A long-lost son, back in the city that bore me. Welcome home.

And the work was going well. A new *Donatus* had been set. Learning from past mistakes, we cut notches in each shank so no letter could be laid upside down. We also brought a higher science to our alloy, mixing the metals in exact proportions – of 28 pounds, 25 should be of lead, two and a half of tin, and one half-pound of antimony – so that the types, when cast, would never break or bend (that alloy was worth more to us than gold). Then there were refinements in the ink, which we found reached its right consistency when a heated drop, having been cooled on an oyster-shell or suchlike, clings to a finger. On the page, the ink was black yet shone like a river under moonlight. I would have liked more room in the workshop: with finished copies to keep, and supplies of paper and ink (also a cat to stop mice nibbling through the pages), we were running short of space – and funds. But a cousin of mine by marriage agreed to lend 150 gulden. And with *Donatus*es mounting up for sale, and designs begun for the Bible typeface, the business seemed secure.

By the evening of my visitor, then, I could not have been more comfortably settled in. And though the man shown in by Lorenz was far from a pretty sight, there seemed nothing ominous about him. He looked my age, perhaps a year or two older. Broad-shouldered, thick-haired, stubby of hand, vast of stomach, he might have passed for a pigman or dyke-digger. But his face, bloodshot to start with and now sweaty from climbing the stairs, told me that here stood a person used to sitting, while the worn fingernails spoke of one who made his living by counting coins. His mouth was red and open as a furnace door. In one hand, he carried an alder walking stick, in the other a feathered hat: the very image of a broker. The stick he laid on my table as he stepped towards me. He did not seem to be lame.

'Herr Faust,' I said. 'Delighted to meet you.'

'Fust.'

'Pardon?'

'The name is Fust.'

'Of course, *Fust*. My apologies.' A sharp look passed from me to Lorenz, who was better at running errands than delivering names.

'Johann,' he said.

'That is correct,' I said. 'And your name?'

'Johann.'

'Yes?'

'I too am called Johann.'

'Ah, I see. Not Jacob?'

'Jacob is my brother.'

'So we are both of us Johanns together.'

My confusion may be forgiven, since I knew already of a Jacob Fust, treasurer to the city council, and had had thoughts of meeting him, given that I might one day require a loan and he, in his position, could help. The brother, this Johann, I therefore greeted warmly, hoping to use his family ties. While he took a seat, Lorenz fetched a jug from the cellar, my own being just drained and the cellar amply stocked since my arrival. We sat across from each other, two solid Johanns.

'Were we not at school together?' he asked.

'At St Viktor?'

'St Christoph.'

'I was there till I was nine,' I said.

'You remember the Henzer brothers?'

'I remember the name.'

'Martin and Matthias.'

'I think not,' I said.

The vice of Matthias's arm. My arm plucked like gooseflesh. The red-faced tubby chanting 'Gensfleisch' over and over. Surely . . . A nervous silence fell. I glanced at Fust, who looked down at the floorboards, the old cracks dividing us.

'And when you left school?' I asked.

'I became a goldsmith like my father,' he said.

'Here in Mainz?'

'Here in Mainz.'

His work now tended more to 'selling and lending', he said. With the city council run by the guilds, there were more prospects for the likes of him and his brother. I took this as a tilt at my own class, and braced myself for a sermon on how the city had been bankrupted by old families. But if he thought this, he showed no sign. His spleen was aimed at the clergy, who had lent money to the council and were demanding interest back – and who if not soon repaid would refuse to serve at ceremonies.

'Baptisms we can do without,' said Fust. 'And men and women need not be wed to lie down together. But to die without last rites . . .'

'The priests will condemn us to purgatory,' I said.

'For the sake of a few gulden.'

'And meanwhile make our lives hell.'

'They have us over a barrel.'

'Can I fill your glass?'

So we ran on. I was happy to grumble an hour, over a jug. Still, there is a time in any meeting when he who has called it must come to the purpose, lest the other grow restless and make to leave. And that time swiftly arrived with me. As host, I could not depart – where would I go? But in my head I was wandering off, and from this began casting my eyes about, impatient to have done. These hints Fust finally took and steered the talk where he wanted it to go.

'All of Mainz is speaking of your enterprise,' he said.

This surprised me. I had said nothing except to a few who might lend me money. But I did not show my alarm.

'Do they approve it?' I asked.

'They say you are an alchemist.'

'It is nonsense.'

'Of course.'

'With the same breath, they denounce me for dabbling in black arts.'

'People are ignorant.'

'It is honest labour. With hands, metal, ink, paper, wood.'

'I have worked with metal myself.'

'You understand, then.'

'I also deal in manuscripts.'

'Even better. What is that phrase the masons use? "I found it wood and left it stone." I would like people to say of me: "He found it goosequill and left it metal."'

I kept a *Donatus* in my room, for meetings such as this, thinking to impress any man of business. Deciding Fust, for all his puffing, was one such, I brought it out.

'Here is our first book, see. No magic conjured it, merely science.'

'It is handsome work. A scribe could not have written it better.'

'And I sell it at half the price, which no buyer can resist.'

'You sell only in Mainz?'

'I have connections too in Erfurt and Strasbourg.'

'But the number of buyers is still small.'

'For now, yes.'

'Listen. Next week I leave for Paris. I have business at the university – with the bookseller there. If you had a *Donatus* to spare, I could carry it as a sample.'

'You are taking manuscripts with you?'

'Yes.'

'And this *Donatus* could be slipped among them?'

'Yes.'

'Without a word of how it was made, so that the bookseller can first judge the quality, not knowing it comes from a press. And if he likes it, you then astonish him with the cheapness of the price, saying the book is artificially written thanks to a new invention.'

'And he then asks will I bring him more.'

'Which you say you can.'

'His mind by this point running ahead, for though it costs him only half the price of a manuscript version, he sells it no less dear, and keeps the profit.'

'But I too will profit, because where that book came from it is easy to make more.'

'If you would let me take other copies, to show in towns along the way . . .'

He did not seek a commission, explaining he would earn sufficient from his manuscripts. My *Donatus* was a bold and lovely experiment, he said, which, should it succeed, the city of Mainz stood to gain esteem from. Therefore he was happy to perform me this service, more than happy, proud, proud to the sole of his boots, as who would not be helping to usher a man-made marvel into the world. I did not trust his pretty words – indeed I thought them so much horse-piss in the gutter. But what had I to lose?

By the time the jug was empty, he had agreed to take twelve copies with him. Any more he could not have carried. Besides, I liked the number, which made me feel these books were my disciples, going forth to spread the word.

I did not think there might be a Judas.

*

Fust's journey kept him away four months. I pitied the mule that had to bear his huffing rump, and marvelled it did not take a year. From Paris he sent a letter, all ink-blob and misspelling ('The seler in Paris is miteily eeger for moor'). I had thought that to deal in books a man must on occasion peer into them. Not so Fust, who thought Ovid a work by Homer and who said of my praise for Petrarch he could 'see no market for foreign cook books'. Did Fust's lack of learning make me underestimate him? Perhaps. A man can be good at sums without knowing the alphabet, just as one who has broken commandments can make a Bible. But I had no cause at first to be mistrustful. Fust had run me an errand. His travelling brought new orders. The *Donatus* would clear my debts and fund a typeface for the Bible. We set new editions and pressed ahead.

Fust hoped to return before June was out. On the twentieth came an invitation to supper next evening. Midsummer Night. Since the time the Devil squeezed me in the graveyard, it was a feast-day which I had held in little affection. But I was older now – almost fifty – and my star rising, and in Mainz and all around the sun shone kindly down. Poppies and buttercups among the corn. Dandelions and cow-parsley in the yard. I remember picking through alleys to Fust's address, a more modest one (given his airs) than he must have wished, close to where I had moved with my mother. The young had gone to their *danse macabre*. Old men sat playing cards on the pavement. Their wives were cooking suppers of sausage and kale. The evening dust smelled of honeysuckle. I felt at ease. I even said the words out loud to myself: *at ease*. Almost at once, as if needing shadow, I found it. If you are at ease, Gutenberg (so I addressed myself), why do you have no fond expectations of the evening ahead? It was true. I did not. Fust, I knew, was married, and doubtless his wife would be shrewish, the food deadly plain, the wine acid-sharp, the talk a tub of dully unslanderous gossip. With luck, any Fust children would be gone to the fair. But even this might fail to spare me. On the contrary, in the absence of offspring, I was certain to hear more than any childless man would care to know of the son who *takes just after his father*, of the daughter with a talent for *playing any musical instrument put in her hand*, of the infant capable of *walking at nine months*, and of the baby who *now sleeps through the night*. Forgive me, but when on occasion I have sat through tales of infant miracles I have found myself thinking fondly of King Herod. No doubt it is my being unchilded which makes me curmudgeonly. But where lies the consolation in knowing that, since the state is itself a stab of pain, or was for me that night. At ease, Gutenberg? I berated myself. Where is Ennelina, then? Where is the wife you might have had? Where are your heirs? Like a murderer approaching the gallows, I dragged my feet towards the Fusts. I had set off in mellow sunlight. But by the time I reached the house – which point I deferred almost to the point of insult – my weather was wholly damp and dark.

I lay this out to show how little prepared I was for the vision awaiting behind the door. It was a Fust child, no question: the brow and nose bore the stamp of his. But there I am pleased to say all likeness ended. She stood taller than him by an inch or so. Her hair hung in black ringlets. Her eyes glowed like mead. The only redness in her face was the blush that spread across it as she gave out her name. Christina. I followed her as she took me to her parents. The face was angelic-sweet, but the swaying hips were womanly. I put her at nineteen.

That children can be miraculous I was ready to believe for once, all the more so upon seeing the mother, a small, stout, pig-eyed woman of forty or so whose imprint on Christina was as blessedly slight as her husband's. Margarete Fust – Grete, as she asked me to call her – was unused to entertaining, or so I guessed from the haste with which roast kid was served us, a cook being summoned to *pour the sauce over* and a maid to *dole it out*. Both must have been hired for show – Grete fidgeted as they moved around the table, as though itching to do the work herself. She was nervous too at using a plate and spoon, as though stewpots and dripping fingers were all she had ever known. This much I took in, but for the rest saw only Christina, who though she added little to the discourse – even less, that is, than myself and Grete – took a lively, head-cocked interest in it, no small achievement when the sole theme was her father's impressions of Paris and they so general – 'a wide river … busy streets … people speaking in another language' – any other city might have served. Mention was made of a Peter Schoeffer, whom I took to be a relative or adopted son, then studying as a calligrapher in Paris (Fust had partly gone to visit him) but shortly due back in Mainz. I might have taken an interest in this Peter, who like me had studied at Erfurt and was said to 'write a brilliant hand'. But my efforts lay in drawing out Christina. Not least I wished to know how old she was and whether attached.

I tried to hide my eagerness. But Fust, raising an eyebrow at me, then arched it across the table at his daughter, like an arrow flying between us. 'What do you make of my Christina, then?' he asked, nudging my arm and mock-whispering so she and Grete could hear. The mother tutted, the daughter blushed. Since the tone was more suited to a tavern than a dining-table, how to answer fittingly I did not know, and silence hovered like candle-smoke. Fust wafted it away by replying for me. 'Beautiful, eh,' he said, less the proud father than a lecherous drinking-companion. 'In her prime too. Next birthday, she will be fourteen.'

At this, the women withdrew, not in protest at Fust's leering tone but to clear the carcass of roast kid (the cook and maid having by now returned to whichever house they had been loaned from). I too stood up as if to go, but Fust – filling my glass – pressed me back into my seat again. To him our being alone meant the start of business. He leaned across the table, man to man, Johann to Johann.

'They liked your books in Paris.'

'So you wrote me. I am grateful for your efforts.'

'The orders must be flowing in.'

'Business is improving, certainly.'

'And when other cities hear of your *Donatus* and how cheap it sells at, then every school and college student will want to buy.'

'There is still a prejudice towards manuscripts.'

'But it will pass.'

'I hope so. My other ventures will be ruined if not.'

'You have other ventures?'

'Yes.'

'Such as?'

'Missals, psalters, dictionaries, even . . .'

Christina put her head round the door. Black ringlets setting off pale cheeks. Mead-warm eyes.

'I am going to bed now, father.'

'Good night, my sweet.'

'Good night, Herr Gutenberg.'

'Good night, Christina.'

For a second her eyes held mine. The earlier revelation – just thirteen! – had rudely prised me from luscious reverie, but now once more she struck me as a woman and pleasing visions of the two of us stroked and stirred my imagination. Yet even as they did I saw too what she carried in her hands as she made for bed – a little wooden doll such as you find in the crèche at Christmas. From the blueness of its gown, the doll must have been the Madonna. The grown woman and the little virgin! Where Ennelina I first took for younger than she was, Christina I had taken as older. Girl and woman: so hard to know which is which and when one has become the other! Perhaps my fluster at this made me careless, for – turning back from the departed Christina – I let it out before I meant, and then heedless rushed on.

'You were saying: even . . .'

'The Bible: I have plans for that too.'

'The Bible! Now that would be an enterprise.'

'We have already begun designing the type.'

'It will look different from the *Donatus*?'

'More elegant.'

'And the *Donatus* is but a few pages, whereas . . .'

'The Bible will run to twelve hundred.'

'And you have the resources?'

'I will raise money.'

'Who will lend for something so uncertain?'

'I can think of several in Mainz,' I said, though it was a lie.

'But to win their confidence,' said Fust, 'you will have to reveal your art to them. And then your secret will be out.'

It was true. Since coming to Mainz, I had hired no men but Heinrich and Berthold, to keep it hidden. Likewise, the fewer loans I took, and the more within my own family, the less would be discovered of my enterprise. For this alone, I was ready to listen to Fust. But he had more.

'Suppose one man could lend you all you need?'

'It would depend.'

'On what?'

'His interest rate.'

'If that were standard – five or six per cent?'

'There would have to be a written contract: not every broker can be trusted.'

'Nothing more?'

'If I should tie myself to one man, I would need to trust – beyond the written contract – he had my interests at heart.'

'He would have to be a friend?'

'Or family. Yes.'

'Look no further. You have found him.'

'It is kind of you, Herr Fust. But the sums involved . . .'

He bristled at this, as if I meant to question how a man like him could find the funds. And I did question it. I had in mind a sum of several hundred, which when a working man had to live off ten gulden a year, and even the city clerk earned less than 150, was a sum far beyond a Fust. To lend to me he would have to borrow, no doubt of it. What was the benefit, then? Any interest he earned, he would himself be charged. Any profit would be small. I could only think he had miscounted, or in his fever to join my enterprise was ready to take a loss. It puzzled me, but I had seen before the gleam of money in men's eyes: the later the hour, the deeper the jug of wine, the brighter it shone. Fust must be a fool. His greed or vanity had got the better of him. He knew nothing of my debts in Strasbourg. If I played it canny, I could gull him.

'How much do you need?'

'The lowest? To scrape by with? Six hundred gulden.'

'And to work as you would wish?'

'For four presses. A new printshop. A workforce of twenty or more. Eight hundred.'

'Eight hundred would do it?'

'Yes.'

'I will have it for you next week. Let us shake hands.'

'I should ponder overnight.'

'Come on, shake on it. Why do you hesitate?'

Why did I hesitate? Not out of fear. No bell tolled in my ear to warn that this scene would *plague* me for ever. Rather, an instinct that more could yet be wrung from him – that if I hovered long enough at the gates, he would grant me the freedom of the city.

'Give me your hand,' he repeated. 'Is the money of a Fust not good enough?'

'It needs some thought.'

'Have I not made you welcome at my table?'

'I am grateful for the kid. Please give my thanks to Frau Fust. But now in all conscience . . .'

'Sit down a moment. I too have ambitions. My export business is growing and I will need a partner. And then Christina – soon I must find a husband for her. A partner and a husband: if these two could be one and the same, a businessman of standing as well as a sire to my grandchildren . . . A family enterprise. You see, Johann, how my mind is tending. It would not serve my interests to loan you at a crippling rate, since I aspire to tying you closer. Do you catch my drift?'

I did. If I let him lend me money, he would throw in his daughter. Has a man ever been made a fairer offer? I laughed, knocked my wine back and shook his hand.

16. Peter

A lecture given by Johann Gutenberg to his assembled workforce at the newly opened printshop of the Humbrechthof, circa 1450, as recollected by himself and dictated to his scribe fifteen years later.

'*Guten Morgen, meine Herren.* And I am pleased to see you *are* all men, else something must have gone amiss with my recruitment. A printshop may be a fine thing, especially in so spacious a house as this, but it is no place for women. Those few of you who worked with me in my other premises, which I have kept on while renting these, will know the torrent of noise when we go at it – the roar of the furnace, the chiselling of punches, the hammering of copper, the dabbing of inkballs, the slam of the platen on the bed. I hope all here can bear the hubbub, for you are good workers and I am pledged to pay you well – twelve gulden a year, the highest wages in Mainz. But you must take care to add nothing to that noise. Use your tools, yes, but do not loose your tongues. There is a Rhine of sound already here, and if you stir fresh rivers of discourse our ears will burst and our minds be flooded out. This is why I have hired no women. The sight of them bearing food and drink for us might gladden our rest-times, the more so if the bearers are pretty and young and not too convent-stiff to withhold their favours. But women, like geese, have a fault in common. They like to gabble. And if women were free to gabble in here, the clacking of their tongues would drive us mad.

'When I say you should not loose your tongues, I mean it half in jest. This is a print-works, not a monastery, and you will need to talk so that each hand knows what his fellow performs. But when the world outside – and this I mean in earnest – asks after your work here, pressing you to uncover what you make, and by which means, and with what tools, and at how fast a rate, and in what numbers, and from which measurements, and to what end, then you must answer as a monk, with chapel silence. I will not insult your good names by making you swear an oath to this. I will simply trust your reason. Our work is copying books. But our method for copying is the first ever in the world, and if rivals copy *us* then we are lost. I know some who if they got wind would pass laws to stop us, so as to save the living of scribes. Spies are all around. Snooping strangers lurk to catch you in talk. Silence must be your reply.

'As you see, we have three presses here, two already complete, the other almost. We will need three more, and for this purpose, to save my own resources, it may be I shall borrow money. But do you think if so the man who lends me his gulden will be told how the presses work? No. I will not tell him. He has a right to know I will repay him, but not to know how I spend his money.

'You have seen our *Donatus*. But it is not for a Latin grammar, or any common text, that we have set up shop. It is for one book only, the holy book, the Book of Books, the Bible. Until today, only three among you have known this: Heinrich Keffer and Berthold Ruppel, who have been working with me several years, and my servant Lorenz Beildeck, who goes back to my youth. After today, you all know it. But if I hear it has spread beyond these walls, every one of you – innocent as well as guilty – will lose your jobs. We cannot have traitors in our midst.

'You see here in my hands the manuscript Bible we will work from. The labour will be long and arduous. Some of us may barely see it out. Can I justify it then? Human advancement is its own reward, perhaps, but let me pitch it lower. This Bible runs to twelve hundred pages. Writing a page a day for the two hundred working days in a year, how long would it take a scribe to copy it? Six hundred days, did I hear? It is as well you are my inkman, Otto, not my accountant. Six years? Bravo, six years it is. So, if it takes one scribe six years to copy the Bible, how long will it take three scribes? Correct: two years. I do not wish to crush you with numbers, but by my estimate, with twelve hundred pages, forty thousand types and a ton of paper and ink, it will take the twenty of us just as long. So no advance is made, you say? We may as well cease now, before we start? Wrong. Once the scribe has finished copying, he must begin all over. Once we have set the pages for one Bible, we can print as many as we like. The first copy will take two years, but so will the next hundred.

'After arithmetic, lesson two: beauty. To those who buy our Bible, the greatest merit will be its cheapness. So if the words are legible, a plain typeface with lines marching like drunk lead soldiers will serve? Wrong again. These are God's words. When the priests mutter against our Bible, and say the Devil wrote it, our sole reply can be its beauty. We must make it look better than one copied by hand.

'What other lessons should I teach you? Divinity: "In the beginning was the Word, and the Word was with God, and the Word was God." Obedience: "If you abide by my word, you shall be my disciples indeed, and you shall know the truth and the truth shall set you free." Those two sentences come from the Book of Johannes. This Johann before you – he too will make a book. But I will not call it mine or leave a mark on it, and nor will you. We are not Authors but Makers, working in humble service of God's ends.

'What else? Moral philosophy: this teaches us to respect our brothers, as all here must each other if our enterprise is to succeed. Geography: the world is large, but thanks to us Mainz will one day be its centre. Science: it is the laws of mechanics that guide us, and we must follow them as steadfastly as we do God's.

'But I am here to feast with you, not to preach. My servant Lorenz is presently passing among you with a jug of wine. Please fill your cups. And after we will eat veal together. On this paper I have the names of every one of you: Keffer, Ruppel, Beildeck, Gotz, Von Spyre, Mentelin, Neumeister, Eggestein, Spiess, Krantz, Drach, Stein,

Remboldt, Renner, Wolff. To these, before we finish, when the presses are working, will be added several more. I must mention, too, my distant cousin, Henne Salman, who has kindly rented me this building. We will not shout our names out to the world. But when God meets you on Judgment day He will not forget. Your prize will be to dwell with Him for ever.

'But enough: my tongue begins to wag like a woman's. A toast, then: "to the work of the Book".'

Forgive me if I pause a moment. My stomach eats at me and swims with bile. It is from thinking on the feast before the famine. Or else from brooding at how I overreached myself. I was content once. Had my best years not been given to the Bible, I might be still. Plain fare and modest portions are safest for the belly. But the Bible was a vast banquet running on.

There is a chapter in Revelation where Johannes asks the angel for a book. I should look it up and quote it at you. And yet there is no need, since it is graved inside me: 'And I took the book out of the angel's hand, and ate it up; and it was in my mouth, sweet as honey; but as soon as I had eaten it my belly was bitter.' So it was with me. The Bible was manna while I ate it. But later it ate back. And my life became a bitter ache.

I try to keep this poison from the page, but cannot pretend it is not in me.

I should have known, with Fust's loan, there would be a *kick* in the tail. He was a donkey, how could it be otherwise? Since what he asked was not written in our contract, I might have refused. But for the same reason, I could hardly object. It was more by way of a favour. The favour I granted, but I did not feel bound by it. If it proved a burr, I would shake it off.

Peter Schoeffer was returned from his calligraphy in Paris. Fust had spoken warmly of him often enough: 'He is like a son to me.' Though Peter was but five-and-twenty, it was an old acquaintance. He had, it seemed, come young from Gernsheim and, his father and mother being dead, Fust adopted him and gave him lodging. His notion now was that I take this Peter into my employ, as an engraver. I smelled a rat, of course. Fust had high praise for his art, but what would Fust know about art? The prodigy was doubtless a prodigal, the golden boy a lump of lead. Still, I agreed for Fust to bring him along, with samples. A working day was first proposed, so Fust could see the printshop and how his gulden had been spent to furnish it. But I feared he would behave as if he owned the place, which I did not want my men to witness (they being unaware of Fust's loan), so a Sunday was agreed instead. 'And why not bring the Mistresses Fust?' I added, pushing the occasion in a happier direction, for though one Mistress Fust I could well live without seeing again, the other, Christina, I had often thought of, willing her to reach an age where I might woo her as her father wished.

The Sunday shone early, a blue and pealing-bell morning. I arrived at the Humbrechthof an hour ahead, to look over the latest types and proofs. The design of the face had progressed at a snail-crawl, but this slowness had not vexed me. First we chose a manuscript Bible accurate in text and fair of hand – one whose script looked squarely old-fashioned so any reader would feel at ease. Then we traced from it the best examples of every letter, as many as ten of each. Last we carved these letters on punches, from which matrices and castings could later come. With so much else to watch over, I was content to leave the engraving to Heinrich and Berthold. Now, in the silence and bare light, I saw their letters – and was disappointed. True, the letters were small and sweetly shaped (by trimming their heads and tails, we hoped to get more lines to a page). But they lacked the scribe-perfection I sought. On metal, their strokes and curves looked slender as any girl; but printed, from the ink being squeezed between face and paper, the letters came out like fatboys, puff-faced and thick of limb. I did not blame Heinrich and Berthold, who were trusty and hard-labouring. But they had reached the far end of themselves, and whatever hours they might spend would never do finer than this. The dawning of this knowledge sunk me in a gloom. It was as if God had put before me a little door, leading to riches and majesty, but I could not push it open.

So lost was I in reverie before this door, I did not hear the knocking on my own. When I did hear, and knew it must be Fust, I approached heavy of heart to unlock it, for all that I would see Christina again. The light was blinding when I swung back the door and I could not at first observe her. She was behind her father, whose bulk and bustle near obscured her though not so well as to prevent me catching her mead-warm eye, which capture then made her blush. This cheered me while I bowed at the mother and then shook hands with Fust, who afterwards passed Peter to do the same.

Peter. Has any man in my life outshone a woman? Could any man eclipse the glow of a female blush? If so, it was only then, with him. The feel of his hand, first, which after the sweating fat of Fust's was like slipping into some long cool stream. Then the eyes: slate-blue and deep, like those fjords I had once glimpsed far to the north. And the blond arch of hair, that lit him like a halo. But more than these, it was as if some tremor or nerve ran through his body that made him skip from foot to foot, as if he could never see and know and do all he wanted fast enough. Meeting someone, we know nothing but by instinct. What instinct told me of Peter was that some life burned in his mind and body that did not burn inside the Fusts.

We stepped on to the work-floor, I leading the way, but Fust commanding me from the rear. It was as though he were the captain and myself the helmsman steering to his course. The presses, the hand-moulds, the composing cases, the inkballs, the vellum: like a priest on a balcony holding up his relics, I showed them all. At each display, Fust

nodded and aah-ed with approval, content to see his gulden
wisely spent. I was careful not to explain too much. Fust had
once worked as a goldsmith, and though he might be a
donkey I feared him carrying off my art. As for the ladies,
who found the reek of ink and metal an offence, I did not
wish to burden them with facts that had no bearing on their
life at home in kitchen and bed. Sparing of detail though I
was, the eyes of the three Fusts quickly fogged over. Only
Peter's were like a mirror taking all in. I do not think he
ever blinked, such was his fear of what he might miss if he
did. The colour of his iris made me think of the Virgin's
robe, but the faith that shone there was less in a celestial
ever-after than in a heaven of art and science below. Among
this little pilgrim-band I showed round my print-works, he
alone asked questions: how this and when that and in what
numbers those? For the first time in my life, I recognised a
man in my own *mould*.

By and by, we reached the proofs and types, which I had
kept till last, not wishing to revisit my earlier gloom. I tried
to make light of my doubts, but Peter pressed me on them,
and when I shared some small dismay at the roughness of
the product compared with our drawings, he agreed and –
with shyness not from malice – pointed to further defects I
had not mentioned. We put our heads together at the stone,
like men looking for ants buried under grass blades. Fust
was impatient with us. He could not see, he said, why such
fuss should be made about a typeface. That sample page I
had shown him any man might read with ease. Surely the
work could now be fast advanced. I bristled at this, angry at
the father for poking his oar in my water but not wishing
the daughter to see my rage. When Fust began to prattle of
the hopes he harboured as my *investor* (a word he spoke as if
it meant master, not moneylender), the urge welled up in
me to cry out against him as a dolt, a leper, a mule, a
donkey, a buffoon. But before this roar could escape my
mouth, Peter spoke and checked it, saying a book like this
that was the first of its kind in all the world must be worth
every pain it took and would *repay* the slowness of the
labour. These words gladdened me, and I was struck by the

spirit in them. Being adopted and lodged by Fust had not cowed him in the least.

By now I was minded to take Peter on, and not only as a favour to Fust, so I asked to see his samples. He reached into his bag. It was a bag such as I had lugged round when young, the kind carried by scribes. And since some scribes looking for work had lately called on me carrying similar bags, and none of them men worth hiring, I had little hope of what Peter would draw from it. 'I have a page of Aristotle, two from a psalter, and the alphabet in different scripts,' he said, which too was commonplace, and my heart sank a little more. But then he unrolled his sheets and laid them out. They were magnificent. I had not often seen my own penmanship outmastered. But the hard grace of his letters, the valley-bed straightness of line, the balance and Rhine-flow of the finished page: I at once yielded place to him. 'Have you learned goldsmiths' skills?' I asked, and he said he had but had not practised them of late. 'We will start you tomorrow,' I said, vowing to myself that if he showed the smallest knack for it I would assign him to refining our future typeface. He was young, which Heinrich and Berthold would resent. But I would make them masters in name, and he their assistant. And if his engraving came close in beauty to his pen, they could not in faith refuse.

The Fusts were all smiles, the brightest of them Christina's, which I took to be her pleasure in me for accepting her adopted brother. Perhaps too she was tired at having him all day about the house, when her mother was tiresome company enough. Whatever the source of that smile, I was happy to see it light on me, and counted in my head the days till she should be fifteen, when I might fairly call to pay her court. I did not pretend she could be an Ennelina to me. Still, a solid marriage would disperse the solitude of the hours when I was free of work, short though those were. (The city of Mainz forbade men working after dark with candles, but this law I defied.) Anticipation of wooing Christina lifted my spirits, and when I showed my pilgrim-band the door I was happier than when they had entered. Christina blushed as I kissed her hand adieu. With Frau

Fust I forced myself to do the same, out of courtesy. Peter's hand I shook warmly. Fust came last, and clasped me longest, his words licking me all over like one of those big dogs the monks keep in their kitchens. Was I not grateful now to have received his loan? he asked. Was I not pleased to see his daughter again? And did I not think his adopted son might find favour with me? To which last, hiding my gratitude to Fust as earlier I had hidden my anger with him, I nodded gravely: 'Let us wait and see.'

Peter was a gift. But my interests would be better served if Fust thought I was doing him a favour.

Peter began. I set him to engraving punches – to filing and polishing letters in reverse on steel. This was a skill I had myself, and which Hans Dünne had in Strasbourg, but Peter brought it to perfection. What Heinrich and Berthold would allow he turned away, wanting to do better. I recognised a kindred soul.

It was the same when he drove a punch in copper. A blow was not enough for him: the impress must be minutely inspected, and filed to correct the smallest bulge or skew. So too with alignment. Our letters had always danced a little – this one above the head of that, and the next below, like a choir of monks filing to the altar. With the *Donatus*, a schoolbook, it did not matter, but for the Bible, the Book of Books, and our future resting on it, the letters – as Peter said – must be steady, upright, drilled in line. He had an eye for this like a calligrapher, and spurred me to ask more of our compositors, so that nothing blurred or crooked was let by. I had thought to hear some muttering against his youth. But his quiet way of looking on, his patient ear for what men told him, the shyness with which he nudged them to it ('Could we this time try it slightly otherwise, just to see?') – so gentle was his manner he won them over.

With Peter overseeing the typeface, I shifted Heinrich to set the pages, in which labour he blissfully sank himself, like a bee inside a flower. He worked a sentence at a time to keep the river-flow of sense. Even the best compositors will leave words out or put them twice, which is why we have need of proofreaders, but Heinrich made fewer errors than most. He used none of those gestures that fatigue men and lose time – throwing out an arm, nodding the head, ticking letters against a rule. Wide white spaces (pigeon-holes, as we call them) he accounted poor workmanship and took pains to avoid. His art, he said, was not one but four – to read, to set, to space and to justify. He could tell by its feel, without looking, if a letter was damaged or worn.

Berthold likewise I moved on, to the hand-mould, to which he brought new art. The trick is to be swift when ladling in the molten metal, so that it runs to the heart of the matrix. But Berthold found that some letters form better with a jilt of the wrist – if the letter be small, a harder shake works best – and he taught this knack to others.

Meanwhile, I went about looking for buyers – through Germany and even beyond. With the *Donatus*, I had entrusted such travelling work to Fust. But he being such a donkey at it, with the Bible I did my own selling. Thanks to Nicholas of Cusa, a number of bishops and abbots knew of my work, and agreed to meet me. Nervous at giving affront to scribes, they were men not easily swayed unless some hours were first spent over a jug. But in time I had gathered over a hundred orders. Between meeting clerics, buying paper, mixing metals, checking proofs and urging my men, I scarce had time to sleep, and shortened my bed-hours from eight to five. Yet I was not weary. Peter, by his presence, breathed life in me and fired my will.

He did more. I confess it. He knocked at something hidden in my heart. If he was working at a vice or workbench, I would hover close. His blue eyes fastened themselves unblinking to the task. His blond curls glowed as though God was lighting the air around him. Most vivid of all were the movements his hands made. You have seen perhaps those shadow-shows at fairs, when dexterous men make animals of their hands on lighted screens. Peter was just the same. When he chipped and graved a punch, he was a pecking wood-pigeon. When he struck it in copper with rolled fists, a jabbing thrush. When he filed, a darting wren. And when he pulled on the press (for this I sometimes let him do, to show our pressmen how a smoother image might come), he was like a muscled ape lowering itself to the ground from a hefty branch. I never tired of lingering near him. And if his neck ached, which from that ceaseless banging and grinding it often did, I would lay my hands on his shoulders and knead. This action, so he said, took the pain off. He was pleased by it and I pleased to render him service. But I think if I speak candidly we both of us enjoyed it for itself.

Love between men is in our age a matter not much broached. There is some unnatural fear of it, which the Ancients never had. For why should love of one man for another be sinful? And why should men not innocently touch? Anton here will tell how he and I sometimes break off from my narrative to link arms about the garden. It is our custom, whenever he comes or leaves, to kiss each other on the cheek. He has felt my hand rest on his shoulder and when his neck aches from writing he lets me knead it, just as I did with Peter. Why, even as I dictate these words I have laid my hand on his thigh, which he seems to find a rhythm that aids the work, my fingers gently urging him on as he strokes my thoughts across the page. I think he likes it – deny it Anton, if you dare – and why not? He is young and vigorous and this compact between us a touching-innocent one, such as it was with Peter. If God allowed, Anton would not be here with this old ink-striped badger but in the bed of that girl he sometimes walks home at dusk – there, his blush betrays it and the thought disturbs his pen. But in the meanwhile, he is here with me, whose ancient heart leaps highest at the sight of a pretty woman yet beats smoothest with a handsome young man. Fellows who rub along together: there are many among us like this, yet the priests cannot see it and imagine something dark, and condemn it, and lay penances. It is some narrowness, a part of that more general ignorance which I hoped my invention would cure. Anton at least has wit enough to construe me right.

But to return to the business. Within six months of his starting, it was understood by one and all that Peter had become my right-hand man. If away soliciting orders, I left him as overseer, knowing no harm would come in my absence. We were by now deep into typesetting, and the proofs we pulled cheered us greatly. Having set the early pages with forty lines to each, we tightened the spacing to accommodate forty-two, which saved on paper and – Peter and I were of a mind about this – enhanced the look. Less happily, we abandoned printing large initials in red. This distressed Peter, whose designs for them were exquisite, but we could find no means to mix black ink with red. So he instead sketched these letter designs in pencil, to be inked in later by the buyer, which went against the grain but saved on labour and expense.

There were other savings. But to make the perfect book, the Book of Books, did not come cheap. Soon enough, Fust's eight hundred gulden had been swallowed up, as I confessed one night to Peter (the only one among the workforce I could talk to freely). We were drinking in a tavern. A candle lit his face. He set his mug down and frowned at me.

'Already spent? But we have only just begun. We will be working for months yet.'

'A year, by my reckoning.'

'So . . .'

'The *Donatus* will bring some money in.'

'But in the long run . . .'

'I must borrow again.'

'Who will lend?'

'Getting money off folk has never been a problem of mine. There are many in Mainz with more gulden than wit.'

He inferred from this a gibe at his adopted father, and sulked, and would not speak. So I told him I intended no insult at Fust, who had dealt fair with me, and to whom I owed gratitude, not least – here I cast an arm about his shoulder – for the gift of Peter himself. At this he blushed and smiled, as if mollified, and we changed the topic, and had another drink.

In truth, I was too foolish-fond of Peter to tell him what I thought: that Fust was a simpleton, a clumphead, a sweating tub of lard, whom I delighted in having robbed of eight hundred gulden and hoped to rob of more.

17. Christina

What I thought of Fust I also kept hidden from Christina. Girls that age are enamoured of their fathers, and it would have been cruel and against my interests to disenchant her till we were wed. Wed? Yes, my intent in this had grown now I had passed the age of fifty and she fifteen. Fust having made clear his own wishes at the time of the loan, I had expected him to press me about marriage. But since Peter had been taken on in the enterprise, we had seen little of each other, and those few times we met at supper, in the company of Peter, Grete and Christina herself, the matter was not raised. It occurred to me that Grete had ordered Fust not to nag me in the business, for fear of raising false hopes in their daughter. After all, why should a man of my standing be enticed by one such as her? For all they knew, I might have no scheme to wed at all, let alone to wed a Christina. Yet the girl had made an *impression* on me. And though my sands were far from run, I would soon be of an age when the point of marriage would not hold up for me. So it was that I wrote to Fust announcing my intention to call on Christina the following Sunday. A seemlier man would have let a day pass before replying, but he replied in sweaty haste to give his blessing, adding that 'given the disparity in your ages, I do not see the need for a chaperone'. I was a touch offended by this insolence, and briefly contemplated escorting Christina to some remote spot where I could overman and deflower her, so as to teach Fust to make less presumption of my waning vigour. But I had some softness for the girl, and could not abuse her merely in order to disabuse the father.

We walked by the river. Where else? Sunlight, a pretty

woman on my arm, dark water running swiftly to the sea: the best of life has been in such moments. No wonder an old man wants to revisit them. Why a river goes with wooing has no reason, and yet it seems to. It must be the rushing forward, the water pulling you along to somewhere new. And then the light that skims and flickers off the surface, crossing the face of the one you are with. And the lap-slap of waves against the shore, as opposite elements – earth and water, male and female – gently meet. To give due tongue to it is beyond me (making words was my business, uttering them never), and I would be pushed to justify it to a master of logic. But so I feel.

We walked a mile upriver talking of nothing, till Christina slipped her arm in mine, where it rested at first a little awkward (perhaps her mother had instructed her to do this, and she felt shy about it), but then more happily, as though we were merely – which indeed to any onlooker we must have looked – a father and daughter out walking. What words we spoke I have no memory of. But at some point further, I stopped and took her hands in mine, and briefly looked into her face, and then at length addressed the parting in her hair (for she had cast her eyes down, all demure), saying I was fond of her, and liked our discourse, and hoped she would consent to see me more. I did not ask in so many words if she would wed me, thinking this a matter best left to myself and Fust. But when she raised her face, I saw from her eyes she had been softly crying, no doubt in pleasure and gratitude, so I knew she had understood.

Did I love Christina, then? Why ask it so accusing? Do you say I am inconstant for having loved twice in my life – thrice, if one of my own sex can be counted? How narrow-rutted if you think so, how *unlived* of you. Why should a man be let to shoot only one arrow? My quiver contained several more. And then the darts that were shot back – is the fault my own if more than one wounded me? In love one has no choice and small protection. No walled fort can keep it out. No vigilant sentry, either. It creeps up invisible and catches you offguard. Once caught, you are helpless.

Whatever noble aim you have in life, whatever work you intend, it keeps you from. It is like hunting in a wood for the rumoured beast: you have tracked it hard and have it almost in your sights, and if you kill it the world will be a safer, better place. But then some shy doe appears from nowhere through the trees and lifts her limpid eye and flares her nostrils and teeters on her ankles and trembles to see you standing there, till you are smitten utterly, so that, forgetting the catch you came here for, you swing your bow around and aim instead at her – but miss, or are yourself snared in flying after her through thorns and thickets, the pursuit lasting an age and sapping all your strength, which if you were sound of mind you would resent, but since you are fevered, and worship the very ground she treads (as though each twig that broke under her feet were a holy wafer), you go on unrelenting till you have her, or she has you, and you fall together to the ground, and lie with each other, and the little death comes, or the large, a resolution at any rate, an ending to the chase, which ending may be happy or may be sad, but was so far from your thought when you first – in all innocence – entered that wood. This is what love is. Ennelina had taught me that. It is a feeling that humbles a man, since he knows, once he has felt it, how little of the world – not even his own heart – he can command.

So I say again: love comes unbidden, and can arrive several times in one life. But if I am truthful, my love for Christina was not the same as that I felt for Ennelina. Along our walk by the river, I thought to persuade myself it was, or could in time become so. But she was too much the child to drive away the memory of my former passion. Those womanly hips, that bosom, the artful polish of her lips – I saw them and yet did not. Blanking them always (like a tympan over a page) was the memory of her at the parlour door carrying her little virgin doll: 'I am going to bed now, father.' I wanted children – dolls of our own – which she might help me to. But I had no goatish visions of Christina lying naked and abed. She was too much the child. I loved her for her sweetness. But not as I had Ennelina. Not as a man loves a woman.

Back at the house, our river-walk ended, the mother served us cake. A cat scutted about the kitchen. Hams hung from the beams, beyond its claws. Grete said little, Christina nothing. I was bored with making all the talk. Then Peter came in. Though it was Sunday, he had been all afternoon at the print-works, and we talked of what he had done there. Christina brightened up, and was attentive, pushing cake on him, which he ate between mouthfuls of print-talk. Her sisterly fondness spoke well of how she would conduct herself as a wife. Once she knew me better and we were contracted, I looked forward to her fawning over me.

Then Fust beckoned me into the parlour 'for a quiet drink'. I had expected this. So burning was he for the marriage, a solitary walk would be cause enough to prise a vow and date from me. Being stubborn, I planned to make it hard for him. But I would not be so rash as to refuse. Against the dismal thought of Fust as a father-in-law was the prospect of milking him for more gulden, for surely he could not deny his daughter's husband.

'I hear you have spent my loan,' he began.

Though it surprised me we should start with gulden, I was not unhappy, since it would save me the effort of steering him to them later. Nor was I vexed with Peter, who must have told Fust of our recent discourse. It bore witness to his sweet and loyal temper that he had done so. And since I had not bound him to secrecy, why should he not be open with his adopted father? He had no doubt been preparing Fust to look kindly on the notion of a second loan.

'It is true,' I said. 'I shall soon be looking for new investors.'

'Are you not anxious to keep your venture secret?'

'I would prefer it, but the work is well advanced. No rival could now leap by us.'

'Peter brought home some pages to show me.'

This somewhat did vex me, since I liked to keep Fust's

nose out. But I knew Peter must have meant it for my advantage.

'And you admired them?'

'They made me think my investment well spent. They made me proud too. We are spreading God's word together.'

I did not care for 'we' and 'together'. From where he sat with his furnace mouth and pouring stomach of fat, Fust seemed to think of himself as God, with me as Moses bringing down the tablets of stone. It was not how I saw our arrangement, and I was minded to tell him so, till discretion held me back.

'There are many in my printshop who can also take pride,' I said.

'And yet the work proceeds so slow.'

'Perfection is not fast attained.'

'The first copies were to be ready by now.'

'The scale of the endeavour is larger than we thought. Making sufficient type alone has taken a year. We have only so many men.'

'You said my loan would hire all the men you needed.'

'Then there are materials.'

'You had a budget for those. Eight hundred gulden was supposed to cover all.'

'The cost of paper and metal has risen. To go faster we need two more presses. And some of the men are pushing for higher wages.'

'So what do you need? Two hundred? Three?'

'More.'

'How much?'

I had lately done some sums, like this:

> 6 presses at 30 gulden: 180
> Typecases, frames, hand-moulds: 70
> Handwritten Bible to copy from: 70
> Rent for Humbrechthof (reduced family rate) over 3
>   years: 15
> Heating: 125
> Steel, copper, lead and antimony: 60

Ink: 30
Paper for 150 copies of Bible: 300
Vellum for 25 copies: 150
Wages for 12–20 men over 3 years: 500
Total 1,500 gulden

Though these were but rough, they gave an idea. With the eight hundred Fust had already loaned, and some money still of my own, a further five hundred might suffice. But with him puffing so hard to make me his son-in-law, I did not see the need to scrape by. And since my business was *copying*, I loved the notion of doubling him. So . . .

'I would need another eight hundred.'

'Impossible.'

'I do not expect it of you. There are other men in Mainz who . . .'

'It depends.'

'On what?'

'The speed of the work. How fast you sell the copies once ready. What price you fix them at.'

I had likewise done my sum for this, based on undercutting handwritten Bibles by 50 gulden:

150 paper copies at 25 each: 3,750
25 vellum copies at 50: 1,250
Total 5,000 gulden

These numbers I now slimmed down for Fust, since I did not want him seeing my true profits.

'I will sell at twenty-two gulden,' I said. Making three thousand five hundred in all.'

'That is a healthy return,' he said.

'Any moneylender could feel safe,' I said.

'Half the copies sold would repay me.'

'I did not mean to presume on you. For a man in your position to raise another eight hundred . . .'

'. . . would be possible. If the terms were right.'

By 'terms', he must mean his daughter. I prepared to bargain.

'These terms?'

'Only two. First, six per cent interest. I would not insist on it, of course. But for form's sake, in the contract at least . . .'

'And the other?'

'A formality again, to keep my lawyer happy. That if you cannot repay me in gulden, I take your equipment in lieu – the presses, paper and type.'

'That is all?'

'That is all.'

Christina would not be part of the bargain, then. I was sorry at that. Had she been so, I might have pushed him farther. But I saw no hardship. The terms would suit me well enough. If later they did not, I would ignore them. It was only one more contract among many. We shook hands on it and began another jug.

Another jug, Anton. Not that you should fetch me one now, but that a jug has once more spilled into our text. It is ever thus. When men come together to do business, when they join for pleasure, when they work, when they worship, when they woo, when they eat, when they brood alone – always there must be wine there. It is ink to the spirit, helping words flow out. It is excitation to the flesh. It is a taper lighting the mind. You remember the wine-press in Erfurt, and the notion it stamped on me for a like invention. You have seen my cellar. You know how wine sits *at the bottom* of all I do. Do not then punish me with such looks for quaffing it. It is a balm and joy. What else would you have me drink? Rhine water? Had I supped at that, my veins would be cankered by now, and I not alive to tell my tale.

Wine also goes well with writing. I do not mean your writing, Anton, since a scribe must look hard at what he pens, and keep his mind clear, and to such labour wine is a distraction. But for myself, giving out the writing, wine is a useful heat. Many a day begins with my brain frozen like a millpond. But then wine at breakfast comes up like the sun and melts me, so when later you climb the stairs – the noise of your footstep gladdening me, even before I see your handsome face – my memories are unlocked and I am ready to gabble at you like a goose. And you can trust what I pour forth as faithful recollection. Even when dusk has drawn near, and I am the better by a jug or three, what I dictate to you has true substance – not a phantasm conjured by drunkenness but the lees in the bottom of life's jug. Why then condemn me? Why such frowning? Is it from envy? If I ration you by day, keeping you to swigs for refreshment, it is only so your hand be correct. Any dusk when we have done our work, you know you can stay and we two empty more jugs together. I cannot go with you to the tavern, since I walk too slow there and besides dislike the general company. But we can make a kind of tavern of it here. Bring that girl of yours, Anton. Let the three of us carouse. Though I am jealous of your person, I would not hog you all night.

In the meantime let this book be the jug we share. I think a book, when it reads well, can indeed seem like a jug of wine, making a glow through all the body. Better than a jug, a book is never finished. You can reach the end and it is all still there and always will be, forever replenished like the wine at Cana. To think of men years ahead taking sustenance from this little of jug of ours – that is a pleasing notion, and determines me, while my brain is still fermenting, to squeeze a vintage out, full and candid to the palate.

In my cups you shall know me and all that I have done.

For a month I did not see Christina. Since Fust had failed to enter her in our contract, there seemed no expectation of panting ardour from me. I was busy besides. Work began on two new presses. I also passed a birthday, which occasion I marked with Peter – first at a tavern, drinking among beggars, then at home, with draughts from my own cellar.

Peter was still my haloed hero: a beaver at the print-works, a songbird in the taverns, a lolling bearcub at my house. We were as close as any men who ever lived. Yet I could not put Christina from my mind. It was not herself only (and I hardly knew her) but what she might bring. My birthday had made me ponder my mortality. I wanted children.

Children? Since leaving childhood, I had taken little interest in them. As I had said often enough when shaking the hand of any new father among my workers, the first twenty years are the worst. For what are children but raw, ugly miniatures of adults? And adults being tribulation enough, what lower commendation could there be? 'Ah yes,' these workers would come back at me, glaring from their black-bagged eyes, 'but the point of children is to leave some *copy* of ourselves. And that justifies all the hardships.' This being said in my language would always set me off on some harangue. Conception is not like printing, I would say. The matrix is weak, the casting rough, the bed unpredictable. Mothers intent on pressing out a little Mutti or Papa find their hopes have melted in the foundry. Fathers set on duplicates discover a monster in the cradle, and doubt the seed that sowed it is their own. 'If it is copies you want,' I would tell them, 'stick to typesetting. The flesh does not come close.' My gruffness was an act. I meant a kind of tribute to the variety of mankind, which can never be replicated like type. But these were men in no mood to jest. And my gulling and Herod-ing did not endear me to them.

By the time I passed my fiftieth birthday, my view of children had altered. It was not that I dreamed to leave a copy of me – one Johann Gutenberg in the world was more than ample. But I thought to cheer my waning days with the rock of a cradle, the toddle of little feet, the babble of infant tongues. Or if I lived that long, to give away my daughter as a bride. I wanted children – and Christina, a child herself, was my channel to them.

To navigate that channel I would first have to put it in my name – to wed her. This matter Fust would soon want to broach with me, I thought, the girl now being fit for childbearing and I a son-in-law any Mainzer of Fust's class would want to have. Since I kept Fust from swanning it round my print-works, his chances to waylay me were few. But when at last we came together to sign the second contract, our lawyers, as is their way, having strung the business out so as to take a healthy portion, he asked had I an hour to spare and I, to oblige him, said I had. We turned from the lawyer's house towards his own. But halfway there he led me inside another house, and not a tavern either. The bath-house! The one I had gone to with smiths and chestmakers thirty years since, in my days as Jo-Jo the clown! By the look of the sweating walls, it had grown no more wholesome in the meantime, and I did not relish its putrid water swilling through my toes. But Fust led me off into a back room less filthy than the rest, where we removed our clothes. It surprised me Fust should come here, there being a law against married men using such places. But he slopped unabashed into the water, a tub of lard inside a tub of steam. Two women appeared to wash our flesh. Sweet Sirens of the suds, they sang lyrics as they scrubbed, enticing us to enter deeper water. Fust lay back and closed his eyes, as though dreaming of their inland lakes. From the way they Johann-ed him like an old friend, he must have swum there often before. But with me there they could not tempt him. He asked for a jug of wine, then waved them off to leave us soaking.

'To our contract,' he said.

'To our contract.'

I was in no hurry. Soon enough the matter would surface and I have my arm twisted to choose a day. But for an hour, till my fingers were wrinkled like old linen, Fust talked only of commerce. Marriage seemed to have sunk forgotten. With the wine drained, and still no sight of it swimming up, it was left to me – disgruntled at being the one – to raise the subject.

'That other family concern we once spoke of . . .'

'Yes?'

'Business mixed with pleasure . . .'

'Yes?'

'Touching on someone in your house . . .'

'Ah, Peter. Are you pleased with him?'

'He is the best I ever have had.' This was honest, though what I added was perhaps less true: 'Give him a year and he could run the place.'

'I will bear that in mind,' said Fust. 'I gave you a bargain there.'

'I had hoped to offer a bargain in return.'

'In what way?'

'By agreeing to wed your daughter.'

'It is my fervent wish, as I have told you.'

'Hers too, I trust.'

'I am no keeper of her heart. But a man such as yourself, with a hold on the world, how could she fail to be impressed?'

'Well, then.'

'Young men with prospects may make the pulse of a girl race faster than we older men do, who have no prospects left. But a fat and bulging purse: nothing a young man carries at his thigh can rank with that.'

'Truly spoken.'

'So I am sure Christina, when the time is fit . . .'

'Has it not come?'

'I would prefer her to mature a year, lest her bridal fruit be plucked too soon and not attain its sweetness.'

'And yet to wait too long, and then some sudden blight . . .'

'What blight could come? In a year, your Bibles will be printed, my loan repaid, and that purse of yours, at present so dependent on mine . . .'

'If your loan be an obstacle to marrying, let us tear up the contract. I can borrow elsewhere.'

'It is signed now. And if you borrowed elsewhere, you would still be in debt. I have my daughter's interests to protect.'

'So you refuse her hand.'

'Refuse? No, let us but wait a year, then she is yours.'

It was not love denied that made me climb out of the tub as smartly as I could, but shame from having to scramble at this girl I felt only *aptness* for, not love. Even worse was the shame of being bested by Fust. He had always been so eager to please me – a man that would not say boo to a goose. But today I had sat naked with him, dangling my wishes before him, and he had denied me. Though I had nothing to fear from his contract, and would sooner commit his gulden to the furnace than repay them, I hated how he had played with my desires. I felt like a bead strung on an abacus, pushed hither and thither at his behest. I felt like a songbird in his foxy jaw. For a moment, in my helplessness, I wondered was he so stupid after all.

♪

Despite the honesty of my endeavour, there is in this book – if I may make bold to call it that – a certain falsity. Because its purpose is to recall the past, I allow you to forget my present. If you think of it at all, you imagine my condition as unchanging, just myself and the boy here, Johann and Anton, master and scribe, engrossed together for ever in this room. You see us as a painting on an altarpiece, perhaps, or as a scene depicted in a woodcut – a perpetuity of stillness. But it is not so. Night falls, day arises. The boy comes and goes. I too come and go. The seasons likewise: there have been three since I started this (though you might plough through it in half a day). The woman in the orchard snipping catkins when I set out has since gathered the apples and today prints out her footsteps in the snow. The pigs that once snorted in the yard, then in the autumn fed off acorns, lately furnished our Christmas plates. Icicles like kerns overhang the thatch. My feet are chilblained. Anton puffs like a dragon as he writes. And these are but our local metamorphoses. Elsewhere, the plague spreads and kings are overthrown. And always, bringing goods and visitors and news of how the world goes, the Rhine flows beyond us, with fresh tides and currents every day.

Nor are we physically unaltered. Anton grows brawnier by the week. When I feel his muscles, see – there on the forearms – I find them bigger and harder each time, whether from squeezing at the pen or labouring with spade and sickle who can tell. My own changes are less happy. My heart was once a healthy pat-pat-pat, like waves beating at the shore, but now it pitters weak as a summer stream. My mind forgets itself. My eyes cloud over (and still no sign of those lenses I was promised from Venice). My body shrivels on me, like the corpse of a small animal (say, a mouse cruelly played with by a cat) left to rot in some dusty corner. All this is a pressing matter to me – it is my life, or the coming end of it! But of course you do not wish to hear. You dislike the Now intruding. It is the contract between us. I accept it. Yet I am poor, as you have seen, at keeping contracts. And if I fail today to spare you an excursion on my aged self, it is because, for once, my present has more moment than my past.

I am recognised. I am admitted. I am *paid*. A letter has come from the Archbishop, bestowing a pension on me. My banishment ended some time since, but this honour I had not expected. Why should Adolf make a favourite of me? I find it hard to fathom, but will relish the words of his letter again while Anton copies it down.

'We, Adolf, Archbishop of Mainz, declare and manifest publicly by this document that we have recognised the agreeable and willing service which our dear, faithful Johann Gutenberg has rendered, and may and shall render in future time to us. Therefore by special dispensation, have we admitted him as our servant and courtier. And in order that he benefit, we shall each year when we clothe our ordinary courtiers clothe him at the same time, and also give him twenty *Malter* of grain and two *Fuder* of wine, for the use of his household; and also exempt him graciously, as long as he shall live, from watch duty, military service, taxation and other sundries which we have imposed upon the residents of the said city of Mainz. And about this the aforesaid Johann Gutenberg shall faithfully promise us and personally swear an oath upon the Saints to be faithful to us, to avert harm from us and foster our interest and do everything a loyal servant is duty bound to do unto his rightful master. All the above we promise in true faith to observe. In witness whereof we have attached our seal to this document, which was issued on the day of St Anthony, *Anno domini millesimo quadringentesimo sexagesimo quinto.*'

Swear an oath? I am no man's man, never have been. Does Adolf think by this to have me hover fawning at court? He has honoured the wrong printer, then. If it is greasing he wants, he would have better gone to Fust. Still, I see no harm in putting my name to it. I am not compromised. And the *Fuder* will lie well in my cellar. Two thousand litres a year: it is more, almost, than this house of mine can consume.

Why should Adolf honour me? It cannot be from love. When he took the city, he had me banished. He knows I lent support to his enemy. I would suspect the hand of Nicholas of Cusa, pressing from Rome to have my art enshrined, were not poor Nicholas underground. Maybe Adolf himself has come to see the beauty of print, from the broadsheets run off for him in his battles with Diether. It was my rivals printed them, not me. Yet someone could have tipped him to the source. Or perhaps my situation here in Eltville is what has swayed him. The upper floor of my late brother's house looks straight at the walls of Adolf's summer palace, to which he comes for a month each August. And though I have never met him out strolling, or been forced through some exchange of pleasantries to show more neighbourliness than I feel, it may be that others in Eltville have spoken for me and drawn his attention to my case. I shall at all events take his wine – the clothes too if they sit on me. Not so the freedom of Mainz. I have once or twice sneaked back, but the place dispirited me: the stench, the rats, the brawling young. I am happier in Eltville. Soon in any case I may not walk or see.

I asked the boy who brought the letter: are there many of these? Is there a general dispensation? He told me not, there were no others, the letter was addressed solely to me.

Being alone in the honour gives me pleasure. Doubtless Fust will get to hear of it, and curse and kick the walls and rant himself into a lather at being passed over. I hear he has gone to Paris on business. But word is sure to reach him. I would delight to see his face.

*

To resume. I had my second loan from Fust. But he would not barter his daughter. If I had tied him to a date a year ahead, we might have settled the business. But I would not thus abase myself. This was partly tactic. My error had been to look too eager. If it was thought at the Fusts that Herr Gutenberg might marry elsewhere, they would begin again to value me. I also, to be candid, feared a further refusal. So cold with me was Fust, I wondered had he changed his mind.

His coldness found a mirror in me. If I had loved Christina to the core, I would have gone wooing despite the rebuff, unable to be parted from her longer. But I did not love her in that way. I felt fondness, yes, but no passion. Chiefly she was a conduit. And she, bright enough in her childish way, probably grasped this – saw how I saw her. Which to a girl of sixteen (as now she nearly was, so river-swift had the months passed) cannot have been pleasing.

Despite this cooling on both sides, I resolved at last to pay a visit to Christina – and Fust when I wrote him of it raised no protest. It was May, some warmth back in the earth. The sun shone like a blessing. My hope was that the balmy day would excite Christina with thoughts of love. We walked by the river, of course. Christina had little to say for herself. I found nothing odd in this, except that her shyness seemed even greater than before. She would not look me in the face. Perhaps she was waiting for some exclamation of romance. Maidens like to hear talk of cupid-bows and throbbing hearts and aching breasts, with never a thought that these pretty passions lead only to the birthing-stool. But though I had wooed Ennelina in that fashion, I could not Christina. I had forgotten how to do it. And even had I remembered, I would not make a *copy* of my earlier love. Instead, I talked houses and gulden.

'You have seen my home?' I asked.

'No,' she said.

'You should come visit me with your parents. I have servants, including a cook. A large wine-cellar. A handsome table in best oak – as all the chairs are.'

'The house is yours, then?'

'My late sister came into it, I then owning one in Strasbourg. Now my brother-in-law means to sell it back to me. It is too large, though, for a single man. A family would suit it better.'

At this she blushed, and kept her eyes fixed on the river-bank. Encouraged, I turned my discourse to the print-works, so as to impress her with the scale of the enterprise (and with myself as a man of substance). I feared she might sigh to be cheated of airy love talk. Instead, she looked alert and questioned me closely.

'So how many work there?' she asked.

'Twenty. Ten beaters and pullers working the presses. Four compositors setting the pages. Two engravers filing punches. Two typecasters tilting hand-moulds. One broom-boy sweeping the floor and puffing the furnace. And Peter, who has an art in all.'

At Peter, she blushed and lowered her head again, but when I persevered with mention of him – praising his skill, his loyalty, his eager manner – she looked up and listened keenly and her pupils widened, like two opals set in amber. It occurred to me that, of course, living in the same household, Peter must on occasion have talked with her, and he being closer in age than her parents were, and less of a *Fust*, these conversations must have lit the dullness of her life at home, just as her eyes lit now walking with me. But that was all that did occur. Only later did I understand.

After a mile or so, we turned homeward again. By now, I had run short of print-talk, and circled back to my wifeless house.

'It feels a little forlorn,' I said, 'with no woman in it but

Frau Beildeck. No children either. It is too quiet to make a man content.'

'Do you do no work there? Is all labour at the Humbrechthof?'

'By no means. My two lodgers are goldsmiths. We have an enterprise making mirrors and trinkets – if ever you should want a bracelet ... I have a press too, for jobbing work – grammar-books and calendars. Soon we will print an indulgence. But this is a secret' – here I put a finger to my lips as if mockingly to shush her – 'which no one, not even your father, must know.'

She smiled, her eyes warm mead at last. But when I stepped closer, meaning to take her hand and speak plain of marriage, she looked away, whether from mistaking my intent or understanding it too well I cannot say. Empty-handed, I endeavoured to draw some tattle out of her – about trinkets or clothes or (this I did mindfully plant) who among her friends were due to have babes – but she answered nothing, and after a while I too stummed up. Before we reached her home, anger began to burn in me at having worked so hard at Christina for such little return, when my time might have been spent on next month's budget. We bid each other farewell by the door. I was not invited in, and, had I been, would have refused.

I had some lingering fondness for Christina as an instrument for stamping out my children. But the price of this – the courting rituals – I regarded as too dear. Nor did I think it quite fair on Christina that a man with no deep affection for her should bully to become her husband. If Fust commanded us both to the deed, and we consented, so be it. But I would not in the meanwhile call again.

18. Bibles

One day a priest passing the printshop looked hard into my eye and as he did spat noisily on the earth. I took it as most ungodly and a spit intended at me. The men confirmed it. I had felt welcome in Mainz, a prodigal embraced with open arms. But now rumours were going round about my work, and priests and scribes, fearing for their livelihood, were those most active in denouncing me.

It was said I was the Devil, sent to earth to make a counterfeit Bible which would spread ruin among men.

It was said I was a dabbler in witchcraft and my printshop an alchemist's laboratory.

It was said I had invented a thing more explosive than gunpowder.

It was said I was a heretic, since in my artificial writing the letters were constructed *back to front*. (The charge made me think of how fleshly relations between men and women back to front were likewise regarded as a sin.)

It was said I was a demon, since my books resembled each other in every particular, which was deemed beyond the reach of human skill.

It was said I hated scribes and my invention would dig their grave.

This last, as Anton knows, is a wicked lie. In truth, I wished to save scribes for lighter tasks. For centuries they have been oxen ploughing with blades – beasts of the field, heavy-burdened, made to sow black seeds in the white earth. I dig their grave? They never lived in the first place. They are our nameless ghosts, condemned to a purgatory of oblivion, while those whose words they copy enjoy immortal fame. At least by me scribes are acknowledged. Many have I taken into my printshop – to rubricate or proofread or learn hot metal. No, I do not hate scribes. If anything – this too Anton will tell you – I have loved them to excess.

Still, I did not care for being spat at, and sought audience with the priest at my old church, St Christoph, hoping he would ease my worries, which he did, save for admitting his own doubts about my art.

'There are many in the Church like Nicholas of Cusa,' he said, 'who see how your work will benefit us and who want your enterprise to succeed.'

'I am grateful to know that.'

'Only . . .'

'Yes?'

'For myself, I do not understand your method of copying. Surely to copy words requires a man to think. And this no machine can do.'

I have heard this said many times – that copying requires understanding, else it will lack beauty, order, harmony; that a book copied mindlessly will let the Devil live in its pages. But as I told him:

'With copying, thought does not enter in. The best copyists are often the most stupid of men, whereas a book copied by a *thinking* scribe will be full of errors. Thought is provoking, distracting, disruptive. This is its virtue, but also why the clever make poor copyists. Their minds are always running elsewhere.'

So I said to that priest, and felt better for justifying myself. Next time a man spat at me, I would ignore it.

Time passed – more time than I had reckoned for. I had no complaint against my workers. They were good men, who grumbled sometimes at their wages but did not skimp or idle. Inside our doors was a torrent of noise – a roaring furnace, creaking wood and clinking tin. We took no heed of the world beyond. When Constantinople fell, it scarcely made a ripple with us. Our own wars were more consuming.

The greatest battle was to keep the press slamming down – *again* and *again* and *again* and *again* – a task that made us weary, and might have oppressed us with *tedium vitae*, but for our urge to finish the Book.

No, our industry was not in question. It was the scale that set us back. With the type, each compositor needed sufficient for three pages (the page he was working on, that in the bed of the press, and that waiting to go back in its case). With three thousand letters to a page, that meant nine thousand types for him – times four meant nearly forty thousand, and from letters becoming broken or worn my typecasters were forever sweating to renew them. The straightness of our margins was a triumph, and better than any scribe could do, but this too slowed the compositors. Silky-black print, regular lines, the golden mean: I demanded them unbendingly. All had to pass by me, under my eyes, so I saw that it was good. This was my Genesis, my Creation, and I, as the men said, Almighty difficult to please.

No impiety is meant by this, but I did sometimes think of God as my rival. Being a jealous god, He would not give me the time to finish His Book, since with Sundays and penance-days and saints' days and holy-days we were more often in church than manning the printshop. The Bible was intended to honour Him. But when a page was spoiled or a matrix snapped, I wished I had chosen a humbler form of worship. In my original conception, we would make every last bit of the Book, even the binding, so that each aspect of the work became a matter for us to decide: what quality of cow-hide or pig-skin to lay over the end-boards, and how to decorate them, and whether to edge the corners in brass, and if to fit a clasp to keep out dust and damp, and so on. In time, I saw that these matters were better left to the buyers, and made do with printing texts, not wrapping them. Even so, there seemed no end to our labour. To check for error – and I read over all twelve hundred and eighty-two pages – I used to come at dawn, with light flooding yellow through the window. I should have been freshest then. But from working so late and sleeping so little, my eyes would sometimes veil with cloud, till each page looked like a whitewashed vault with black-gowned monks in it, some walking tall, some waving their arms, others stooping, kneeling, kicking or sitting. So much, I thought, for my invention. I am still in my scriptorium, and no less weary from toil.

By now, more than a year after his second loan, indeed two years fast approaching, Fust was a regular caller at the works. I had always discouraged these visits, knowing how he liked to God it over the men. Listening to his ignorant reproaches – why *this* rather than *that*? why *here* instead of *there*? – was like hearing a drunken cowherd by the Rhine question a shipman's use of the tiller. Even when Fust praised our work and paid me respect as *founder* of it, to have his grunting body about the place and his skin leaking pails of sweat and his furnace mouth breathing out spices was a horrid trial. Still, it was broadly known by now that money of his had gone into the enterprise, and to have kept him from the seat of our labour – he being Peter's adopted father and all – would have been discourteous. There was also the matter of Christina, which I had not yet fully despaired of. Marriage was impossible with money still owed – my worth as a son-in-law rested on it being repaid. But it served me to stay in with Fust. The channel to an heir still awaited me, and I did not wish to poison the source.

Mindful of this, I did my best to make Fust welcome and would have kept myself all smiling grace had not his visits been so many and often. But the more he called, the more he wore the air of one whose solemn right it was to call. Worse still was his wifely niggling as he examined what he called (meaning an irony) 'the progress'.

'Why the delay over this page?' he asked one day, seeing a block of type sitting unattended.

'It needs amending.'

'You fuss too much. What is wrong with it?'

'The reader has marked several errors, see.'

'None of consequence, I am sure. A man can happily read this page already.'

A man other than you, I was tempted to answer, Fust's Latin being slight to say the least. But instead I said mildly:

'We shall soon have it reset.'

'But these delays . . . It will not do, Johann. You had my money in good faith. When can I expect a return? When will the first Bible be printed?'

To calm his anger, I tried to lay on him, as I had with my men, the notions of beauty, harmony, perfection. I had him stroke our smoothest vellum. I even made him sniff the ink. But his snout was too much inside his purse to catch my drift. He had not a brain beyond piggish profit. All art was lost on him. In his mind, I now saw, I appeared as an airy-headed inventor, too priestly-cloistered for the market-place, unfitted for the ware-worn world. That I had conceived the work did not impress him. He supposed I would never deliver myself of it, as though I feared its birth would be the death of me. On the contrary, I ached to be done and get it out. But yes, it was a kind of child to me, and I would not let it go until fully formed.

'Just wait a few more weeks,' I said. 'Every man is working his utmost.'

'Then hire some more men with the rest of my loan.'

'If only it were so easy,' I said, and hummed and hawed of the difficulties of training new recruits, omitting to answer Fust the true reason – that his loan, did he but know it, was all spent. This was no squandering of mine. But Fust would rage and say it was, and accuse me of filling my wine-cellar at his expense, so I thought it better kept from him.

Since he was my partner, I might have been more honest. But did not God tell us to be wise like serpents? Why then, I shall not repent my cunning. It was needed for the work of the books. Goodly ends may come by wicked means.

It was calves that had eaten up Fust's loan. Their skins, I mean. For vellum.

My first plan had been to print only on paper. Since Christendom has more rags in it than beggars, I knew there would be no shortage. From Basel to Bamberg, new paper mills were springing up on every river. Each business had its own mark – a bull's head or whatever. I had visited the mill in Strasbourg of which Andreas Heilmann owned a share, and had seen sheets of paper being conjured from giant vats of pulp. Paper was cheap. It cost a fraction of vellum. What more could be needed for my Bible?

But with some of my buyers lay a prejudice towards vellum. Most abbots thought that anything less than vellum was ungodly, and I met lawyers who kept fancy books as a kind of furniture. 'Paper may be cheaper,' they said, 'but it lacks elegance.' The more these men spoke, the greater profit I saw. Since they were not short of gulden, they would pay whatever price I charged. In the end, nearly a fifth of the orders were for Bibles made that way.

It was more than profit, though, that drew me to vellum. I loved its springiness to the touch. Its velvet nap. The whiff of animal still hanging about it, as though when reading or writing you were living *inside the beast*. I loved the blood-veins running there, under the ink. I loved the brown-white, brown-white run of pages in a vellum book, since however long soaked in lime-water, and whatever sharpness of blade is used to scrape it, and no matter what creature it has come from (calf, goat, pig, sheep, deer – with smaller books even squirrel), hairside will always be darker than fleshside. I loved all this not as a man of business in his middle years but as a boy with a goosequill in a scriptorium.

What I had not reckoned was the number of skins needed – 150 for every copy. With thirty-odd vellum Bibles in all, that meant the hides of nearly five thousand calves. To buy them through a skin-merchant cost too much. The only hope was to go straight to the *source*, and to use Fust's loan to get skins cheaply.

Among my neighbours in Mainz was a butcher. To him I put the notion of a partnership, whereby we would buy whole carcasses together, with him taking the meat and me the hide. He sighed and shook his head. Any carcass from the abattoir came skinned, he said. And so lucrative was the trade in vellum with monasteries, no outsider could break in. Undaunted, I went to an abattoir in Mainz, and found the head slaughterman wielding his cleaver. Two fingers were missing on his left hand. His apron, streaked with calf-blood, was like a rubricated letter M. Could we talk business? I asked. He said he doubted it – his hides went straight to his brother's vellum-shop; the monks then 'hogged them'; the trade was all *sewn up*. When I asked if still we might see his brother, he shrugged, put his cleaver down, took his apron off, and led me next door. We made our way past brindled cow-hides drying hairside-out over wooden beams. Holding a knife shaped like a newly risen moon, the brother was paring hairs from a pelt held drum-tight in a wooden frame. The pelt was so small and pristine-white I could scarcely credit it.

'Uterine,' he said, catching me looking. 'The dearest of all vellum.'

'You abort the calves?'

'It is not official practice. But if a cow, for some reason, should miscarry and its calf be stillborn . . .'

I stroked the pelt's soft silk, then turned to the two brothers. Mean-faced and hatchet-eyed, they looked no more fond of each other than of me – the Cain and Abel of the meat trade.

'I have in mind an order for five thousand skins,' I said.

'Of uterine vellum? Impossible.'

'Not uterine. It is a larger beast I have in mind.'

'You will be needing year-old calves, then.'

'About that size.'

'The slaughtering and skinning would double our labour.'

'If the work were spread . . .'

'It would take us a year at least.'

'I cannot wait so long – unless the price is right.'

'We cannot haggle over price.'

'With an order in such bulk, I hoped to make a bargain.'

'It is no bargain if we are forced to hire more men.'

'I would match what the monasteries pay.'

'You would have to pay us more. With them, it is a steady trade and we can sell the meat to butchers. But with a multitude of calf-skins together, half the veal would go putrid and be wasted.'

I stuck my ground an hour or more, but had no choice but to settle at a price that stretched me thin. Even then, they could furnish only a quarter of the skins. I had to go to other abattoirs to find the rest. Each time the price rose higher. I think word of me went ahead – that they saw Gutenberg coming down the road and knew they could *fleece* him. Thanks to the printing of the Bible, the slaughtermen of Germany were kept busy for months and veal went cheap at my expense. I had reckoned 150 gulden for vellum. But the final cost was 350 – as much as I paid my workforce in two years. Five times as many copies in paper came to less.

I should have kept to rags and pulp rather than flesh and hide. It has become by now a saying of mine: Better strip a beggar than kill a calf. Each time I see a man in rags I give him money to buy new clothes – not from the goodness of my heart but because his old rags will go to making paper. But when I see a calf hung on a butcher's hook, its neck slit and running with blood, I feel sick at it, as an image of myself being drained of gulden.

That the gulden were Fust's did not comfort me. It made me ever more his dependant. And to staunch the losses I was forced to look in secret elsewhere.

♪

I have always been a man for secrets. My new one was a commission from Nicholas of Cusa, to print an indulgence. This was no common indulgence, the kind sold by pardoners for remission of sins; those I had done before for Nicholas, with the prior of St Jacob's acting in between. No, this was to raise money for the King of Cyprus in his war against the Turks. Doubtless it would swell Church coffers just the same, but I had no feeling against that, only a need to replenish my own. The indulgence was but thirty lines on a single sheet – less than one page of my Bible. To do it at the Humbrechthof would not have been wise, with Fust so fiery for a conclusion. The other way was my press at home, which though cruder than the new presses would serve to print a calendar or *Donatus*. I had type already cast, and scraps of vellum for the Bible could be brought from the Humbrechthof and *used* rather than thrown away. My old steadfasts Heinrich and Berthold did most of the work, with me overseeing them in my spare hours. It was mere jobbing, but would ease my current debt. If ten sheets raised a gulden, then with ten thousand of them I could – if so minded – replenish Fust with half his loan.

Heinrich and Berthold were sworn to keep it secret. So was Peter, whom I trusted as myself. But word of it got out – through Nicholas, or his salesmen, or some other. When it reached Fust, he came steaming to the Humbrechthof to berate me. What outrage was this? What venture kept from him? How could I distract myself thus with the Bible not yet complete?

'I did it at home,' I said, quietening him in case the men should hear. 'In my own time.'

'But with my money,' he raged.

'It is a separate venture.'

'Using materials I have paid for.'

'The press is an old one of mine.'

'Already you were behind. Now you stall further.'

'I work as many hours as ever.'

'You do not give your best.'

'I have given the Bible my life.'

But Fust was too choleric to listen, and though he did not ask further how I had funded the venture or whence the paper for it came, even a donkey could have guessed it. Some of my men were now peering over, stirred by our shouts above the printshop rumble. I drew Fust to one side, and to placate him spoke of another indulgence in the offing, suggesting it be done at the Humbrechthof, for our joint profit. This Fust readily agreed to. Indeed, in his own words,

'I insist on it, Johann. You will not double-deal with me again.'

'I have not before. But this is proof of my good faith.'

'Have you no harder evidence?'

'Indeed,' I said. 'Once the Bible is done, I have a grander scheme for us – to make a psalter. Large sales to the Church would be certain.'

'So you have tested the market this time?'

He said this with a sneer, as though to imply I had been careless over the Bible, since two buyers of ours had lately fallen by. I ignored the slight.

'Peter will design it. Then we can print in colour ourselves and save the buyers the cost of a rubricator, for which they will happily pay us a higher price. That way, we make more profit.'

Fust on any other day would have slavered at talk of profit. But he continued grumbling that I had cheated him, said his loan must be repaid once the Bibles were done, and spoke of our contract as 'binding'.

'If need be,' he said, departing, 'I will pursue it in court.'

I laughed inside at this innocence of my way with lawsuits. But I did not like Fust's tone. Though he left the printshop less testy than he had come, the men had meanwhile heard him raging. A few, I thought, talked more brazen to me afterwards, as though I were a man to be wrangled with, not a master. Perhaps I was imagining it. But I worried where Fust's example might lead.

I was right to worry. In the days that followed, his mood looped up others, like a stone thrown in a river spreading ripple-rings far and wide. Peter became distant-cold with me – I suspected he and Fust of conferring at home. And then the men, too, whose wages I had lately lowered on account of a shortage of ready gulden, turned more sullen and mutinous by the hour. I explained that they would shortly reap harvests to compensate for the present famine, and even promised each a finished Bible (to sell or keep by them as they wished). But they were tetchy with me and stirred up, as though doubting my word, and complained of their conditions – the hours, the cold, the food and so forth.

The pressmen were the noisiest. I had little regard for most of them – any beefy tavern-hand could do the job. But my compositors and typecasters had grumbles too, and I did not want to lose them before the Bible was finished. Not after, either – we had the psalter to do, and if any among them left to set up as rivals, they could, with their skills, ruin my business.

One night the men left early. Without full pay, they said, it was not just to keep them longer. Afterwards, I went to Peter.

'The Humbrechthof is full of grievances,' I said. 'What can we offer as an olive branch?'

He put his punch down.

'Pay them a full wage,' he said.

'Is that all?'

'And improve conditions.'

'How?'

'Do you want a list?'

I think he meant it as a sneer, but I made him do one. Though cool to start with, he warmed to the task, and together, under a candle, we drew up a sheet of working practices, which Peter set down in ink. (Here, Anton, I have kept a copy for you to look over.) We called them our ten commandments, and intended them to benefit all parties. Even the first I meant to stand by, difficult though that would be.

Draft for
𝔉𝔲𝔱𝔲𝔯𝔢 𝔚𝔬𝔯𝔨𝔦𝔫𝔤 𝔓𝔯𝔞𝔠𝔱𝔦𝔠𝔢𝔰 𝔞𝔱 𝔱𝔥𝔢 𝔥𝔲𝔪𝔟𝔯𝔢𝔠𝔥𝔱𝔥𝔬𝔣

1: Wages henceforth will be thirteen gulden and twenty pfennigs annually to all except apprentices – that is one gulden and ten pfennigs payable on the last day of each month.

2: Those ladling the metal into the hand-mould should at all times be kept supplied with goat's milk, as protection against the fumes from antimony and liquid lead.

3: Those that rub the type after casting it should wear finger-stalls on the two forefingers of the right hand, lest the skin tear against the sharp greet of the stone.

4: The printroom should be arranged so that the compositors be given the brightest place in it, and so the light comes in on their left hand, for else the light plying between the window and their eyes might shadow a letter they pick up and make them mistake it.

5: The pressmen should be placed on the north side of the printroom, so their hard labour in summer may be the less incommoded by the heat of the sun.

6: Boys being apprenticed in any printshop art should be instructed clearly. Such discourse as is common with us cannot help but be new to them and needs slow unfolding, since in the world outside those words have other meanings and may bring confusion – namely, body, face, bed, coffin, gallows, plank, shank, furniture, hose, cheeks, ashes, winter, balls, feet, cap, garter, worm, toe, tooth, plough, mouth, hag, dressing, male and female.

7: A printshop being a kind of chapel, there must be laws to abide by. In ours we decree as follows:

No swearing.

No fighting.

No giving the lie.

No gambling.

No drunkenness.

No pissing in the ink.

No flame to be left burning at night. (Last man out snuffs the candles.)

8: Fines will be imposed on each of the above offences, according to the case.

9: If these fines be not paid, then the offender shall be taken by force, and laid on his belly athwart the correcting stone, and be held there till he apologise.

10: Should he refuse to apologise, he is to be given eleven blows to his buttocks with a rod, though not with such violence as to make him piss blood.

Such was our list for reformation of the printshop. We left out the last two clauses, which Peter said the men might take amiss. The rest were put to them next day. And with Berthold and Heinrich urging their fellows to 'see sense', all present approved them – and agreed to work full hours.

One hundred pages of the Bible remained. But now we could quickly have them set. The dispute, it seemed, was at an end. We pressed ahead.

How long it was after this I cannot say. I keep no journal, and since all I did then took much longer than foretold, I dare not guess. I recall only Ulrich Han calling me over, he being the best puller and the one entrusted with the task. I took my place beside him. Peter stood there too. It had happened ten thousand times before, but all knew this moment was the one. Even Ulrich turned theatrical, putting his hands together as if in prayer and gravely bowing, till a hush fell through the room. Then a row on the lever, a ship-creak of timber as the platen fell and rose again, and a sheet under the tympan for Herr Gutenberg to inspect. Out it came from the frisket. I stepped forward to look. Straight margins. Upright letters. Silky-black type. As perfect as all the rest. It had happened ten thousand times before. But as I handed Ulrich the sheet, I could not help but hug him, then in turn hug every other. The last page of our Bible, two years late.

For the occasion, I had planned a mighty banquet. Though not by nature a trencherman (indeed I feel some sympathy with the Scottish who count gluttony a crime as well as a sin, and – so I am told – punish any offender by drowning), this was no ordinary banquet, but the crown of fifteen years of labour, and only the richest foodstuffs would serve. Frumenty with venison, beef, boar, stewed capon, roasted cygnet and heron, pike, perch, lobster, bream, baked apple tart, jellies and custard – the menu had long simmered in my head. Sad to tell, I could not bring it to table. I was out of funds still, and no man in Mainz would stand me credit. Peter urged me to go to Fust, and make peace, and invite him, implying that if I did so he (Fust) would give what gulden were required. But since I abhorred his presence, I chose not to run to him but to call on the talents of Frau Beildeck. Wonders have been worked with loaves and fishes. Her art was less miraculous, but she cooked us turnip soup followed by veal cutlets (donated by my good brothers in the abattoir), these swilled down with wine from my own cellar. With the wine drunk and the chomping over, I made a speech. The men should be proud, I said. The Bible was more wondrous than I had dared hope. Soon the world would thank us. Until that day, I would like each man to take this modest bonus – here I handed round a gulden apiece, which I had borrowed from my brother-in-law – to see them through. There came a muttered thanks or two, urged on by Lorenz, but not the rousing cheer this *publication day* deserved. Then the men dispersed into the taverns to spend their coins.

I had given them the next day free. So only I was there when the summons came. Fust's talk of law courts had been no idle threat. At this my moment of triumph, he foreclosed.

Part four

19. Betrayal

I have news to report. Anton has left me. From today, any words you read here will be written by Thomas, my new scribe. Yes, take it down, boy. Since I depend on scribes, I like to acknowledge them. As I named Anton, so I name you. You are a good boy, and welcome here. Even these dim eyes can see the grace with which you write. And I will not keep you long: there is little of my story left to tell.

But let me admit, meaning no unkindness, Thomas, that I mourn the loss of Anton. To start with, his going has cost me months – this is the first in nearly six I have sat here, so long did it take to find a willing hand. And now I can dictate again, I have mislaid all sense of who this book is for. Before I saw my reader as Anton, who had wit, learning, curiosity, laughter, beauty. Now – no offence again! – I write into a pit of nothingness. For when we write, do we not keep in mind to whom we are writing? (Such things I have lately learned, whose life before was the making of books, not the penning of them.) The Lord above, to whom I commend myself, I do keep mindful of. But He, being mighty, cannot be *pictured*. Perhaps you, Thomas – whose only fault is my not yet knowing you – will fill the chasm. But in the meantime I am discomposed. That is my second cause for grief at Anton's leaving.

Then third, to end with (and an end of me it nearly has been), are the rumours. The rumours. You will have heard these, Thomas, or are sure soon to be told. Shameful rumours. Let me not shirk them. It is said I was over-fond of Anton, and he complained, and his mother removed him. The last at least is true: the Mutti is to blame. But let me assure the reader – the scribe, too – that nothing ever happened amiss. If I like a boy to work with, and pat and stroke him sometimes for encouragement (knowing of old how weary it is to be a penman), and even fondle his neck where it aches from bending to the task, this does not make me a Sodomite. I am none such nor ever have been. I think the lady – the werewolf mother who banished the boy – must have heard of my ancient breach of promise suit with Ennelina. And it maybe struck her that my being unwed and childless bespoke a fancy for my own sex. And then Anton, who never meant me malice, likely let slip some mention of our easeful way with each other. And she then pressing him, and he turning silent out of loyalty to me, three was made from adding one and one, and he was ordered on pain of death to come no more. So she exiled him from my room, without the courtesy of telling its tenant. Which on the first morning of his absence meant I sat here like a monument waiting for him to mount the stairs and breathe me into life. An hour passed without my thinking anything amiss, for he had been late sometimes in the past, from youthful excess the night before. After two hours, I sent Frau Beildeck for word of his absence, assuming him sick, hoping it not a fever or the plague. She being slow, that took another hour, by which time I myself was plagued and feverish with fretting, with just cause as it proved, since Frau Beildeck had been told the boy would not be coming again, because his mother considered my conduct unseemly, not to say sinful, towards one so young. What she meant by this I had no notion of, and had to push Frau Beildeck to make it plainer, which she blushed to do, but at last confessed the mother's very words: 'No boy of mine will earn his wage in a house of sodomy.' Frau Beildeck then ranted at the woman over the slander of this, and ranted the same to me, thinking I might be cheered by her loyalty. But I drew small comfort from what she said, since it came out between the rants that because of my spurning Ennelina, and not marrying, and being so loving-close to Peter Schoeffer, the taint of sodomy has long been faintly present, like a shadow forever following me about.

I do not think many believe it – only peasant minds in

Eltville. If word of it had spread as far as Mainz, I would not have been honoured by the Archbishop. Still, it pains me that some mistake my manly friendships. Which is why I put on record for posterity, and for Thomas to know true of his employer, that no such sin of the flesh was committed by me.

Now, with this heart of mine done grieving for Anton, let us to business.

♪ ♪

It was simple-minded of me, perhaps, but after Fust had served his summons I persisted in thinking Peter Schoeffer my friend. But why should I have doubted him? He did not work less hard on my behalf. He showed no signs of turning the men against me, or of making them more restive than they were (sales of calendars and indulgences had at last allowed me to pay them, but not all they were owed). His distant-coldness had abated, and though our relations were not as formerly, he came to drink with me sometimes and let me ruffle his hair. His only reluctance – making his eyes (formerly so steadfast) scurry like a rabbit in search of a burrow – came when I asked after Fust. I meant this in pleasantry, since, as I often told Peter, my view of the 'coming court case' was that it would not come to court at all. Fust and I would bury our differences, I said, which to my mind, though this I did not say, meant that he would have to *cave in*. Peter looked relieved to hear it, but would not talk of his adopted father. Nor would he speak of Christina. This we had done sometimes in the past, not with intimacy, nor of course lasciviously, but as two men might when one is half-betrothed to the woman and the other to all appearance her brother. Now, though, came a vow of silence from him in everything relating to her. What this shyness betokened I could not say, but shyness it was, a blush printing his cheeks when I said her name and his eyes rabbiting again after that burrow.

At work, now our first Bibles had been pressed out (a few,

to my dismay, with pages left blank or printed twice), I turned to the new venture, a psalter. So as to 'suit our market', as Fust put it (I hated the middle word even more than the first and last), it was to be much more than a book of psalms: there would be hymns, songs, prayers, poems, collects, litanies and vigils. The words had to be set large, so that a choir could sing them in chapel gloom, which meant a new typeface. I had long since set Peter to the task, knowing the care he would take, despite Fust's eagerness to 'get the psalters out quicker than Aesop's hare' (Aesop being another author whom Fust cannot have read). Nor did Peter disappoint me. The typeface he made was more lovely even than our Bible's, with decorative initials (some like lilies-of-the-valley) enhancing the look. As to rubrication, we invented a method for tweezering out initials from the inked forme, so they were alternated in red and blue against black text. We could charge high prices for the psalter. And with my pressmen laid off (which saved on wages), and the Bibles mounting up for sale, I saw an end to our present hardships.

So I did not dwell on preparing myself for court. Statements were taken from each of us, and from other 'interested parties', which in Fust's case included his brother Jacob and in mine any workers still loyal to me (there were, despite the difficulties, a few). Our original contract was called for by the Judge. A date was set for the hearing. But Fust's case being manifestly unfair – he was demanding not just the 1,600 gulden he had lent me, but the compound interest on it, 2,020 gulden in all – I knew I would come off best.

Should I have paid Fust back in part, to keep him quiet? It is a question I often ask. By the time of the hearing, my Bibles had been sent out, and my coffers should have been full. But the monasteries were slow to settle their bills. A dozen unbound Bibles had to be given to my best workers, in lieu of wages, which lost me profit. Any other monies I had were put towards the psalter. To repay Fust meant borrowing from my family again, and I was damned if I would rob a cousin to pay a donkey. If he persisted in his notion of doing battle, let him take the consequence.

At last the day of the hearing was set. It was to be held in the refectory of barefoot priors, in front of a judge and city treasurer. The previous week, my punch-cutters and type-casters had been absent, not from sickness but from refusing to work till paid their due. I guessed it was Fust who had stirred them up, to unnerve me into settling with him out of court. But since type enough had been made to keep my compositors going, his scheme did not succeed. On the contrary, like molten metal in a hand-mould, I hardened and clarified. Why yield an inch, since once in court I could not lose? Indeed, so certain was I of winning, and so eager to work with Peter on the psalter, I conceived the wonderful notion of *not attending court*. Ellewibel had been a doughty opponent. So in their way had been the Dritzehn brothers. But the pygmy Fust was of no consequence. To see him off, the statement I had submitted would suffice. Rather than dispute with him, I would send Lorenz on my behalf.

At the back of this, perhaps, lay Ennelina. She had not come to court to do battle with me. And though she had lost the suit, she had won a kind of victory, since I had been left (once the triumph passed) feeling cheapened and guilty. I would copy her conduct, then. Except in one respect. My victory would be more than moral. I would see Fust judged, ruin his standing, and banish him from my business ever more.

⌐⌐

The case was heard at eleven o'clock on Wednesday the fifth of November, 1455. See, Thomas, how it *prints* itself in my memory. All I did that morning I see now like an icicle dangling from an eave. There it hangs in perfect clarity, and I innocently walking below, not seeing the dagger about to plunge.

I went to the Humbrechthof at seven, according to my usual custom, in expectation of a worker or two arriving by eight. When by a half after ten none had come, not even Peter, I thought for lack of something better I might take myself to the courtroom after all, so as to see how fast the Judge would find for me. But as I was throwing a cloak about my shoulders, one of my young apprentices (printer's devils, as we call them) returned from Cologne, with a long discourse on how a large sum owing me from sales of Bibles, which he had been sent there to collect, had still not been paid. By the time I had railed at him to speed straight back and demand part-settlement, the moment for court had gone. I took my cloak off and sat down to work.

By now I was a little gloomy. None of my men had yet come in. Worst of all was the lack of Peter. Whence his absence? I took him to be sick. It did not occur to me he was in court, let alone that he might speak there. But he was, he did – as Lorenz told me, scuttling straight from court and bursting in.

He told me once, then repeated it over. Even then I could not take his story in, and made him copy it word for word again, in hope I had heard wrong and that a kinder version might appear. The case had lasted under an hour, he said. There had been the Judge, the Notary, the City Treasurer (Fust's brother Jacob), a scribe (see Thomas – there are always scribes!) and several witnesses, but not a friar (barefoot or otherwise) to be seen. According to Lorenz, the high drama of it played as follows:

JUDGE: Herr Fust, if you loaned Herr Gutenberg 1,600 gulden, why do you now seek repayment of 2,020?
FUST: Compound interest, your honour. I am a man of modest means and had to borrow in order to lend. In such circumstances, usury is no sin.
JUDGE: And you say he has no intention of paying you back?
FUST: That is right, your honour. He has boasted of cheating me.
JUDGE: Have you witnesses who can support this allegation?
FUST: I have one, your honour – Peter Schoeffer.
JUDGE: Then let us call him.
NOTARY: Call Peter Schoeffer.

Enter PETER.

JUDGE: Could you state your name, age and occupation.

PETER: Peter Schoeffer, aged twenty-eight, printer and chief deputy at the Humbrechthof.

JUDGE: It is alleged that Herr Gutenberg boasted to you of cheating Herr Fust. Is that correct?

PETER: He did not precisely boast ... He did not exactly speak of cheating ... I have great respect for him ... He taught me all I know ... His invention is a miracle ...

JUDGE: Please answer the question.

FUST: Peter, we agreed you must disclose the truth.

PETER: On one occasion, I have to admit, he told me he had no gulden and that if ever he acquired some – to use his actual words – 'I will keep them from the greedy clutches of that fat, sweating liar and thief.'

JUDGE: Meaning Herr Fust?

PETER: Yes.

JUDGE: Anything more?

PETER: No.

JUDGE: Thank you. You may step down. I wonder if Herr Gutenberg has anything to say in reply.

NOTARY: I cannot see him in court, your honour.

FUST: He has not troubled to appear, that is why. This is how he conducts himself in all things – with patrician arrogance.

JUDGE: Perhaps he is waiting outside in the cloisters. Let us call him.

LORENZ: He is unable to be present, sir, but asked me to speak for him and to say that he has nothing to add to his statement.

JUDGE: Are there no further witnesses?

FUST: None, your honour.

JUDGE (to LORENZ): Have you nothing to speak for your master?

LORENZ: Only that he is honest, and means no harm, and that his invention does him great honour, which no man [*looking hard at* FUST] should try to strip him of.

JUDGE: That is all?

LORENZ: Yes.

JUDGE (*having conferred with the City Treasurer, Jakob Fust*): Then I will pass judgment.

NOTARY: Let the court rise.

JUDGE: Herr Gutenberg has made a Bible through his new method of artificial writing, and with it driven forward the business of the Gospel. Perhaps in time a just celebrity will ensue from so bold an undertaking. But the task of this court is to pass judgment in the here and now. We have heard from Herr Fust of a loan made in good faith towards the enterprise, which Herr Gutenberg allegedly treated with contempt. And having heard the evidence, we find beyond all reasonable doubt that an injustice has indeed been done.

The case is therefore awarded to the plaintiff. Herr Gutenberg must pay Herr Fust the 2,020 gulden owing, or if he lacks the funds reimburse him in property and tools. This I will set down more fully in writing. In the meantime, I will require you to attend here tomorrow week, Herr Fust, to swear an oath that to lend money to Herr Gutenberg you were yourself forced to borrow at interest. If Herr Gutenberg wishes to attend tomorrow week also, to appeal against my judgment, he has the right do so, and I hope his servant will invite him to consider it.

FUST: Is my oath to be sworn on the Bible, your honour?

JUDGE: Of course. Have you a difficulty with that?

FUST: No. I will happily affirm to God that I borrowed 1,600 gulden at six per cent interest. But perhaps I might be allowed to swear this on one of the Bibles printed at my own works – and make a present of it to the court afterwards.

JUDGE: That is most kind, Herr Fust. My notary, Herr Ulrich Helmasperger, will prepare copies of my judgment as required.

Exit JUDGE.

FUST (to PETER, *as overheard by* LORENZ): Two thousand gulden will come to everything in the Humbrechthof –

the building, the metal, the paper, the vellum and the presses.

SCHOEFFER: Leave him a press at least. The one in his old printshop is decrepit. Besides, the work of the books has been his life.

FUST: You are too lenient. As a business partner, you must learn to be less yielding. As a husband too. [*Blush from* PETER] But if giving him a press stops the old villain making further trouble ... We will see.

Exeunt FUST *and* PETER.

Was that how it happened? Lorenz was my only witness, and being old by then – he died within the year – his mind may have played tricks on him. So may my own mind now be playing tricks on me. But this is how I recall him reporting the scene. The words Peter said I used of Fust I cannot remember speaking to him, but perhaps in my cups I did so – 'that fat sweating liar and thief' was a mild expression of my judgment. Now that judgment had become a judgment of me, and all I had worked for was lost. In my hands, at the workbench, as I sat listening to Lorenz narrate my downfall, I held a hand-mould. I had longtime pictured myself as that hand-mould – the instrument shaping all. Now I felt like hot metal in the mould of Fust, who had used me while it suited him, then thrown me off.

I left the Humbrechthof before Fust and Peter could return, and retired to bed. It was still open to me to appeal, by attending the next week, and Lorenz urged it, but I would not thus abase myself. What chance had I had at the first hearing, with Fust's brother Jacob present to see that the verdict went against me? And what chance would I have next time, now Fust had bribed the Judge? I would not go. I would not even ask Lorenz to go. In his place I would send Heinrich Keffer and Berthold Ruppel, they being my trustiest workers and the ones who would give Fust the meanest looks.

From my bed, I spun webs of wild revenge – a fire to burn the printshop down, the theft of the psalter typeface, the wrecking of the presses and cases. More practically (for even at my lowest ebb I could not think in earnest of destroying the work), I hatched schemes to garner two thousand gulden in a week. This cousin here, that mintman there, a Jew or two, surely with such help . . . But it was useless. Twice what I owed him would not now pay off Fust. It was my work he wanted, my men, my tools, my future profits, the honour and esteem of my invention. The donkey had proved a fox: perhaps Fust had read Aesop after all. He had plotted, bided his hour, crept up unawares, then sprung. He had outplayed Gutenberg at his own game. He had consumed me.

I returned to the Humbrechthof only once, to collect some notebooks and arrange for the removal of a press (the only one out of six allowed me, though I was careful to choose the best). Fust, as I knew ahead, was absent that day, gone to Rome. But Peter, though he part-hid himself, I caught sight of and waved to across the room. He saw me, I am sure, but pretended not to, as though preoccupied with some object on his bench. Undaunted, I moved towards him. He was working in a murky corner with two compositors, Heinrich Eggestein and Ulrich Zell. To show I bore those men no grudges, I offered to shake their hands – to shake Peter's too if he allowed it. Heinrich and Ulrich smiled awkwardly, with eyes guilty and sad, as they took my hand, but at least it was a greeting of sorts. Whereas Peter – a second time – refused to know me, his eyes scurrying away into the distance, as though I was not there at all. Other men wandered over to speak with me, and to let me know, through their eyes if not their mouths, that I had all their sympathy – they had stood by Fust only because he paid their wages. I asked to see their latest work, and they took me round from bench to bench, but were too embarrassed to say much, as though fearful it might upset me to be reminded of what I had lost. Lorenz had meanwhile been gathering some old tools of mine, and a few new ones besides which he guessed Fust would not miss. At last he was finished and said that we should go, since Lotte would by now have cooked supper for us. Only one man I had not yet bidden farewell to, and now I walked across again to see him. 'Peter,' I said, hoping his name would bring him back from whatever far-off place he had gone to. But his ears would not hear me, his eyes disdained to recognise mine, his hand played busily with type. 'Peter,' I said again, and then 'Peter' a third and last time, but still he would not hear or clasp my hand.

I walked away. My truest disciple had denied me.

♫♫

Was that a tear, Thomas? If I had eyes to study your writing, would I find that last line blotched? Perhaps my readers, if there should be some, will weep as well. They must pity me, I know. For a month, I pitied myself – passed from shock and rage through envy and doubt to chastened wisdom. I had learned from my long life, and from reading the Bible and the Ancients, what it is for a man to lose all. The proverbs rang in my head. How the wheel of fortune must come round. How the mighty are fallen. How fields of grass will turn to dust. Yet knowing this did not help. I was lonely-bitter, and the story too much my own. My art had been stolen from me, my trust betrayed. This was no general plight, but the tragedy of one man once and that man me.

Yet I do not want your pity. Poor old Gutenberg, cheated and destroyed then left to wither miserably to death – it is so much wasted pathos. My downfall was no joy, but I would not let it be the *ruin* of me. Is it ruin to be alive at over sixty? To have a brimming wine-cellar? To sit by our nation's greatest river, a willing and handsome penman at my side? Yesterday two woodpeckers flew down and called at each other and hugged the trunk of our linden, and in the warm air I dimly watched them an hour. If this is ruin, some will likely choose it over their own unruined lot.

Nor was even my work at an end. I had my workshop still, in the basement of the Gutenberghof, which I had bought after Claus had passed away. I housed the old press there, and now a better one from the Humbrechthof. I had Heinrich Keffer and Berthold Ruppel as workers, they out of loyalty having said good riddance to Fust. I had the *Donatus* to print for schools, and indulgences and calendars for the Church. A month was long enough a spell of melancholy. That Fust had planned his suit to be the death of me was like a flame lighting up my life.

Christ says when wrong is done us we should turn the other cheek. So I did, but would not shut my eyes and ears and mouth. Having long kept them to myself, I now preached far and wide the marvels of print – in part to earn commissions, in part to anger Fust. He, I knew, was fearful of the secret getting out. Through adding bolts and walls and oaths of silence, he made the Humbrechthof a fortress to rival Carcassonne. Inside, so I heard (for there were men of his happy to blab to me), he was pressing on with the psalter, for which Peter, before the trial, had designed the face. Since Peter was its maker, it would be a lovely thing – a book my humble presses could not match. Yet my existence was of itself a kind of rivalry, a threat to spread the art abroad. In truth, I did not think Fust should keep it hidden. Had not my press been made to break the cabal of priests, who kept their books under lock and key? If so – and it was so – then the sooner men were taught the art of printing the better. My duty as a Christian was to go forth bearing good news. Old Gutenberg of the clamped lips now became the biggest mouth in town. Before I had been clandestine, for fear of losing all. Now all was lost, I need fear no more.

Even without my help, once the Bibles were out (the last few of them being sold at a book fair in Frankfurt) word of my invention began to spread. And though Fust & Schoeffer (as they now called themselves) tried to rub out my name like a misprint, some knew what was due to me.

To take an instance. Ulrich Helmasperger, notary at the trial, the man who had copied my death-warrant, also acted as a cleric in Bamberg. Falling into talk one day with the bishop there, he mentioned my Bible, and the dispute with Fust, and the injustice as he must have seen it of the verdict. Upon which the bishop wrote inviting me to make a new Bible for him. Since I had but two presses (one of them old), and no resources to build more, I at first refused. But the bishop being persistent, and coming to Mainz to see me in person, and offering to meet all costs of paper and metal, I was persuaded to cast the typeface at the Gutenberghof, with Heinrich and Berthold in charge. In time, the type was carted to Bamberg, and the setting and printing done there, and I paid visits – for a fee – to oversee the work. This Bible was not as handsome as my first. With thirty-six lines on each, it ran to 1,800 pages, which is longer than any book should be. But nor could it now be said that Fust had killed me off.

As well as calendars, indulgences and jobbing work, I had another large commission – for the *Catholicon*, a Latin dictionary many hundreds of times copied out by scribes. The idea for this – and the gulden – came from Dr Konrad Humery, town clerk of Mainz, whom I had met years before at Erfurt. Much of the labour for it was provided by a single Frenchman, Nicholas Jenson, who had been sent to Mainz from the court of Charles VII in order to be instructed in my art. Nicholas was no Peter, but he showed willing and learned fast. With a small workforce and three presses, we had the *Catholicon* finished in two years, using new methods to set it and squeezing it to seven hundred pages. Dr Humery urged me to put my name to it, as Fust & Schoeffer had put theirs to the psalter. Though tempted to leave a mark, I did not think it right. If the names of scribes are rarely given, why give those of printers? Is not the work we do nameless obeisance to the glory of God? While Fust & Schoeffer paraded themselves like fairground hawkers, I offered this colophon instead: 'By the help of the most high, at whose bidding the tongues of children become eloquent and who reveals to the lowly what he conceals from the wise, this noble book was born in the year of our Lord 1460, from the mother city of Mainz of the renowned and illustrious German nation, without help of reed, stylus or quill, but by a wonderful concord, proportion and measure of punches and forms.' Or some such words. The tone was humble, the print uneven, but the *Catholicon* filled me with pride.

I thought of printing another dictionary, this time in German, giving words spoken by the mass of men. There is some priestly compact to pretend that Latin is the sole language on earth – as though the more tongues men speak and write, the more sins they do. But to me the Tower of Babel is no Devil's construction. In a fashion, I built such a tower myself. Let all manner of words be set free! But when I put my dictionary notion to investors, they frowned: 'Why collect low words?' To which my answer was – and is – that the manner in which we Germans truly speak may be coarse to hear but cannot be so low as to deserve oblivion. A vernacular dictionary is a record of the words that fly from men's mouths, and without it they are gone and lost in air, whereas to set them down is to catch and name them like birds. And who knows how such knowledge might one day be of use.

I have not yet done it, Thomas, and now I fear it is too late. But this my testament is given in German. Write in it if you will that I have made two things in life which any man might be proud of: a Bible to spread the word of God, and a dictionary to spread the words of men.

20. The Visit

Word would often reach me of Fust & Schoeffer, and the triumph of their psalter. But of Peter and Christina I heard nothing. It was known they were in love and engaged to marry. I felt foolish not to have seen it. To a degree I *had* seen, only not acknowledged it. For years they had cooed and nuzzled at each other like a pair of ring-doves. Yet only after the court case would I admit this mutual fondness, which Fust of course had used against me. I mourned the loss of Peter first. But Christina being my hope for children, I mourned her too. Their deceit did not bear thinking of. Still, to my knowledge they were not wed. And with some years gone, and still no wedding-feast, I began to think Fust must be playing old tricks. What impossible target had he set his business partner to put off the day of Peter becoming a husband? Would Peter be bribed then gulled as I had been? Would another take his place as he took mine? Would Fust delay so long that Christina (fast approaching five-and-twenty) became too old to bear children? I did not raise my hopes, but it did me no small pleasure to think there could be pain and mischief hereabouts, and that my enemies might be suffering.

As to myself, I was sixty by now – not too old to marry, but too old to see the fruits of marriage mature. What point in getting wed unless to have children? And what point in children, if you cannot watch them grow? The loss of the lawsuit, and then my debts and low spirits afterwards, had for some years made me unfit for marriage. But in time, thanks to Dr Humery, I was a man of wealth again, and might have frolicked with some twenty-year-old along the Rhine, as many an ageing widower does on a sunlit afternoon. That I did not was in part on account of my shyness but more because my vision was clouding over, which made me worry I might choose a woman who was ugly. For myself, I could have lived with such an error (it was only the marriage-bed I wanted her for, and the marriage-bed is dark), but I would not risk the consequences for my heirs. Any children of mine must be pretty or handsome – how otherwise, in this world, could they prosper? – and this was an unlikely outcome if their mother looked like a weasel or a frog. Understand, it is not that I number myself among God's beauties. But nor am I warty or hunchbacked, nor do I sprout a bulbous nose. No, I would not mingle my flesh with an unknown maiden's, for fear of what the act might spawn. Bitter as I was to sense my eyes going, and to think my days at the press might soon be over, I refused to console myself by rushing at some girl I could not clearly see.

Any doubts about this were finally settled when one August day in Eltville, at the house where I now sit (to which I came each summer), I received a visit from two nuns. Properly speaking, they were not nuns but Beguines - lay sisters in gowns and head-dress. Several had called before, to beg for alms or bread. If dirty of foot and vagrant in spirit, they would at once be sent off by Frau Beildeck. This pair, though, were admitted, having struck her as refined. More, they asked to speak with me in person. Frau Beildeck came up the stairs and pressed their suit. And I, with a groan, ready for my purse to be lightened, agreed they should be brought up.

'Herr Gutenberg,' the shorter of them said on entering the room, and she began at once to tell me of the work the Beguines did, their sick-nursing and kindness to the poor. It was a lecture I could have done without but felt I must endure, since to make ready too quickly with my purse would look ill-mannered – and would also mark me out as one so spendthrift as to be worth often calling on again. While the smaller nun proceeded backwards from present charity to the history of the order since its founding, I had time to regard her companion, as best as my misted sight allowed. No less greying than her sister, she looked taller by some inches and prettier of visage, with eyes – if this was not a delusion of mine – that lit with something sweeter than Christian devotion. Seeing me stare, she blushed, and regarded the floor, then raised her head again, and to my astonishment – to the astonishment also of her sister, who was just then describing the original Beguine community in Liège and how 'women of wealth were admitted to be bountiful among it' – and even perhaps to her own astonishment, since she stammered as she spoke it, said:

'Johann. Do-do you-you not recognise me?'

I did not. Yet the voice, under the stammer, seemed familiar, and I searched her face like an astronomer tracking planets in the sky. Those streaks of apricot in the grey, that sapphire gaze ... The hairs rose on my flesh. I began to believe it might be. Yet still she shocked me when she said it.

'It is your Ennelina.'

The 'your' was the greatest shock of all, since it betrayed a fondness I had supposed was missing from her heart. The companion-sister, too, must have noted it, for she conferred and then – saying there were calls to make on other houses – withdrew and went downstairs and out the door. Left alone, Ennelina and I clasped each other's hands and stood there, lost for what to say or do. After a time, this made us shy. Since there was nothing in that room to sit on but a single chair – my throne, as Frau Beildeck called it – and the weather outside was kindly, I suggested we go into the air. Ennelina looked hesitant at first but then agreed, knowing of course the river lay nearby and hoping perhaps, as I did, that its fluency might help us speak more freely.

It was I who talked first, as was proper, being man and host. I did not speak of what touched me closest: my guilt over the breach of promise suit, my regret at not marrying her, the hum of self-reproach which had never, despite my efforts, been drowned out by the rushing years of work. I spoke instead of my outward life after my quitting Strasbourg and all the people in it: Nicholas of Cusa, Brother Konrad, Brother Ruprecht, Fust, Peter, Lorenz, Heinrich,

Berthold, Konrad Humery and so on. Christina I left out, not from fear of making Ennelina jealous – that this ageing nun might envy any romantic dalliance of mine seemed unlikely – but because to mention it would have insulted the memory of my first love. Ennelina listened close, but later admitted she had heard some of it before – rumours of my Bible were strong in the convents at which she lodged during her missions for the Beguine sisterhood. I had supposed her calling on me to be mere chance, but now began to conceive it differently.

'So when you came today to Eltville . . .?'

'I hoped to see you. I had been told where Herr Gutenberg dwelt.'

'But the sister with you . . .?'

'I did not tell her of our connection. Even to myself I had vowed to say nothing – just to do our business, hoping you would be charitable, then go away. But when you looked at me, I could not help myself.'

'And your becoming a Beguine . . .?'

'Is a long story.'

It was, some of the details too burdensome to set down, and some in any case forgotten by me, since the heart of it – and Ennelina spoke more frankly of her heart than I had of mine – was what held me more. If you will license it, and trust me to recall her words in rough, I will tell the story as Ennelina spoke it that day.

♪♪

'Is it because we come from their wombs that we cannot see our mothers straight? Does that first darkness blind us forever after to their faults – to their virtues too? Remember, Johann, how you used to rail against your own mother. Against mine too. Indeed against all the mothers in the world. What was it made you angry with women – every woman, so it then seemed, but me? I never understood it. But I did feel it was your mother who had made you all you were, for both good and bad.

'What I feel about my own mother, now she is dead, I cannot say. But I see much more clearly how possessed she was by the thought of marrying me off. From my birth, she eyed the world in search of likely husbands for me. And once I reached twelve, she began to lure them to our house. You were not the first. You were not, I blush to say, the last. Even while she laid the lawsuit against you, she was reckoning likely others. I cannot blame her for it. Nor, after all these years, should you. My father being dead, she could not provide for me and wished to see me settled with a man of wealth. There was herself in it too, all her own yearnings, being a widow and still young. If a man could be found for me, why then a friend or brother of his might be found for her. So she thought, I think. There was a desperation in her I did not feel myself. Nor was it only wealth she sought. For her, a woman could not be made whole but by marriage – unwed, unringed, we were half-souls crying in purgatory. I did not see it thus. I did not need any man to complete me. For though I loved you, Johann, I had – as you did – aspirations for more than marriage. Did you think, once wed, to wall me up at home? You could not have done so. There was another man in my life – He whose message was to go forth and do good. I barely knew what it meant, but He seemed to want it of me, in this world not the next. A woman can feel close to Christ because she knows what it is to shed blood, as He did on the cross. Even before I met you, I had begun to go about on His behalf: an errand for an ageing neighbour, broth served on winter evenings to the poor and vagrant, a child rocked in a cradle while its mother had an hour of sleep. I told myself I did these things for others, not to bask in the glory of my own goodness. Of course, I also did them to escape my mother. Even so, I must have sounded pious to you. No wonder you did not listen when on our walks I tried to tell you of my aspirations. Your own work held you too close. You would never unclench to hear of mine.

'My purpose is not to chastise you for that, but to explain why I felt no haste for marriage. Because of the work I did, and a desire to travel, I would happily have waited. Even after that time ... even when I allowed ... even once we were intimate, still I would have waited – but for my mother pressing me. Not that I ever told her what happened in the farmhouse. Nor did I say you had promised marriage. I said only it was understood between us, which it was, or so I thought. When my mother lost patience and took you to court, it was not at my bidding. On the contrary, I tried to dissuade her, knowing it would enrage you. I cannot blame you for that. But why did you not relent once my unhappiness was plain? If you loved me, could you not have saved your reputation without destroying mine? You could, I think. You could have won the suit but then married me right off. You could have won it and set a wedding-date ahead. You could have contrived to lose it. You need not have fought it at all.

'It is too late for reproaches, and I intend none. But it was how my mind ran at the time. Do you wonder at my mistrust? What else was I to think? I could not blame you for fighting a case my mother had trumped up. But to give no reassurances, to turn cold towards me, to cease to visit, to humiliate me about the town by denying our courtship: scorned as I was, I knew you no longer loved me. You shake your head. I only tell you what I felt. Without a drop of kindness from you, I entered the desert of unlove.

'And unlove soon turned to hatred. I doubted you had ever cared for me. Our intimacy, not a sin to me before, now became one, because no earnest love compelled it in you. I saw you had tricked me to it, through artful words and stealthy movements of the flesh. I had given myself from passion, and you had taken me in cunning. I was not with child, at least. But I felt as open to the world as if I had been – my fall for all to mock at. You too walked mocking through my dreams. Worse, I saw that I disgusted you. That in your mind the ardour I had shown had become cheap, sweating, whorish, depraved. The ardour had been for you and you alone, and so innocent was it I willingly defied God's law. To what end? To be despised by you. And now to despise myself.

'For months – years – I dwelt in a kennel of madness: the

straw and barkings of my own head. Even my mother turned against me, since no man in Strasbourg would I consider as a husband. Not that I still loved you – in time I was consumed with murderous hatred. But I took all men to be as bad. My deflowering was a secret still, even from my mother, and I did not suppose, wicked though you were, that you would boast of it. Yet it was no secret from God, and I felt ready to confess and do penance. But this meant confession with the city priests, for which I was not ready, they being gossips or worse (I had heard of one who with sins of the flesh favoured 'atonement through replication' – that is performing the act again with him). In my troubled mind another notion formed, of entering a convent. The prospect pained me, since it meant leaving my mother, who was ill from some wasting sickness. And would they give sanctuary to one such as me? Also it meant surrendering hope of you, Johann, for though full of hatred I had some fancy of you dropping from the clouds on a white steed with a thousand pardons for your conduct and a vow to serve me with loving humility evermore. I shied away from leaving. But in the kennel of my head I howled ever more madly, and I knew I must act or die. Slowly my resolve grew. I would enter a convent far from Strasbourg, where no one would know my name and past. Just before I was due to leave, you passed me in the street – remember? There was no white steed, nor time for pardons to be said, but it was you. Afterwards I walked in turmoil half the night. Had it been a sign from God that I should stay? Or the Devil tempting me to further ruin? I decided the latter, and took the boat as planned.

'I had hoped the convent would cure me, and the nuns indeed were gentle and kind. I had a wooden bowl for food, my own straw-pallet and the leisure to pray six hours a day. At confession, to unseen mother superiors behind the screen, I told what God and I already knew, the sin committed with you. No crack of doom greeted my tale, no burning sword, not even a plaint or sigh. All I had was coaxing sympathy and modest penance. I guessed that other girls in the convent had the same story to tell – that even those behind the screen (whom I imagined to be twice or thrice my age) had first put themselves into a nunnery from fleshly shame. This should have consoled me but did not. I wanted to be punished – and combed the scriptures for dreadful martyrdoms. That which seized me most was Saint Cecilia's, who on her sentence to be beheaded took three sword-blows to the neck and died in agony of them over days. To be tormented slowly to death became my greatest longing. I resolved to contrive a fatal sickness.

'You shake your head, Johann, in disbelief. But I hoped by this to burn all sinfulness from my body and to suffer as Christ did on the cross. Life had no joy, death held out no fear, so why not will a fever on myself? It was simply done. By starving myself of food and sleep, I began to shiver and fade. The nuns fed me water and herbs, but I pushed them off: this was my Passion, and must not be disturbed. The third night of my fever, they agreed I would not last till morning and said last rites. Already I felt numb and dead below the waist – God's punishment for my sin. Cheering at this, that he had struck at me at last, I asked to be moved to a sitting position, with my head against the wall, so my heart could more freely beat its exequy. The mother superior was summoned. My eyes were fixed on stone, and I could or would not speak. She held a wooden cross, which she set before my face, saying "Daughter, look on this image and be saved". Then the room fell dark about me, like a gown slipping off, and I saw myself naked before the Lord. He was clothed in goose-white light, and the Virgin stood in blue by his right hand, and on his left hand stood Jesus, bleeding red from his crown of thorns. The Lord entreated me to live and serve Him on earth, which I had little wish to, since my hands had fallen to my sides, and my blood had stopped running, and my sand was almost sunk. But though I thought I must die, in that instant my suffering left me, and I was cured throughout my body, and slipped into a long and wondrous sleep. The sleep lasted two days. Within an hour of waking, I was up and eating heartily of bread and broth.

'That was twenty years since, Johann, when you were

forty and I just twenty-six. After some months in the convent, I returned to Strasbourg and nursed my mother to her end. Inside a cooking-pot one day, I discovered your letter proposing marriage, which must have come during my absence and which my mother, still hating you, had hidden away. I knew then that your heart was truer than I thought. But when I went to your workshop, they told me you had left Strasbourg, and were being pursued for debts, and no one knew your whereabouts. I consoled myself that your love had been sincere at least. And the way you look at me now confirms it – that the act in the farmhouse was not some brutish slight encounter on your part.

'Since then, I have lived and worked as a lay sister. I thank God for having spared me to be His pilgrim. You too, I know, have served Him well. I have heard some priests denounce the printing press, but they are the exception and you must not mind them. Your book – which I have seen in Bamberg – is a wondrous thing. On our walks, you tried to excite me with descriptions of your invention. I listened as best I could, but was too young to see what righteous use it might be put to, as happen you were also, since you spoke then more of gulden than of God. Now I do see it. To me Christ is a book written on the skin which I carry forever with me. But there are men whom God's word has never touched, and your Bibles will send it forth to them. Whatever pain you have suffered has been for Him. He will reward you hereafter. The rewards of this life are nothing – let Herr Fust have them, while you in eternity rejoice.

'I also mean by this that I forgive you for our breach. I cannot be sure how much you loved me at that time, and do not wish to, since either way, deep or little, would only hurt me. But since I know you love God, that He alone was my rival (for it is said in Mainz you are unmarried still), I feel no bitterness. What lovely children we might have had, what talk together, what joys, what intimacy. But we are not wholly lost to each other. Be at peace, thinking of that. Though not husband and wife, we have been joined in service of God. Look, even now, my arm is linked with yours and we are treading the same path.'

Not again, Thomas. This habit of tears ill becomes a scribe. Let ink be your only liquid. It does not mix with the fluids of the heart.

Besides, my ending will disappoint. Your head is full of knights and damozels. But look at me. I am old. Ennelina is grey and living in a distant city. We write each other twice a year. But we do not meet. When her Beguine sister broke in on us by the river, and told her they must leave to catch the boat, and Ennelina shook my hand, and I looked in her eyes as best I could (my own – I admit, and therefore absolve you – being more than usually misted), and she waved adieu to me from the orchard wall, that was the last time. Yes, I could go to her now and ask her hand. But that is not what either of us wants. Put away your Cupid's bows. Save your harping for other hearts. By the time we found each other again, Ennelina and I were too settled in our ways, too wedded to our separate selves. Let the young race to the altar. When we old are carried to church, it is in a slower cart and for an earthier ceremony.

No, if it is wedding bells you wish to hear, then think of those that rang (not long after Ennelina's visit) for Peter and Christina. Why they took so long to peal is a mystery. Perhaps some contract for another book was imposed on Peter as a prior condition. Perhaps Peter spoke up at times for his old master, and this so angered Fust that he would not give his daughter. To get round this, Peter might then have threatened to start a rival business of his own. Or perhaps he got Christina with child – and to avoid the shame of the babe being born out of wedlock Fust relented. Whatever the reason, he did finally let them off the rack. The wedding-feast was large and, so I am told, cost more than the vellum for my Bible. I thank the Lord they did not ask me to it, nor to the christening of Fust's grandchild. Yet I am glad for them. Christina, so I hear, is now with child again. I do not begrudge her it – her husband neither. Let that be your happy ending.

As for old Gutenberg, you have seen for yourself that I live solitary and unwed. But I am content. You need not pity me. It is enough to have been reconciled with Ennelina. Love healed us before we died. No one could ask more of it. My life has had much pain. But joy has done its best.

21. Exile

After Ennelina's visit, I returned from summer idleness in Eltville to the workshop in Mainz. My eyes dimming, I was less active now, and could not tell a ꝃ from a ꝟ. There were consolations in being half-blind. To have gazed full-eyed on my *Catholicon*, and then to measure it against the psalter done by Fust & Schoeffer, might have dispirited me to death. Dr Humery, keeping me in gulden with new commissions, was benevolent as a saint. But I had not the men. I had not the materials. I had not the art and purpose of old.

From Rome came a letter in the name of my old friend, Nicholas of Cusa. He was now returned there from Brixen to aid Pope Pius II, of whom he wrote despairing: 'He is my good friend, yet uses me as a tool to further his ambition and will not hear me when I tell him what goes on in curial circles: that everything is corrupt, no one does his job honourably, and all are out for advancement and greed. If ever I speak about reform these days, I am laughed at. It is a poor world, Johann, where no one takes the Church to heart. I had hopes your press would aid me. Perhaps in time it will. But meanwhile, the way to mend lazy priests and broken laws is with stronger leadership from Rome.' Nicholas was my friend, but I did not approve this last. For years, Rome had looked upon us Germans as barbarians, though our blood and toil had made her queen of all the world. Already, our nation had been reduced to poverty and servitude. If the Pope meant to bear down on us, this could only worsen our condition.

So I then thought. Soon nearly all in Mainz thought it too. Popular feeling had been stirred by our new elected

Archbishop, Diether, whom the Pope did not approve. When asked to surrender powers and taxes to Rome, Diether would not bow to it, for which he had our gratitude and love. For a time, Diether had the winning of this battle. But then the Pope plotted with some in Mainz to plant his own man, Adolf von Nassau, as Archbishop, this Adolf being as quick to do Rome's bidding as goats are to devour a garden. For nearly a year it was the war of the archbishops, with Diether refusing to bend to Rome, and Rome recognising only Adolf, and confusion on the throne. Dr Humery was for Diether, as I was, and to this purpose we printed a broadsheet taking his part. But other broadsheets flew for Adolf, some of them from Fust & Schoeffer, who printed for anyone who would pay them – Diether, Adolf, they danced to either tune, with never a care about the rights. Perhaps they laughed to see words used for war, supposing that no one dies by them and that metal type is safer than the sword. But for myself I did not doubt that if these paper wars went on, an iron battle would follow. And so it proved.

The plot, so they say, was hatched in Eltville by men hoping for honours from Rome. Rumours reached us in Mainz that Adolf's party was planning an attack. Some said we should strengthen the city walls, or hire mercenaries to protect us. But the council, deep in debt, had not the funds to act. For a week we lay uneasy in our beds. Each gust of wind against the roof-tiles exploded like an enemy cannon. And whenever a dog barked we thought that it had scented Adolf's men. But when the siege began one Thursday morning, close to dawn, near the Gautor, the air was silent and the city asleep. With scouts using ladders to scale the walls, five hundred soldiers slipped through the city gates. Three thousand more were waiting outside. At last, the alarm bell sounded from St Quintin's tower – when it woke me, I knew what it must mean. But having fought battles enough in life, and being too frail to bear arms in my old age, I stayed at home, barring my windows and doors. Those of Diether's party were soon armed, and fought a brave defence, among them Jakob Fust, who was struck and later died of his wounds (even I felt pity for him and his grieving brother). During these skirmishes, Diether escaped over the Rhine, promising to come back with reinforcements from nearby fields or distant towns. But by the time he returned, the battle was lost – and four hundred of our citizens were dead. That night and the next, Adolf's soldiers turned to rape and fire and looting. I was known to side with Diether. And when a band of mercenaries came beating at my door, I feared the worst – not my death so much as their burning the presses and wrecking the type. But seeing me in the rushlight, a half-blind hermit trembling in a nightshirt, they did not enter, merely bade me come to the market-place next day.

There I went at twelve, with Frau Beildeck – eight hundred of us circled by Adolf's soldiers, like sheep in a pen. From the steps, stern and long-bearded as Moses, Adolf barked mad-dog at us for disobedience to the Pope, for which he said our lives must be forfeit. Frau Beildeck whimpered and clutched my arm. To me death held no demons. Besides, I suspected Adolf of playing Moses so he could later turn mild as Jesus. Which at last he did, saying if we surrendered all possessions to him he would temper justice with mercy, and merely banish us rather than have us slain. Frau Beildeck fell for him, kissing the ground, offering praise to God above, and pushing her few jewels at the nearest soldier when with some guile she might have saved them, as I did a hundred gulden in my boots. Still, the greater loss was mine, since I had to give up my house, and the presses in it, which Adolf handed to a supporter of his, Conrad Wilvung. Robbed of all we owned then handed half a gulden in payment, we were made to walk between Swiss crossbows and Adolf's swaggering boys. Spits on one side, kicks and curses on the other. Two by two they made us go, like the animals to Noah's ark, ready to face the flood. One red-eyed mercenary kicked me as I hobbled by him: 'Hurry up there, old man.' I shuffled faster, afraid he would hear my gulden jangle. But he gave no sign and let me go. At the city gates, two scribes sat taking down our names, and demanded half a gulden to let us by.

So we were banished with nothing but what we stood in. Except that many had sneaked out jewels and gulden – and a few the tools of their trade. As we gathered by the Rhine, I met several workers of mine, past and present, who had punches with them, and hand-moulds, and compositors' cases, they having smuggled these away the night before and hidden them in the bushes and rivergrass. Where best to go now, they wondered? For me it was easy, my sister-in-law's haven in Eltville lying close by. For them, the journey would be longer – to Cologne, Nuremberg, Bamberg, Utrecht, Antwerp, Prague, Leipzig, Basel, Paris, Lyons, Rome, Venice, Florence, Seville. I did not see Peter Schoeffer, nor Johann Fust (who was perhaps tending his brother, yet undead), and did not know if these my enemies were among the banished. But since they had printed for Diether as well as Adolf, I guessed they were. And even if not, their art would now be at a stop, since from the number of beaters, pullers, inkers and engravers collected by the Rhine, they had lost their workforce. On another day, I might have smiled to see my rivals vanquished, their business broken up. But I had lost too much myself to take pleasure in their downfall.

As I boarded the boat to Eltville, a flock of geese flew over, and I thought, hearing their call: Now the secret of print is truly out! When we walked through the city gates, the secret flowed with us. Fust & Schoeffer had tried to dam it up – to keep it to themselves. But now Mainz was sacked and burning, and its ashes blowing through the world. Berthold Ruppel, Heinrich Keffer, Albrecht Pfister, Johann Neumeister, Heinrich Eggestein, Anton Koberger, Johann Sensenschmidt, Konrad Zeninger, Ulrich Han: these men – these print-pilgrims – would take my invention far and wide. Out across Christendom they were carrying the word of Johann. And books at last would fly like doves.

♪♪

Do you recall that Italian – Rimaggio – with his promise of

lenses? Perhaps you have forgotten him. Certainly I had. You, Thomas, will not have heard of him to start with. He appeared in the first days of my dictating this, before your time. But you see these two lenses that perch upon my eyes: he brought me them last Monday. He brought two other pairs as well, but these best help me see. I feel like Lazarus, having crawled out of darkness into light again. Where I saw before only eagles, I can now make out a wren. It is a miracle.

I should be happy at my rebirth, and I am. It is hard to part me from my lenses, even in sleep. Ask Frau Beildeck, who found them dangled across my face while I lay snoring in this chair ('Do they help you see better in dreams?' she asked). I am more fond of them than of any man living. Yet I confess they have twice upset me already, and I worry, if I live longer, what shocks may lie ahead.

To take the first, which is the simpler. I hooked them on me yesterday while I walked out from the orchard to the river. The lovely Rhine: scratched and fading though my eyes have been these latter years, I have never lost sight of it. That strong brown flow, the boats hugging its tide, the swans gliding – many an hour these floating images have cheered me. What ecstasy to see the river clear again. Yet my rapture was short-lived. I had forgotten what noisome matter floats along it. Rotten fruit, cabbage-leaves, dead cats, dead birds, half-eaten fish, peelings, nutshells, turds: all came floating by. In my blindness, I had been picturing the river too kindly. My two lenses showed it true. For comfort I took them off a moment, and only with reluctance replaced them.

My second upset was and is more grave. I have been perusing that heap of papers near where you sit, Thomas, the pages of my testament, those you lay aside when covered with words. And seeing them in detail has filled me with anger and dismay. Calm yourself, boy. This is no reproach to you, whose art – so these lenses have confirmed – is perfect elegance. No, it is your predecessor I am vexed with, young Anton, he of the dragon mother. Not that penmanship is his error, either. You will forgive me for saying this, Thomas, but his hand, being more practised, is even more graceful than yours. The art of a scribe, though, is first of all to copy correctly. And though Anton's as and bs are finely shaped, he has not always set down what I spoke. I have read but a few pages, and perhaps I was unlucky in my sampling. Yet I find many a word has been missed out, so that the meaning is hard to unpick. Worse, far worse, are sentences – whole passages even – that have been added, with words of mine I surely never spoke.

I am old, of course, and have no memory of exact speech. Even were my memory perfect, it could not recapture the flow and matter of each page, since the heat of dictation – or composition, let us call it – is like a kind of trance which afterwards leaves no trace of itself in the mind. (Or let me picture it as an island in the river of time. Or a vision out of daytime logic, a kind of dreaming.) All I spoke to Anton and speak to you, Thomas, is the truth. But *how* I speak it, what words I use, the other words drawn unexpected behind them and leading elsewhere – this is a kind of mystery. Might my words then have journeyed to places which, now I look at them cold, I do not recognise? It is possible. Yet there are passages so foreign to the way I have lived, and to how my mind works, not even in a fit could I have spoken them. Which makes me think that Anton made them up.

I mean especially – though to spare your blushes, Thomas, I will not detail this – certain passages about my youth and private self, unrelated to the work of the books, where Anton has let his mind run off with him, as wild as Aesop's hare. Perhaps Anton did this when he was bored. Or because as a scribe he hated my invention and all things mechanical. Or else he thought me niggardly in my payment of him and took revenge. Perhaps his dragon mother put him to it out of malice. I do not know, nor have I the will to make emendations in my hand. Though these lenses would allow it, in the short time left me upon earth the labour of correction would be too great. So I must let the pages stand and hope the reader, guessing between my true confessions and those devised by Anton, will know me for who I am.

The sorry business of mistranscription has a long history. I have read of other scribes as unscrupulous. Bernard of Clairvaux had one – not Geoffrey, who served him faithfully, but Nicholas, his predecessor, who wrote letters to one and all expressing his views in Bernard's name. Now Anton has done the same, illuminating my text with beasts of his own imagining.

This my new lenses have helped me to see. They are lynx-eyed and miss nothing, not even treachery. I thank them for their clarity. Yet it makes me wish for blindness, or death.

So I was ruined again: banished from Mainz, kicked and spat upon by enemy soldiers, my house seized, my materials confiscated, my men dispersed. But many others were ruined worse. And since I had been ruined before in Strasbourg, and at the monastery, and again by Fust, this my fourth ruin had no sharp sword-blade. I welcomed it like an old friend.

Soon enough, besides, I was rising from the dead again, this time in Eltville. From Mainz were also banished Heinrich and Nicholas Bechtermünze, whose father I had known in the days of Frilo and Ruleman (my twin cousins, Thomas, long since dead). Their cloth business having been ripped apart, Heinrich and Nicholas were game to begin some new enterprise, and had the youth and will and gulden for it, which I did not. Would I help them? they asked. I named a price. It meant me getting my hands inky, but I was glad of an occupation. In time, the mood eased in Mainz, with Adolf and his Popish crew taking full charge. And though I chose not to return, my friend Dr Humery prevailed upon the city to have my tools released to Eltville, including presses, punches and hand-moulds. So new types were cut, and we began printing calendars and indulgences, as of old. To assist was the Frenchman, Nicholas Jenson, who had followed me from Mainz in hope of further instruction. Not that, by this time, he needed it: he had almost the skill of Peter Schoeffer, and was eager to spread the word. Later, Nicholas moved to Marienthal, where they are building a monastery. He is there still. The brother scribes intend to exchange the pen for the composing stick, and Nicholas is teaching them. I have myself twice been called there to advise. The air above its hill is sweet with pine, and breathing it I feel at peace.

These days my discourse with the world is mainly through letters. In one that came the other day, the bishop of Bamberg writes me that the Pope has now been apprised of the origins of type – and knows the founder was not Fust. What greater solace can I ask? It helps me forget the other letters, those I receive from Strasbourg (yes, the City fathers have tracked me down here) asking for repayment of certain loans. The imperial court at Rottweil has been informed, they warn. In their impudence, they are even demanding compound interest – which over twenty years comes to a princely sum. Well, they can set their dogs on me, but I will not pay them back.

The rest you know – even you, Thomas, know it. Three days a week I attend the Eltville printshop, for though my eyes, before these lenses at least, could not see to shape a matrix or read a proof, yet there were ways I could assist by mind and mouth. Now I am visioned like a lynx, I might be more in attendance, but doubt I will, because the effort of walking there, even with a stick, becomes more of a struggle each day. I like, besides, the pattern of my other days: two to read, study and contemplate; one to pray; and one to dictate here by the window. Soon I must pay to earth the debt of humankind. This tattered body will be a garment cast away. The prospect does not frighten me. When we die, it is as if a page has been torn from the book of life. But every page blows up to heaven, where God sits binding them up, so we all are assembled in His library. One day I will be a volume in eternity.

22. Making an End

You thought I had nothing more to say. I thought so too.
Yet here is news indeed. Fust is dead. Frau Beildeck heard
of it at the flax-market two days back, but did not want to
tell me, in case it prove untrue. Now a letter has come
confirming it. He had gone to Paris on business, selling his
psalters and Bibles (my Bibles!), and there the plague took
him. They said a mass for him at St Viktor, so Peter
Schoeffer writes.

Yes, a letter to me from Peter, which is news no less
remarkable than Fust's death. I had no lenses about me
when it came, but even through the fog I recognised his
hand. How long is it since I last saw him at the workbench,
that day he would not see me? Ten years, eleven, twelve?
Why reach out to me now, after this time? Perhaps his
father-in-law's death has released him from a vow of silence.
As a condition of their partnership, Fust doubtless forbade
him to speak to me. Or Peter's own guilt at his betrayal
might have prevented him from approaching me till now.
He states nothing of this in the letter, which is brisk yet
flowery, saying 'Deeply saddened to have to do so but
feeling certain any who loved him would want to know, I
write to inform you of the recent death in Paris of my dear
father-in-law, much loved father of Christina and grand-
father to Gratian and Johannes.' Felt certain I 'would want
to know'? Assumed, more like, I would rejoice to know. Yet
it is too late for rejoicing. Fust's death is no sweet revenge,
nor does it heal my ancient hurt. I am too old to cock-a-
doodle over the death of a fox. My end is only hastened by
the ends of others. After one Johann has gone, how long
until the next one follows? This Peter ought to have seen.

Still I cannot be wholly angry with him. He did not need to write, nor to add for my eyes only, below the news doubtless sent to many others (for ease, he should have had his letter printed), that he hoped my health was good and 'Next time I am in Eltville, if this is not a burdensome prospect, I should like to call.' Burdensome? It lifts my spirits to think of seeing him. And yet the lumber of hurt pride, the lead weight of grief, the cornsacks of betrayal – they are a burden, right enough. He must know to have written this how great an injury he did me. But which pain does he think the worse? The betrayal at work, or with Christina? He may feel the guiltier at the last, assuming I loved her when him I loved the more. I should like to straighten Peter on this, *justify* him even, tell him he is welcome to his wife. As to the work, who knows how his conscience stands. He may think Fust seized what was owed him. That the press stamps better without me. That some other was the true inventor of the art.

And perhaps indeed some other is. Dr Humery told me last week – having had it from Ulrich Zell in Cologne – that a man from Haarlem is going about with claims I robbed the art from him: I am accused of jobbing in his workshop, then stealing his types one Christmas Eve. And another in Avignon (this I heard from Nicholas Jenson) says he printed in metal ten years before my Bibles. 'The impudence!' said Dr Humery. We laughed together at it over a jug. But alone I have been prey to doubt. To be stripped of my business ... banished from home ... and now these rumours that Gutenberg was not the first. Who can judge the matter? I am too old for it. I thought by this book to stake my claim. But perhaps I have no claim to make. Now all I wish is to be left in peace.

But first, let Peter visit me here in Eltville. Or if not I will call on him in Mainz. Having pressed it for months, Dr Humery has finally persuaded me to go there – once I am strong enough, as soon as this cough of mine abates, I will take the boat. If I do go, there are other men besides Peter I ought to visit. But I would like to hear his voice again. Watch his lips move. See his eyes, his hair, his hands.

I hope if Peter does come, he will bring his children – for preference the second one, Johannes (who we will pretend was named in honour of myself). Any child of his must still be small, but will soon outgrow him. It is like that today, children rising tall as nettles while we old stoop low as cowslips. When I was young, many believed (as the priests taught) our race would shortly die out. We were too plague-ridden, too sparse, too sunk in sin, and God in anger would soon have done with us. So they said. I never thought it. Now I think so even less. Perhaps it is these lenses, but to me the world looks stronger and brighter. It is like leaving behind the innards of Mainz – the cobbles, the alleys, the strung-up clothes, the gutters running with piss – and coming here to Eltville: wide horizons, nothing to close a man in. Each day we see a little further. New mills grind and scientists discover new truths. It is like some great coming of knowledge, or rebirth. You, Thomas, shall live to see if I am right. I hope myself to watch it from heaven.

Yes, this world as I leave it looks better than when I entered in. But much remains to do. Give me longer, and I would find a way to make the Rhine run my press for me – for does it not drive mills and pestles and mallets and wheels? Give me longer and I would publish not dusty Ancients but men of living flesh and blood. Give me longer and I would print in ruder tongues, for as the birds of the field sing in several voices, so men do – there is no one language for truth. Give me longer, and I might make an instrument the opposite of the printing press, so that instead of paper being pushed against inked type, inked type might strike itself against paper. A machine like a man swinging a pick. And if each letter should have its own rod and axis, as though a line of men with picks should strike in turn . . .

Of such dreams for making books, there is no end. But I am not Prometheus, bringing in an instant the gift of heavenly fire to all mankind. As yet, even the rudiments of my art are known to only a handful of printmen. To that purpose I am tempted to add an afterword here, with guidance in such matters as kerning and ems. But I am weary and will not stretch this out.

Next Sunday when you come, Thomas, you must gather up the papers from the floor, and set them neatly in order on the desk, and begin copying them out afresh. This way, you will achieve a fairer text, one which a compositor might work from, so my friend Dr Humery can set it in type. And even should he decline (saying no man alive would wish to read my book), still your time will not have been wasted, since there will be two written copies for posterity, which can be stored in different places (the neater in a strong-box), thereby doubling the chances of this my Justification living on.

Let us make an end, Thomas. You are quill-sore, and I have nothing left to give. Myself I have bequeathed. A potage of flesh and blood spilled on paper – is that all it is? I regret I have not made myself more seemly. But worse would be to stand in city squares, six feet of marble rectitude, a beard hiding my face.

Let us make an end, Thomas – before the worms make an end of me. Outside, evening is falling, as it has a hundred times since we began. But it is a different evening from those: the last, the very last. Fust, Peter, Christina, Ennelina, Ellewibel, Anton and all the other ghosts – I must let them go. There are cygnets in angel feathers on the Rhine. The sky is lowering its blue heaven. The wind through the linden bids me hush and be at peace. There is more, much more, I might have *pressed* on you. Life was riches and I have minted only a pfennig. But let us make an end.

Author's Note

After the fall of Mainz in 1462, and the death of Johann Gutenberg in 1468, the art of printing spread rapidly across Europe. By the end of the fifteenth century, Germany had some 300 printshops, Venice alone had 150 (producing 4,500 titles) and, according to one estimate, as many as twenty million books were printed – more than those produced by all the scribes of Europe in the previous fifteen hundred years. In England, William Caxton, who learned of printing during a visit to Cologne, brought out Chaucer's *Canterbury Tales* circa 1476, some twenty years after the publication of Gutenberg's Bible.

Gutenberg himself remains a shadowy figure. The date of his birth is uncertain. None of his printed works bears his name. No portrait of him was done in his lifetime (later paintings and statues show him with a beard, but it is now thought unlikely he had one). The little that scholars do know they have deduced from a handful of legal documents (concerning business disputes, loans, annuities, interest defaults, wine-tax payments and a breach of promise suit) and from the forty-nine surviving copies of his Bible. For much of this novel, I have had to make things up.

Albert Kapr's *Johann Gutenberg: The Man and the Invention* is the standard biography, and I am grateful to its English translator, Douglas Martin, a distinguished book-designer and print historian in his own right, for his help in answering questions. My thanks, too, to James Mosley of the St Bride's Printing Library, to Hans Eckert in Mainz, to Gavin Bryars (whose notion of an opera collaboration first got me interested in Gutenberg) and to Alison Samuel, Frances Coady, Ian Jack and Pat Kavanagh.